REVENGE OF THE DOG TEAM

WILLIAM W. JOHNSTONE
WITH J. A. JOHNSTONE

PINNACLE BOOKS
Kensington Publishing Corp.
www.kensingtonbooks.com

PINNACLE BOOKS are published by

Kensington Publishing Corp.
119 West 40th Street
New York, NY 10018

PUBLISHER'S NOTE
Following the death of William W. Johnstone, the family is working with a carefully selected writer to organize and complete Mr. Johnstone's outlines and many unfinished manuscripts to create additional novels in all of his series like The Last Gunfighter, Mountain Man, and Eagles, among others. This novel was inspired by Mr. Johnstone's superb storytelling.

All Kensington titles, imprints, and distributed lines are available at special quantity discounts for bulk purchases for sales promotions, premiums, fund-raising, educational, or institutional use. Special book excerpts or customized printings can also be created to fit specific needs. For details, write or phone the office of the Kensington special sales manager: Kensington Publishing Corp., 119 West 40th Street, New York, NY 10018, attn: Special Sales Department; phone 1-800-221-2647.

PINNACLE BOOKS and the Pinnacle logo are Reg. U.S. Pat. & TM Off.

ISBN-13: 978-0-7860-1995-7
ISBN-10: 0-7860-1995-7

First printing: July 2009

10 9 8 7 6 5 4 3 2 1

Printed in the United States of America

ONE

Night and the desert.

Nevada is mostly badlands, arid, sunbaked flats ribbed by jagged mountain ranges. Located in the central part of the state, the Black Sand Desert is one of the baddest of the bad. By day a bleak inferno, by night it's even more dangerous, a place shunned by honest citizens. Avoided by law enforcement except when absolutely necessary, and then the authorities come well armed.

A good place to do dirty business: gunrunning, dope and people smuggling. On this night in June, a deal was going down, the kind that's best done in the hours of darkness, far from the haunts of men.

Choey Maldonado was taking delivery of a quartet of female sex slaves.

They couldn't even be called whores, because that term implies a certain amount of remuneration, no matter how minimal, and sometimes even a degree of choice. Aspects that were absent in the case of this unhappy foursome.

The meeting place was a flat west of the Tres Hermanos, the Three Brothers mountain range. So named because the triple peaks, standing in single file running north-south, resembled with their rounded tops and hunched shoulders a trio of cowled monks, monastery brothers—or so they had seemed to the conquistadors who first penetrated these lands five hundred years earlier, in search of fabled cities of gold.

They found no cities, no gold. A number of silver veins and lodes were scattered among the hills, but they eluded the invaders. The indigenous native tribes had had their own name for the triple-peaked landmark, but what it was is unknown, since nobody had bothered to record it before the locals were exterminated by the conquerors.

A canyon mouth opened in the western slope between the middle peak and the southernmost; through many a twisty turn, the passage wound its way through the rocky mass clear to the other, eastern side. On the west, opposite the pass, the flat was studded with boulders, some house-sized, others the size of cars. Cactus clumps filled in some of the empty spaces. An old dirt trail snaked through the rocks, running roughly parallel to the hills. To the south, it stretched all the way across the border, deep into Mexico.

In the lee of a rocky knob as big as a church, a campfire was burning. Nearby stood an old beat-up pickup truck and a mammoth, late-model

SUV. The pickup was the delivery vehicle. The SUV was receiving the consignment.

Two men, Esteban and Bronco, belonged to the truck. The SUV yielded three men: Choey Maldonado, Fierro, and Gomez. The women were named Lina, Amparo, Carmen, and Marisol. Carmen, the oldest, was twenty; the youngest, Amparo, was fifteen.

The men were all armed with handguns. That was a matter of course. They would no more have gone about unarmed in this wasteland by day or night than they would have gone about without wearing a pair of pants.

There was a sawed-off shotgun in the cab of the pickup truck and an assault rifle in the SUV, but those were reserved for any unanticipated problems on the road, not for the meeting at hand. Heavy firepower was not required for tonight's venture. This was a friendly meeting, a routine business deal. This land belonged to Clan Maldonado, affirmed not by title or certificate but by force of arms.

Esteban and Bronco were *coyotes,* people smugglers. Esteban had a pompadour hairstyle and a pointy goatee; Bronco was flat-faced, thick-featured, squat-bodied. Their boss was a long-time Maldonado family associate. This was merely the latest of a series of exchanges that had gone down dozens of times without a hitch.

So simple was it that clan chieftain Rio Maldonado had sent younger brother Choey to handle it, figuring that not even "the kid" could screw it up. Still, as insurance, he'd sent along Fierro, a trusted lieutenant and a professional gun. Gomez was the driver. Between the two of them, they could probably keep Choey from doing anything stupid.

Choey, twenty-one, had a slender frame, but too much booze and soft living had already left its mark with a puffy face, soft belly, and flabby limbs. A shiny, chrome-plated semiautomatic pistol was wedged into the top of a pair of too-tight jeans. His untucked shirt was worn bunched up at one hip, the better to show off his fancy gun.

Fierro was middle-aged, lean, his face as gaunt and hollow-cheeked as the hand-carved wooden image of some martyred patron saint of a pueblo church. Gomez was fleshy, moon-faced, and pear-shaped. Fierro handled the money; Choey couldn't be relied on not to try to divert a few bills into his pocket. Fierro handed the bill roll to Esteban.

Esteban went over by the fire and started counting the cash, several hundred dollars in well-used twenties. Not a lot of money for four young women, an outsider might think, but in these parts, fresh flesh was cheap. The supply of girls looking to cross north over the border was inexhaustible, and for the fresh, good-looking ones who fell into the grip of the *coyotes,* it was a buyer's market.

Choey bridled, said, "What's the matter, don't you trust us? The Maldonado never shorted anybody." His tone was offensive.

Esteban ignored it. He knew Choey. He said, "Sure, I trust you. It's just that Max, he don't trust me." Max Alacran was his boss. Esteban spoke without losing track of the count.

Fierro sidled up alongside Choey, ready to intervene in case he did something stupid. "It's business, Choey." He tried to keep his voice flat, level, but into it crept a hint of a sigh. Playing nursemaid to an overgrown juvenile was part of the job, but it was wearying.

Gomez knew better how to defuse the situation. Waddling into the firelight with a bottle of tequila they'd been passing around, he raised it to his lips and took a swig from it.

That caught Choey's attention. "Hey," he said, "save some of that for me, you pig." He grabbed the bottle, fastened it to his mouth, and up-ended it.

Esteban finished counting and caught Fierro's eye. Fierro replied with the slightest of nods. Esteban pocketed the cash. The deal was done.

When Choey took hold of the bottle, it was more than half full. When he unfastened his mouth from it, little more than a swallow or two remained. It was not the first bottle he'd taken the lion's share from on tonight's venture. His face was flushed, his eyes glittered. His wet-lipped mouth gaped slackly open.

Esteban and Bronco were already crossing to the truck. "All right, you're done here," Choey called after them. "You can go."

The *coyotes* knew how to deal with Choey, not even bothering to ignore him. Bronco got behind the wheel of the pickup and started it up. Esteban stood at the passenger side, hand on the opened door. Nodding to Fierro, he gave him a quick two-finger salute before climbing into the cab.

The truck made a K-turn, nosed south on the dirt road, and drove away, trailed by a feathery plume of dust. Only the parking lights were on, shedding a fuzzy, feeble glow on the path ahead. That, the starlight, and the beams of a half-moon that had only recently risen above the mountains to the east would provide the only illumination needed or desired by the *coyotes* as they made their way back to home base. Out here, head-lights would stand out like a neon sign.

Gomez reached tentatively for the bottle in Choey's hand to possess himself of a final taste. All that did was focus Choey's attention on it. He drained the dregs and threw the empty bottle in the direction of the pickup truck, already well out of reach. Choey swayed, taking a wide-legged stance to better maintain his balance. Fierro indicated the SUV with a tilt of his head, said, "Might as well get going."

"What's the rush?" Choey said. He turned toward the women, wobbling a bit as he did so.

They stood in a clump, huddled together. Heads bowed, eyes downcast. It had been a long, hard trip north; they'd been brutalized and as-saulted virtually nonstop by their transporters pretty much from the start of the illegal crossing. They'd been passed along by several sets of cap-tors before falling into the hands of Alacran's captors. They held no illusions about their im-mediate and future prospects.

Choey said, "Let's take a better look at what we've got. Get those bitches over here, into the light."

Fierro's tight-lipped mouth turned down at the

corners, but he said nothing, just stood off to one side with his arms folded across his chest. He knew that if he pointed out that Rio was waiting for them back at the rancho, Choey would delay their departure all the longer, just out of spite. So he kept his mouth shut and let Gomez play the flunky. That was part of the fat man's job.

Gomez herded the females in closer to the fire. "This way, girls, don't be shy," he said, chuckling lewdly. He lined the women up so they stood shoulder to shoulder between the fire and the boulder in whose lee it was sheltered.

The fire was built from pieces of deadwood, twigs and broken branches and such gathered from the nearby brush and stunted dwarf trees dotting the area. Thin gray wisps of smoke were aromatic, smelling of mesquite and dry sage.

The women wore T-shirts or sweatshirts, jeans, and sneakers. The desert night air was cool, chilly, but it was warm where they stood, with the fire's warmth radiating off the tilted plane of the rock face behind them. Even so, they shivered.

Choey lurched toward them. The nearest was Lina. She stood unbowed, staring straight ahead into the darkness beyond the crackling flames. Long straight black hair hung down on either side of her oval face. She kept her expression blank, but her eyes were wide and dark. Her breasts were high and full against a lime-colored T-shirt.

Choey, swaying, gripped her shoulder in one hand to steady himself. The other hand squeezed and groped her through the shirt, not gently. Lina squirmed, breathing hard through clenched teeth, biting her lip at one point to keep from crying out at the rough handling. All the while, she kept staring over his shoulder into space.

When he let go of her, she choked back a shuddering sob. Choey took a step back, grinning. He caught sight of Gomez, frowned, and said, "More tequila!"

"It's all gone," Gomez said.

"Like hell! Don't give me that. I know you, you drunken pig, you're sure to have an extra bottle or two stashed away somewhere."

Gomez assumed what he thought was an expression of heartfelt sincerity; he looked like he'd just been caught stealing from the church poor box. He began, "Choey, I swear to you that that was the last of it—"

Choey rested his hand on the chrome-plated pistol sticking out of the top of his belt at his hip. "Make it quick before I put a hot round into that fat ass of yours!"

"Maybe there's one left in the SUV. I'll take a look," Gomez said, scuttling away toward the vehicle. Without hesitation, he went to the passenger-side door, opening it. The dome light went on, throwing a tilted yellow square of brightness out the side of the cab and across the gritty, charcoal-gray sands.

Gomez bent over, leaning forward from the waist and sticking out a rear as wide and round as a garbage can lid as he pawed urgently under the passenger seat.

Choey said, "What a target, I can't miss!"

"Wait, wait!" Gomez straightened up and

turned around, holding a bottle by its long neck. "I found one!"

"Big surprise," Choey said.

Gomez hurried to him, masses and mounds of flesh all a-jiggle. He had less than a dozen paces to cross, but by the time he reached Choey, he was panting and heaving like he'd just finished running a marathon.

Choey snatched the bottle away from him, saying, "Give me that before you drop it, you fat fool."

Gomez was too out of breath to speak. Choey uncapped the bottle and tossed the cap away. He lifted it to his lips and drank deep, making significant inroads into its contents.

His bleary gaze fell on Amparo. She was slight, girlish, with a sharp-featured birdlike face. Her eyes bulged like a pair of black olives, her lips were compressed into a thin white line, and her pointy chin trembled.

Her fear was palpable, and Choey seemed to expand physically under its impact. He stood there for a moment, savoring it, while the cowering girl shrank from his nearness. Groggily noticing the bottle in his hand, he looked for someplace to put it. Gomez had caught enough of his breath to volunteer, "I'll hold it for you—"

"Keep your filthy paws off it or I'll shoot them off," Choey said. He set the bottle down on a rocky outcropping.

He reached for Amparo. "There's not enough of you to make a meal out of—" He grabbed a fistful of her shirt and pulled, tearing it away down the front and baring her chest. "A scrawny chicken!" he cried, laughing.

He grappled his hands onto her breasts, one in each hand, pulling and twisting them. Squealing, she sank to her knees, her fluttering hands feebly trying to fend him off.

Fierro said, "Rio paid for her, she belongs to him—"

"Shut up," Choey said, not looking up from what he was doing. His hands worked harder, more viciously, Amparo's shrieks shrilling. She clawed at his face, and suddenly it was Choey's turn to howl. His grip broke, and she sank in a heap at his feet, the rock face behind her propping her up into a half-sitting position.

Choey half turned toward the fire, revealing a set of four bloody furrows that Amparo had clawed into his cheek. An expression of wonderment showed on his face as he gingerly, almost delicately raised a hand to touch the afflicted area. He held his hand to the firelight, ruby droplets of blood beading his fingertips as he fought to focus his gaze on them. A shadow flickered across his face.

Roaring, he turned back toward the girl, thrusting his arms down and grabbing her neck in both hands. He jerked her to her feet and held her up in the air, throttling her. His expression was maniacal. Noises escaped from him as he strangled her.

The only other time Fierro had heard noises even remotely like that, they had come from a man who was burning to death in a house on fire.

Amparo's small sneakered feet thrashed in

empty air as Choey held her at arm's length, wringing her neck. Something snapped and her feet stopped kicking.

Gomez stood there open-mouthed, motionless, staring stupidly. Cursing under his breath, Fierro started forward.

Marisol, standing to one side of Amparo, picked up a softball-sized rock and slammed it against the side of Choey's head. It made a wet, chunking sound.

This time, Fierro cursed out loud. In a lightning-like flash, he could see his entire life before him if a fatal blow had indeed struck down Choey Maldonado, whose brother Rio had charged Fierro to protect Choey at all costs. A flash was all that was needed, for what would remain of Fierro's life was sure to be short and unpleasant.

Choey was still on his feet. Amparo had fallen from his suddenly slackened grip. Marisol, a study in grim determination, raised her arm to deliver another blow with the rock.

One thing Fierro didn't have to think about was gunplay. That was his stock in trade. In one smooth blur of motion, he drew his holstered sidearm and, firing from the hip, triggered three quick blasts into Marisol's middle. Any one of the shots would have been fatal; the three of them nearly cut her in half.

She went down without so much as a whimper. Choey, still standing, started screaming. From the way he was carrying on, it seemed like he was the one who'd been shot. He looked like a crazy man, eyes bulging like they were going to pop out of their sockets.

Fierro knew better. He was a dead shot and when he fired at something, he hit it. He knew his shots had all gone true. Choey was being hysterical, that was all. Fierro found his shrieks deeply reassuring, since it meant he wasn't dead or unconscious.

Choey fell silent, his open mouth gazing. His eyes came back into focus. He shook his head, as if to clear it. He looked around the scene. Fierro, Gomez, Lina, and Carmen all stood frozen in place, like images from a still photograph.

Marisol lay sprawled on her back, face upturned. Amparo lay in a huddle on her side, head twisted at an angle no living person could attain.

Choey's face convulsed, features scrunching up. He looked like he was going to burst into tears. Instead, he started laughing. Howls of mirth escaped him, belly laughs that doubled him up. Big gusts of laughter that were almost as hysterical as his screams a moment before.

That broke the spell. Gomez went to him, gripping him by the arm to help keep him up on his feet. "You okay? Choey, you okay?" said Gomez, who looked like he was going to be sick.

Carmen was a picture of shocked horror. Lina quivered with tension, dark eyes flashing as she looked for an opening, an opportunity to make a break. She made eye contact with Fierro, who shook his head no. She let her breath out slowly, shoulders slumping with resignation.

One side of Choey's face glistened wetly reddish-black with blood from where the rock had struck him in the head. Gomez still clung to his arm, repeatedly asking him if he was okay.

Choey's laughter subsided. Snarling, he tore loose from the other's grip. "I'm okay," he said.

Gomez piously raised his eyes heavenward. "The Holy Father be praised!"

Choey's eyes narrowed, peering around until he found what he was looking for: the tequila bottle, which stood undisturbed on the rocky shelf where he had set it. He took a long pull from it, guzzling it, draining it dry. He tossed the empty to the ground. He looked crafty, malicious. "You know what we have to do now," he said, speaking to Fierro. It was not a question.

"We've got to get rid of the other two. Can't leave any witnesses alive," he said.

Fierro nodded. He knew it was true. Lina and Carmen could tie him to the murder of Marisol. And Choey to that of Amparo. Oh, they'd swear by the cross and the rosary and all the saints never to breathe a word of what had happened here. People will say anything to save themselves. But the eternal truth applied: Only the dead tell no tales. He realized that he was still holding his gun leveled hip-high, where he'd been holding it when he shot Marisol.

He swung the muzzle toward Lina, shaking his head sadly. What a waste! Trust Choey to screw things up so it had to come to this. No way around it, though. What had to be, had to be.

Something hit Fierro with the force of a thunderbolt, and before he realized he'd been struck, he was dead. Stone dead before he hit the ground.

The flat crack of a rifle report sounded somewhere in the black hills east of the campfire.

Before the echoes fell still, there was a second shot. Simultaneous with it was a juicy thud like a sledgehammer hitting a side of beef, the sound of a round tagging Gomez. The impact knocked him sprawling, gut-shot with a tennis ball-sized bullet hole.

Fierro and Gomez had been downed one-two, one right after the other, bang-bang! Came a pause then, one lasting several heartbeats, not long, just long enough for Choey to realize what had happened to his sidemen and to grasp the implications for himself. Not long enough for him to do anything about it, though.

One might almost have thought that the unseen shooter had done so deliberately, to let Choey know that his time had come. Choey looked around madly for cover, for some avenue of escape. He opened his mouth to scream.

Bang! The shot tagged him dead center, knocking him back against the boulder. He bounced off it and measured his length facedown in the dirt.

The third shot's echoes died away. In the silence, the wood on the campfire hissed, sputtered, and crackled. That was all.

A hundred yards or so to the east, from where the shots seemed to have been fired, the stark black foothills and the slightly softer black of the canyon mouth remained unbroken by a single gleam of light or hint of motion.

Time passed; the stillness remained unbroken.

The phantom shooter was just that—a phantom, unseen as the wind. Choey Maldonado, Fierro, and Gomez were dead. Lina and Carmen were alive, alone with night and the desert.

Night, the desert, and Death.

TWO

Too many cooks spoil the broth, or so the old saying goes.

And too many hunters?

That was the question for Steve Ireland. He had time to think it over, plenty of time, because he was on a hunt and the one thing a hunt requires is patience. Hunting is mostly a waiting game, waiting for the time and the place and the prey to align in the optimum combination for a sure kill.

Steve's hunting ground wasn't a wilderness far removed from civilization, not this time, although in the past he'd tracked his prey in jungles, forests, mountains, and deserts. Tonight, though, he was doing his hunting in a big city; in the nation's capital, Washington, D.C.

He was a manhunter but no lawman; at least, no lawman officially recognized by any civilian judicial authority in the land. He wasn't the type who brings 'em back alive either.

Steve Ireland, a few months short of thirty,

was six feet, two inches tall, rangy, long-limbed. Lean to the point of gauntness, he was hollow-cheeked with sharp, jutting cheekbones. His hair was dark and needed a trim. His face was stiff, strangely immobile, all but the eyes. Deep-set eyes were alert and darkly glittering in that clean-shaven, frozen face.

He wore a lightweight utility vest, baggy T-shirt, wide-legged pants, and sneakers. His clothes were dark-colored but not black; they looked more dingy than sinister. Tucked into his waist-band over his left hip was a 9mm Beretta semiau-tomatic pistol worn butt-forward, for a cross-belly draw. He liked it that way for a city kill.

The untucked T-shirt was worn over the piece, an impediment to speedy access but necessary for concealment. The utility vest also cloaked the weapon. Some spare clips were tucked into the pockets; at the back of the neck, a custom-made sheath held a long, slim, stilettolike throw-ing knife that ran down vertically between his shoulder blades. He was a dead shot who hap-pened to also have a real facility with knives.

Whether the prey be man or beast, hunting is hunting. The rules are the same. The predator goes where the game is.

Steve stood in an alley between two brick build-ings, across the street from the main entrance of a topless bar. It was after midnight on a midweek June night.

Washington, D.C., is a place of many parts. When the average citizen thinks about the capi-tal, the first impression that usually comes to mind is a vista of stately white monuments, broad thoroughfares, and massive government office buildings. The bar wasn't located in that part of town.

Washington is also the site of a sprawling inner city, an urban ghetto of teeming tenements, dire poverty, and rampant crime, including one of the nation's highest murder rates. The bar wasn't in that part of town either.

It was in a fringe area near the river but not in sight of it, a seedy, rundown marginal industrial zone on the edge of the warehouse district. There were a lot of gas stations, auto parts stores, some machine shops, a couple of trucking company lots, a tire regrooving place, and the like.

Doors were made of solid metal, windows were netted by protective antitheft grilles, walls and chain-link fences were topped with strands of razor-barbed concertina wire. After dark, the legitimate establishments were locked up tight, alarm systems switched on, and their personnel made fast tracks for points elsewhere.

A lack of residential properties and a broad-minded local zoning board had encouraged the rise of a number of leisure-time entertainment venues generally not welcomed in more finicky neighborhoods: a head-banging heavy metal music club, an adult emporium peddling triple-X-rated magazines and DVDs, some gin mills, and a couple of strip joints.

One of the latter was being dogged by Steve Ireland. No mere hole-in-the-wall dive, it aspired to a certain kind of gritty grandiosity. A one-story, shoebox-shaped structure with a flat roof, it and its adjacent parking lot occupied most of a city block. One of its narrow ends fronted a four-lane boulevard; that's where the main entrance was located. Above it, a red neon sign bannered its name: The Booby Hatch.

Unlike most of the other buildings in the area, the club's parking lot was not fenced in. It didn't need to be. The management was wired into the territory's organized crime syndicate and paid for protection. Muggers, thieves, vandals, and other malefactors knew better than to ply their trade here. Crooks being what they are, though, every now and then one would be too dumb or greedy or strung out to obey the prohibition; swift retribution was sure to follow, and another corpse would be found in a vacant lot, to be labeled by police and press as a "gang killing" and just as swiftly forgotten by officialdom, if not by the lawbreaking elements at whom the object lesson was directed.

A parking lot attendant stood on watch during operating hours, mostly to make sure that no hooker tricks or drug deals were consummated on the grounds. The syndicate had an in with the cops, but there was no percentage in allowing the kind of action that gives the vice squad and liquor-licensing authorities a pretext to hike the going payoff rate.

Some hustlers were allowed in the club, as long as they were reasonably discreet and presentable and took their johns off premises to do their business. That okay came with an obligation to kick back a certain percentage of their fees to the management. They were a draw, too, bringing in male clientele and getting them to spend plenty on overpriced, watered-down drinks. Club dancers weren't allowed to date customers as a matter of policy, to keep management from catching heat from the vice boys. Although back rooms were maintained for select dancers to intimately entertain special friends and associates of the owners.

The street outside was well traveled day and night, mostly by cars and trucks in a hurry to get somewhere else. Police cars cruised back and forth at regular intervals, pausing to roust street hookers and pick up falling-down drunks and cart them off to the city jail.

When prowl cars came rolling along, Steve Ireland faded a few paces back from the alley mouth where he was keeping vigil, melting away into the inky darkness that dwelt in the narrow passageway between two buildings. They were commercial buildings, closed for the night, with narrow slitlike windows set high in brick walls, pale oblongs wanly glowing from dim lights burning within.

The boulevard was lined with heavy-duty street lamps that flooded it with a harshly unnatural, blue-white-tinged glare. But it penetrated no more than a few feet into the alley, which was stuffed thick with black darkness.

The wall on Steve's left was lined with a couple of trash bins filled with cinder ash and metal scraps and shavings from the machine shop within. He ducked behind them when patrol cars came making their slow, sharklike glide along his side of the street.

His car was parked nearby where he could get

it into action fast. He could have kept watch from inside it, but he preferred to be out here, where he could move around and stretch his legs. A lone man sittting behind the wheel of a parked car in this neck of the woods would attract too much attention from the law and street people.

Besides, until recently, he'd been cooped up for months in a small room in a private clinic, recuperating from critical injuries sustained during an overseas mission. He'd had enough of that to hold him for ten lifetimes.

It felt good to be outside in the fresh air, such as it was. Washington is built on what used to be swampland, and flaunts its origins throughout most of the year with heavy humidity. This late June night, the air was so thick and damp and hazy that it plastered haloed rings around street lamps and headlights.

There were dark bands of wetness under his arms, and his shirt hung limp with sweat. From long habit he went jungle-fighter style, wearing no undershorts beneath his pants and hanging free and loose.

The occasional street hookers who went strutting along the sidewalks took advantage of the sultry night air to peel down to the minimum, tube tops and short-shorts, the better to flaunt what they had. The turf was more or less off-limits, but a steady stream of them trolled the pavement, gambling on getting picked up by a cruising john and getting in his car and away before attracting the notice of a cop. They were on fairly safe ground as long as they kept moving and didn't linger in doorways or on street corners.

Other denizens of the nighttime world made the rounds: winos, crackheads, lush rollers, bone thugs, penny-ante drug dealers, homeless derelicts, and crazies. Now and then, they would wander into the alley, nearly stumbling into Steve before becoming aware of his presence. When they did, they got out fast. One look was all it took to realize he was up to serious business they wanted no part of.

His vantage point gave him a clear sightline on the club's front and parking lot. The front entrance was the only way the customers entered and exited the building. There were fire exits in each of the long side walls, and a back door that opened onto a loading platform, but they were off-limits to all but staffers, to prevent any deadbeats from trying to beat the house after running up a hefty bar tab. The oversized, hulking goons that served as bouncers and club personnel weren't being paid to let anyone pull a fast one on them.

The parking lot had a single entrance/exit that accessed the street. Steve knew the layout of the club; he'd been in there earlier tonight while dogging his quarry, and he'd made sure to survey the layout of the joint. Not that he expected his man to execute any evasive maneuvers; Quentin simply wasn't the type. He didn't know he was being followed and even if he did, he wasn't built for any kind of action that might scuff up his expensive, Italian-made tasseled loafers.

Durwood Quentin III, to give him his full monicker. A multimillionaire with a kink for the down-and-dirty side of the street. With his money, he could have been playing around with high-fashion models or high-line, five-thousand-dollar-a-night call girls.

Instead, he prowled the low-down side of the capital's nighttime world, making the rounds of strip clubs, titty bars, and hustler dives, the raunchier the better. He also had a tendency to top off the evening by picking up street hookers and knocking off a quickie in his car. With some of the hard skanks he'd been dallying with, he was lucky one of them hadn't cut his throat for his wallet and watch. Which would have saved Steve Ireland some trouble.

Steve had become an instant expert on Quentin's wayward ways because he'd been tailing him on his forays for the last few nights, after first drawing the assignment to neutralize the financier.

Know your target, learn his pattern to find his point of maximum vulnerability, and strike. That was how Steve Ireland operated, and he was very good at his job. Or at least, he had been, before the hazards of war had put a serious hurting on him and laid him up in a recovery ward for the better part of six months. He was just getting back into harness with the Quentin sanction.

It wasn't until tonight, though, that he'd learned that someone else was also on Quentin's trail. A combination of luck and skill had caused Steve to spot the interloper before the stranger had spotted *him*. It takes one to know one, and Steve had tagged the other as a hunter, too.

Earlier, when Quentin had first exited his expensive Georgetown townhouse and pulled away in his car to begin his nightly prowling, Steve had been surprised to notice a second car take off after Quentin's Cadillac and start following it. The newcomer was a black Crown Victoria.

Steve nosed his machine in line after the other two and brought up the rear. The night air was hot, muggy, but the air conditioner was off and the windows open. He liked it better that way. It kept him in closer contact with his surroundings than if he'd been sealed inside a closed car with the AC on.

Quentin drove across the Rock Creek Bridge into the city proper, trailed by the two tail cars, the Crown Vic and Steve's machine, a nondescript dark-colored late-model sedan. There was plenty of traffic and Steve was a skilled shadower, so he had no trouble keeping tabs on his quarry and the unknown second party who'd interjected himself into the scene. Steve didn't even have to stick too close to Quentin; all he had to do was keep his sights on the Crown Vic that was following the Cadillac.

The three cars threaded a maze of streets named for the letters of the alphabet and the states of the union. Steve used all of the shadower's tricks, sometimes fading back, other times passing both vehicles and letting them overtake him, occasionally pulling over to the curb and switching off his lights for a few beats to make it look like he'd reached his destination, then falling in behind a van or truck and using it as cover to switch on his lights and resume the pursuit.

Several times, he caught a glimpse of the Crown Vic's driver and lone occupant, a big guy with close-cropped dark hair and a mustache. Only a glimpse, though; he didn't want the other guy to get too good a look at him and realize that the tailer was being tailed. Steve had an advantage in that he'd followed Quentin for several nights previously and had a pretty good idea where he was going; the sequence of stops might vary, but the ultimate destination remained the same.

Like an iron filing drawn by a magnet, the Cadillac traced a course away from the blocks of federal office buildings and well-lit monuments, arrowing toward the raunchier side of town, a vice district in all but name.

Of course, that was all a matter of perspective, Steve sourly reflected; to the taxpayer, the whole governmental apparatus could be considered a vice district, the difference being that unlike the politicians, the screwing the hookers gave you was a lot more straightforward and honest.

The shadow man who was tailing Quentin injected a new variable into the equation, one that Steve didn't like so well. He'd already gotten a feel for Quentin's habits and rhythms, and had pretty well worked out how and when he was going to carry out the sanction. The newcomer was a complicating factor, and that never boded well for an operation. For one thing, it indicated that a third party was involved.

Steve was operating solo on this assignment, but he was part of a larger apparatus; the same could be true of the stranger.

Durwood Quentin III was a person of interest to any number of outside interests, official and otherwise. He had a blueblood pedigree. His people were Old Money; he'd attended the right prep schools, graduated from an Ivy League college and postgrad business school, and been slotted into a fast-track position in a prestigious Wall Street brokerage house. He'd married a former debutante, the heiress to a considerable fortune herself, and fathered a couple of kids on her. He belonged to the right clubs, played a good game of tennis and a fair game of golf.

He'd had all the advantages, but inevitably, his true nature had asserted itself and brought him to his present delicate condition. He was a plunger and long-shot bettor with other people's money, namely his clients' financial accounts. He had the temperment of a degenerate gambler, always doubling up and redoubling on ever riskier speculations, finally descending to outright fraud and chicanery.

He'd posted spectacular profits at first, at least on paper, but came a day when he couldn't make a margin call, and the entire towering pyramid of options and hedges and credit-default certificates and junk bonds had all come tumbling down like a house of cards.

His family were big-money contributors to the current administration in the White House; their clout had kept him from being prosecuted by the Securities and Exchange Commission for stock fraud. By then, his marriage was already long defunct; his compulsive womanizing had seen to that.

The Quentin name and family conections still counted for something, Durwood using them to land himself a post as CEO of Brinker Defense Systems, a Washington-based defense contractor. There was no such person named Brinker associated with the company, as it turned out; the name was an inside joke cooked up by its founders, alluding to the fact that they skated on the brink of solvency and legality.

Quentin made a perfect front man, exploiting his contacts with a clique of civilian political appointees in the Pentagon's procurement department to land Brinker some nice fat contracts. Brinker's products proved to be of the same quality as the bad paper Quentin had been pushing at the brokerage house: defective, when not actually nonexistent.

The sweet ride had hit a speed bump when Brinker landed a deal to supply weapons to Iraqi and Afghani police forces that were being trained and equipped by the U.S. Army. The company couldn't just stiff the Army; they had to deliver something. Operating through some accommodating defense ministers in a tiny Balkan state who served as front men for the transaction, they bought a quantity of arms and ammunition from the People's Republic of

China. The matériel, surplus equipment left over from the Korean War, was transshipped to Afghanistan and Iraq. So haphazard and slipshod was the operation, that much of the delivery was still packaged in cases bearing the PRC's original labeling and Red Star insignia. The pistols and rifles were too rusty and antiquated to ever actually hit a target; that is, assuming that the cartridges could even be made to fire.

Brinker might have gotten away with it at that, considering that their high-level civilian friends and co-confederates in the Pentagon were equally minded to sweep the mess under the rug and make it go away.

They hadn't reckoned on the tenacity and single-minded devotion to duty of one Colonel Millard Sterling. Sterling was career Army and posted to the same procurement department in the Pentagon that had brokered the Brinker arms deal. He might have looked more like an accountant than a warrior, but in his way he was a strike trooper straight down the line.

The contract had been granted despite his opposition, thanks to the influence wielded by political appointees, and he was determined to expose the whole rotten mess. He couldn't be bluffed, bought, or scared. Pressure came down from above, giving him the time-honored bureaucratic screw job, relegating him to the Pentagon's version of Siberia and career limbo. Sterling stubbornly kept at it, building a file of relevant documents and affadavits, collecting a damning paper trail that led straight back to the malefactors. He kept going through channels, filing reports, bombarding the higher-ups with the naked facts. Worse, some officials were starting to take him seriously.

That's when Colonel Millard Sterling was found dead in the garage of his modest home in a Virginia suburb, his head virtually blown off by a blast from a shotgun clutched in his hands.

Suicide, his detractors said. It proved he'd been delusional from the start, causing him to construct a paranoid fantasy about alleged irregularities in the Brinker arms deal and, ultimately, take his own life. His grieving family swore he'd never owned a shotgun, but that was sloughed off as the understandable blindness of relatives unable to come to grips with the fact of their loved one's self-destruction.

The Brinker affair seemed to have died stillborn, only to be revived some months later when a long-term congressman and high-level member of the House Armed Services Committee involved with military procurement was arrested by the FBI in connection with an unrelated bribery investigation.

Under intensive grilling and with the threat of a lengthy prison term, the representative spilled his guts, unloading his inside account of a massive criminal conspiracy between defense contractors, legislators, and federal officials to defraud the United States government.

Among those implicated were members of the Brinker board of directors. The company went bust and some of its officers went to jail, but not Quentin Durwood III. Having learned his lessons since his brokerage house days, he'd been careful not to leave his tracks on the dirty dealings that had gone down during his tenure as Brinker's CEO. His accomplices who'd been nabbed pointed the finger at him, but the uncorroborated testimony of convicted felons was inadmissable as evidence.

He looked guilty, was guilty, but the government couldn't prove it in court, so he walked away from the Brinker scandal and collapse free and clear.

So far. Investigations were still continuing, and there was always the chance that prosecutors might unearth some new angle to nail him, though as yet they hadn't come up with anything particularly promising.

One item that had come up during the probing indicated that Quentin had been complicit and possibly instrumental in arranging through party or parties unknown the murder of Colonel Sterling. The information was based on hearsay evidence of a confidential informant, and was too thin and tenuous to justify the expenditure of time, money, and manpower, so it was never followed up.

One of the federal agents who was privy to this lead was an army veteran, a former military policeman who maintained contact with former colleagues who were still on active duty, including a high-ranking officer in the Counter-Intelligence Corps. The G-man passed the information along to his buddy.

In due course, it came to the attention of an army special investigating unit whose specialty lay in investigating such matters. Due to national security concerns, its name was unknown to all but a few. Suffice it to say that the SIU had considerable resources behind it, including sophisticated electronic eavesdropping and communications interception capabilities.

They started digging, unhindered by an excess of red tape or concern for the legal niceties. The lead was authenticated and verified. Durwood Quentin III had indeed contracted for Colonel Sterling's death. This was proved to a moral certainty.

Due to issues of due process, jurisdiction, and some of the extralegal means used to acquire said proof, irrefutable though it was, it could never be admitted into a court of law. Quentin was guilty of an army officer's murder and legally untouchable.

Which is where Steve Ireland came in.

Few if any nations will openly admit to using assassination as an instrument of policy. Most if not all of them use it; they just don't care to admit it, because to do so lifts the curtain a little too much on how the world really works.

The United States government has publicly proclaimed a prohibition against state-sanctioned assassination of foreign political leaders. Since the terror attacks of 9/11, that position has become somewhat equivocal in theory; in practice, no official in any governmental agency or clandestine service wants to sign their name to documents initiating such a project. That doesn't mean that the deed isn't done; it just means that nobody wants to leave a paper trail signing off on it.

The military's job is to make war. That capability is the core of deterrence and national security. The individual service member must, if necessary, be ready, willing, and able to kill the enemy. Whether that function is carried out in bloody hand-to-hand combat or by the push of a button to launch a missile, is unimportant. What matters is the intent.

Assassination is warfare by other means. That is why the Dog Team was born.

In the shadowy half-world of clandestine ("black") operations, the Dog Team is one of the blackest of all black ops. Knowledge of its existence is classified Above Top Secret and restricted to a select few. Theirs is an awesome responsibility, one not given or taken lightly.

The Dog Team is the U.S. Army's assassination arm, its killer elite. Its members are authorized to "neutralize," that is, kill, persons whose elimination is deemed vital to the national security. This includes enemies both foreign and domestic.

Terrorists, spies, and traitors are not the only foes. Sometimes, the threat comes in strange and unfamiliar guises. Many and oddly assorted are those who seek to make covert war on the republic. Sinister political cabals, corporate cartels, and organized criminal elements conspire, singly or in combination, in a ceaseless effort to suborn the Constitution and seize supreme power by any means necessary.

They may be beyond the reach of the law—but not of the Dog Team.

Brinker Defense Systems had cheated the Pentagon out of many millions of dollars. This in itself was not unusual. The multibillion-dollar defense budget has long been viewed by many unscrupulous plotters as a cash cow to be milked by hook or crook. That's a given, just part of the way the system works. If every public- and private-sector chiseler who defrauded the U.S. taxpayer was marked for liquidation, the slaughter would be prodigious.

By setting in motion the murder of Colonel Millard Sterling, an honorable officer who was doing his duty, Brinker prexy Durwood Quentin III had crossed a threshold and entered the Dog Team's gunsights.

Team member Steve Ireland had drawn the sanction. Now somebody else was trying to horn in on the game.

Who?

Less than an hour earlier, Quentin's Cadillac had rolled into The Booby Hatch's parking lot. The Crown Victoria that had been following it continued southbound to the next intersection and turned left into a side street.

A few cars behind, Steve Ireland's sedan cruised through the cross street and kept on going. Glancing left, he saw the Crown Vic's red taillights come winking on as it braked to a halt in the middle of the side street. In his rearview mirror, he saw the vehicle make an illegal K-turn back onto the main drag, so that it was pointing northbound toward the club.

At the next light, Steve turned right, then right again, putting him northbound on a street running parallel to the one where the club was located. He followed it for a couple of blocks, made another right, then another, emerging southbound on the boulevard a long block above The Booby Hatch.

Pulling in at the curb a couple of car lengths past the corner, he parked the car and killed the lights. Rolled up the windows and switched off the engine.

The overhead dome light was switched off so that it wouldn't light up when the car doors were opened. Steve got out of the car and locked it. It was on the opposite side of the street from the club, a good hard stone's throw away. The neighborhood was pretty crummy, but there wasn't much danger of the car being broken into or stolen, not on The Booby Hatch's Mob-protected turf.

Reaching under the left side of his utility vest, he surreptitiously adjusted the flat pistol tucked butt-out in the top of his pants against his hip so that it sat the way he liked it. On a hot night like this when everybody was wearing light-weight summer clothes, wedging the gun in his waistband was less conspicuous than wearing a shoulder rig or clip-on belt holster.

He made sure his T-shirt covered the rod. It would slow his draw, but life is trade-offs. The flap of the utility vest reached down below below his hip and added to the concealment.

He strolled along the sidewalk, toward the club. The economy might be in the toilet, but you'd never know it by the mass of parked cars crowding The Booby Hatch's lot. The witching hour was near, tomorrow was a work day, but the joint was jumping. It just goes to show people find the money for what they really want, Steve thought.

The building throbbed with the muffled beat of electronically amplified, bass-heavy dance music that thudded like war drums in the night. Loud as it was, it couldn't drown out the buzzing and crackling of the neon sign that spelled out the club's name over the entrance. The lurid red glare splashed the front and sidewalk like the blaze of a burning building.

Knots of men milled around, both blue-collar working stiffs and suit-and-tie office drones. From the noise they were making and the seething restlessness of their movements, it was obvious that more than a few of them had a load on.

Steve kept on walking. Further down the block, he spotted the Crown Vic parked on the same side of the street as the club. It was empty.

Two attributes his trade demanded were sharp eyes and good night vision. He spotted a man standing on the corner of the side street where the Crown Vic had made a K-turn. The man stood in a patch of gloom, but the street lamps were so bright that there wasn't much shadow to be found.

A big guy, with short dark hair and a mustache. The guy from the Crown Vic. He was talking to a woman. Steve couldn't make out too much detail, but from what he could see of her figure and how much skin she was showing, it was a sure bet that she wasn't a recruiter from the local mission making a midnight run to save souls. Their heads were close together, but their body language said that they weren't a couple, at least not in the usual sense of the term.

Steve checked for traffic, turned, stepped down off the curb, and crossed the street, angling back toward the club. It was easy to melt into the swarm of drunks and loudmouths clustered on the sidewalk and in the parking lot. The neon sign buzzed, the red glare seethed and flickered, the electro-beat was a physical thing that vibrated through the pavement.

Nobody paid any attention to Steve. Covering behind an SUV, he looked for the couple on the corner.

They must have come to a parting of the ways, because the woman was walking along the sidewalk toward the club, while the man hung back on the corner, idling in place. She moved like she felt right at home, striding boldly, confidently, breasts bobbing, hips swaying, long legs flashing. As she neared, Steve got a better look at her. She was the kind of woman used to being looked at, and worked hard at it.

She had long hair and wore a dark, low-cut sleeveless top, a skirt whose hem barely reached the top of her thighs, and knee-high shiny white high-heeled boots. As she closed in on the club, the click-clacking of her high heels against the pavement beat out a percussive rhythm that made itself heard over the clamor of the dance music, the buzzing sound, and the hangers-on crowding around in front of the building.

The loiterers started buzzing louder than the sign as they became aware of her presence. Heads swiveled around so fast to take a look at her that some of their owners risked whiplash. Eyes bulged or narrowed, depending on their owners. Gawkers nudged their buddies to get an eyeful of the newcomer.

She was an eyeful, all right. In her high-heeled boots, she stood about five-nine. Her red-hair was cut in bangs across her forehead and hung down at the sides to mid-chest level. Her hair was cherry red, and from its uniform straightness and the glossy artificiality of it, it looked like a wig.

Her skin was bone-white, her features bold. Wide dark eyes were ringed with enough mascara to give them a raccoon aspect; a bold, red-lipped mouth turned up at the corners, though not necessarily in a smile. She was broad-shouldered, narrow-waisted, wide-hipped, and long-legged. Her breasts were strictly from implants, and the cosmetic surgeon hadn't stinted on the silicone on the day they were installed.

Catcalls and whistles, hoots and hollers vented among the loiterers as she moved among their midst. A car was pulling out of the parking lot, causing her to pause to let it pass. Steve used the opportunity to take a couple of pictures of her with his cell phone camera for future reference. The street was almost as well lit up as the crowd, allowing the camera to catch a pretty sharp image.

The car braked to a halt, blocking the sidewalk. The driver's-side window rolled down and the driver, a curly-haired fat-faced guy, stuck out his head. He must have known her, because he called familiarly to her. "Ginger! Hey, Ginger, it's me, Sal! C'mere, doll!"

Ignoring him, Ginger walked around the back of the car, making her way toward the club's front entrance. Sal rolled down the passenger-side window and leaned across the front seat, continuing to call to her. "C'mon, let's go for a ride! Ginger!!"

Wriggling eel-like through the knots of males, not looking back, she kept on her hip-swaying way. With practiced ease, she avoided the clutching hands of guys trying to cop a feel.

"Ginger, Ginger!"

Another car was trying to get out of the lot, but Sal's car was blocking the exit. The driver of the second car leaned on the horn hard. Sal gave him the finger and shouted what the other could do to himself. The second car had four guys inside; a couple of them opened the doors and started to get out. Sal saw them coming. His car lurched forward into the street, just as suddenly slamming to a halt to avoid plowing into an oncoming car.

The new car held down its blaring horn for a long time as it sailed northward on the boulevard. Sal punched the gas, tires squealing as he turned left, crossing the centerline of the road and bulleting southbound.

His taillights were vanishing red dots by the time the guys in the second car climbed back inside, laughing and crowing that they'd sure showed him.

The press of male bodies grew thicker as Ginger neared the club's front door. A wise guy grabbed her right breast and squeezed it clown-like, like he was honking a horn. She leaned into him and she must have worked a knee, because the joker went white-faced and open-mouthed as he crumpled up like a crushed beer can.

Ginger brushed past him and disappeared inside the club. The guy she'd kneed lay curled up on his side on the pavement, gasping for breath, clutching himself with both hands between his legs. His face had gone from white to green.

Those nearby, including the guy's buddies, thought that was funny as hell and stood around yukking it up. They didn't think it was so funny a moment later when a club bouncer came barreling out the front door, looking more than ready to do some bouncing.

He told the joker's buddies to get him the hell out of there. They hauled the disabled man to his feet, holding him up with their hands hooked under his arms. He was still using both hands to hold his privates. His pals half carried, half dragged him across the lot and loaded him into their parked car.

The beefy bouncer stood there with meaty fists on his hips, watching them as they drove away. He went back inside the club.

Steve had paid little attention to the distraction, focusing on the tail man, the Crown Vic driver still standing on the corner. Steve stood where he could watch the other without being seen by him. Five minutes passed before the other made a move, starting up the street toward the club. He made a beeline for the entrance. Steve got a good look at him.

The tail man was big, with a bodybuilder's physique, one that had been augmented by megadoses of steroids. He would have made the club bouncer look modest-sized by comparison. Fortyish, he wore his dark hair cropped close to the scalp, as close as a three-day beard. His blocky head seemed as wide as it was long. His brows were thick dark vertical lines; he had a thick black mustache of the type that Steve for some reason always associated with firefighters and cops.

The tail man didn't look like a firefighter, but he didn't seem the type for a shadow job either; he was too broad-beamed to be unobtrusive, to pass for just another face in the crowd. If a subject once caught a look at him, he wouldn't be forgotten. He was a big bastard. Appearances be damned, though; a tail man was just what he was. A tail man and what else?

He wore a dark sport jacket, tight T-shirt, and baggy slacks. He wore a gun in a shoulder rig, and from the size of the bulge it made under his left arm, it must have been some cannon.

At first impression, Steve would have tagged him for a cop, an undercover cop maybe. That would have jibed with the Crown Vic he was driving; the machine had a major-league mill with mucho muscle under the hood, and was favored by a lot of police departments around the country.

Steve checked out the man's shoes; shoes were a tipoff. Cops, even undercover ones, tend to pamper themselves with a certain kind of shoe: wide, thick-soled black oxfords that are comfortable for those who spent a lot of time on their feet. This guy, though, was wearing heavy-duty work boots with reinforced toes; they stuck out from beneath wide-legged pant cuffs. Footwear that was good for kicking down doors or giving a stomping.

Whoever he was, before he stepped through the club's front doors, a couple of head shots of him were snapped by Steve's cell phone camera.

Steve wasn't much for fancy gadgetry when he was on assignment; the fancier the gadget, the more that could go wrong with it. Should he be apprehended by the authorities, it wouldn't do to be found in possession of sophisticated hardware that could be sourced back to the military and compromise his cover.

Nowadays, everybody has a cell phone, and even the most basic models come with built-in cameras. Steve's cell had a few refinements that weren't exactly standard option, such as an encrypter-decrypter, scrambler, and several other security devices, including a fail-safe destruct mechanism that would activate if any unauthorized personnel tried to tamper with or investigate the unit, turning its hardware into a fused lump of slag that looked like the results of battery leakage.

The communication mode was now switched off; when Steve was on the hunt, there was no distracting taking or receiving of calls.

The tail man smelled of cop, but it didn't figure. Durwood Quentin III was in deep shit, but it was all on the federal level. No federal investigative agency, not the FBI or ATF or any of the others, tolerates heavy steroid use by its personnel, and this guy was seriously on the juice. That was obvious at a glance; even his muscles had muscles. Legitimate bodybuilding can do only so much and no more; you can be sure that anybody built like a comic book superhero got there with some chemical assistance.

The same generally went for state cops. A county or city cop could get away with it maybe. But why would they be interested in Quentin? The tail man's acquaintance with the likes of Ginger could indicate a vice squad operation. Or a criminal one, either Mob or independent. Or who knows what . . . ?

Whatever it was, Steve didn't like it, but for now he'd play a waiting game. He decided against going into The Booby Hatch for a look-see. He didn't think the tail man was on to him, and didn't want to risk tipping him off by nosing around too closely.

Steve hung around outside the club for another five minutes before slipping away. He crossed the street, taking a circuitous route to an alley he'd noticed earlier and filed away mentally as a good potential observation post.

Certain that he was unobserved, he eased into the passageway between two buildings, where a few paces swallowed him up in blackness. From the alley mouth, he could see the club, its parking lot, and down the street where the Crown Vic was parked. He stood around for a couple of minutes, letting his eyes grow accustomed to the lack of light before giving the alley a quick once-over. The passageway didn't run clear through the block of buildings to the next parallel street; it terminated in a kind of courtyard behind the backs of the two buildings fronting the street, and was used by both businesses as a parking lot. It was empty now of all but a white delivery van.

The back of the space was hemmed by an eight-foot-high chain-link fence; beyond lay a long gravel strip ten feet wide that bordered the backs of several one-and two-story commercial buildings separated by driveways and walkways that accessed the street parallel to this one.

That was good. No locals were going to be using the alley as a shortcut between the two streets. Steve settled in for stakeout.

About fifteen minutes later, the tail man emerged from inside the club. The crowd of loiterers was thinning, though the lot was still about two thirds full of parked cars. He stood off to one side by himself, smoking a cigarette.

Ten minutes later, Quentin came out through the front doors, hanging all over Ginger, an arm draped across her shoulders. Loose-jointed, disheveled, his red flushed face plastered with a sloppy grin, he seemed to be feeling no pain.

The tail man was in Quentin's field of vision, or would have been if Quentin hadn't been busy trying to look down the front of Ginger's top. He didn't have to look hard to see much; that plunging V-neckline put plenty on display.

Ginger and the tail man made eye contact for an instant, no mutual flash of recognition passing between the two. Quentin steered Ginger into the parking lot, making for his car.

The tail man turned, walking south, moving briskly but not running. When he was about halfway to the Crown Vic, Steve Ireland stepped out of the alley and headed north, quick-time, toward where his car was parked facing south.

He entered by the passenger-side front door, climbing over the transmission hump and into the driver's seat. He fired up the engine, its muffled but powerful rumblings sending a shudder through the car, a shudder that died down to a shiver. He rolled down the front windows to let in some air and get a feel of the night, but kept the headlights dark.

Not far from the street's southeast corner, a pair of headlights flashed on: the Crown Vic's.

A couple of minutes later, Quentin's Cadillac rolled out of the parking lot, its right rear wheel going over the curb, thumping the undercarriage against the asphalt road surface. The machine moved northbound, picking up speed. It passed Steve; inside, he could see the outlines of two silhouette heads, Quentin's and Ginger's.

The Crown Vic pulled away from the curb and into the lane, following. When it passed, its driver's head was facing front toward the road ahead, not so much as glancing in Steve's direction.

Steve looked left, right, left again, not seeing anything that looked like a police car, at least not a marked one. A couple of cars, one of them an SUV, came rushing along northbound. When they flashed past Steve's sedan, he gunned the engine, whipping the steering wheel around hard left.

The sedan made a screeching U-turn across the white line and headed north. Getting into the lane behind the SUV, using its bulk to cover him from being seen in the Crown Vic's rear-view mirror, he switched on his headlights.

Traffic lights were green for a long way along the straightaway. Rows of street lamps lit the thoroughfare like a stage set. Jockeying past the SUV, Steve pushed the sedan along at a quick clip until he caught sight of the Crown Vic. It was sticking pretty close to the Cadillac, which was about a half-dozen car lengths ahead.

Steve switched lanes, slowing to allow the SUV to pass him on the left. The SUV's driver must have taken being passed earlier as some kind of personal affront, because he punched the accelerator to zoom past the sedan. Moving up fast, it caused the Crown Vic to glide right into the next lane to allow it to pass.

Good; that would momentarily distract the tail man from the vehicles behind him. Thanks, Speedy, Steve thought, grinning without mirth. The SUV bulleted onward, crossing lanes to pass the Cadillac on the right, then flashing ahead, its taillights rapidly dwindling out of sight.

Steve nestled in with a knot of three or four vehicles, using them for cover while keeping the Crown Vic and Cadillac steadily in sight.

A quarter mile further on, red and blue flashing lights came into view, slowing traffic on both sides of the roadway. The SUV was pulled over at the side of the road, a police car standing behind it. A uniformed cop stood beside the driver's side of the SUV.

Steve grinned again, this time meaning it. Tight grin. An instant's passing amusement, and then he was once more all business. He, the tail man, and Quentin and Ginger all vectored north toward a final destination unknown, imminent, and inexorable. And for some, perhaps all—terminal.

THREE

Not more than ten minutes drive north of The Booby Hatch, Quentin's Cadillac quit the avenue, turning right on to a street running east-west. It was far enough removed from the main flow that the traffic lights at the intersections flashed only amber caution lights.

Steve Ireland had to lay back even more to avoid tipping the tail man in the Crown Vic that he was being tailed. Out on the avenue he'd just left, there was a lot of traffic to provide cover; here, not so much.

That was a funny thing about roaming late at night in the city. Especially in a city like Washington, D.C., basically a company town whose main industry was government. At quitting time, the office buildings emptied out, their occupants making a mass exodus to their homes outside the city. Of course, there were plenty of eager beavers to be found toiling, putting in extra hours, but usually by ten P.M., even the diehards had packed it up and called it a night.

One might assume that after midnight the streets, except for the main thoroughfares, would be more or less deserted, but that wasn't the case. There was always a lively hum of activity from folks abroad in the wee hours—not just the obvious ones like party people, police, firefighters, EMTs, hospital caregivers, night shift workers in general, and road crews doing repairs that would have tied up traffic during the daylight hours. There were plenty of citizens to be found out and about, going to or coming from whatever mysterious assignations and rendezvous had called them out when most folks were at home tucked safely in their beds.

It was a phenomenon that had served Steve well in the past, not only in Washington, but other cities as well. It was good to have other fish swimming around in the pool to provide the cover of relative anonymity.

Now, out here off the main drag, his caution would have to be doubled. This was a quieter part of town, the quiet of abandonment and neglect. One thing he had working for him was the stink-o state of the economy. Like everybody else, the city was hurting for money. That meant fewer police cars to be deployed, with more of them being assigned to the obvious trouble spots and fewer for routine patrol along the routes less traveled.

This street was quiet but not dead; a scattering of vehicles traversed it in both directions. Steve hung back a good distance from the Crown Vic, so far back that sometimes he couldn't get as good a look at the Cadillac as he'd like. That was okay. The tail man would keep it in sight, and he'd do the same for the Crown Vic.

He still couldn't figure where the tail man came into this. The guy wasn't federal, that was for sure. He could have been an undercover cop or a crook; going strictly on appearances, it was sometimes hard to tell the two apart. The Crown Victoria was a car model in use by a lot of police departments, both as marked and unmarked vehicles; on the other hand, its automotive muscle recommended it as a good getaway car, too . . .

As he went eastbound, the north side of Claghorn Park came into sight on the right. The left side of the street was fronted by several blocks of long-abandoned brick factory buildings. The city didn't want to spend the money to tear them down, so they'd been boarded up, padlocked, and forgotten. Somehow, they'd survived the best efforts of the local vandals and arsonists.

Named after a skirt-chasing, bourbon-swilling Southern senator of yore, the park was a lopsized oval the size of several football fields lumped together; its long axis ran north-south. Its west side was parallel to the avenue where the strip club was located. On the east, it was bordered by a narrow street that ran alongside a highway, beyond which lay the river.

It was quartered by two roads, one running through its long axis, the other crossing it at right angles at its midpoint; shortcuts for those not wanting to detour the long way around the park. Access and service roads also wormed through it, eating up more land.

The grounds featured a broad open flat dotted by several paved courts, some outbuildings, and a duck pond, all ringed and streaked by lumpy patches of scrub brush and skinny, sickly-looking trees. It was the kind of park that savvy parents warned their kids to steer clear of even in broad daylight.

The Cadillac slowed to a speed of a few miles an hour, causing the Crown Vic and Steve's car to do the same. The lead car poked along as if it was looking for something. Farther back, the Crown Vic pulled in to the curb, halting at the corner of a street that bordered the park's west side.

Steve kept rolling, passing the Crown Vic, not giving it so much as a sidelong glance. Continuing east, he passed the Cadillac. It stood facing the mouth of a gravel service road that ran through a park field into some brush.

About 150 feet ahead lay the public entrance to the park. Before reaching half that distance, Steve looked in his rearview mirror and saw the Cadillac enter the service road and head south along it.

Behind it, the Crown Vic was in motion, its headlights swinging right as it entered the street on the west side of the park.

Steve drove to the park entrance, the head of a two-lane road that cut the park in half lengthwise. A sign warned that the park proper was closed for use after ten P.M. That prohibition didn't hold for the road, which was a through route.

Steve turned into the park road, a straightaway

lit at intervals by lampposts whose globes looked like a string of shiny pearl onions. The road was empty of vehicles in both directions. Trees and brush banded the western rim of the park; through them, he saw occasional glints of light that might have been from Quentin's car making its way toward the south end of the park.

Acting on a hunch, Steve wheeled the sedan around in a U-turn, exiting the park and turning left, going back the way he came. Approaching the street bordering the west side of the park, he glimpsed red dot taillights off in the distance. The Crown Vic, he assumed. Hoped.

He turned left, into the street. Its east side bordered the park, its west side was lined with two- and three-family wooden houses separated by driveways. Most of the homes were dark save for lamps burning above the front doors and backyard garages. The curb was lined with parked cars.

Steve couldn't see the Crown Vic's taillights, but to be on the safe side, he switched off his headlights and cruised south down the street, creeping along at a snail's pace. Street lamps provided enough light to see by. No other moving vehicles were in view, no pedestrians, not even a stray dog walker or drunk.

The trees edging the park formed one wall; the houses lining the opposite side of the street formed another. He could smell foliage and earth smells. The street was several hundred yards long; nearing the midpoint, he saw the mouth of a road on his left.

Steve paused at the entrance, looking in: a

two-lane road that crossed the park east-west. It was bordered on both sides by a knee-high metal-strip guard rail, and lit at intervals by those pearl onion-globed street lamps. About a hundred feet in, the roadway rose up, cresting a low humped hill whose top was twenty-five feet above the fields that made up most of the park.

On the flat, a gravel service road emerged from a clump of trees, meeting the hillside at right angles. A tunnel underpass ran through the hill, allowing the service road to go through it and continue its course on the opposite side. The paved road ran over the top of the underpass.

The Crown Vic stood idling in a narrow shoulder of the eastbound lane at the bottom of the near side of the slope, its emergency flashers blinking.

Street lamps nicely lit the scene. The driver got out, walked around the back of the car, and stepped over the guard rail on the south side of the road, onto the grassy field. He rounded the base of the hill and vanished from sight.

Steve put his car into park, got out, and crossed to the roadway mouth, standing behind the cover of a clump of bushes. It was very quiet. He could hear the whoosh of unseen vehicles driving somewhere in the distance.

After a pause, a couple of pops sounded from the direction of the underpass. They sounded like firecrackers going off. They were accompanied by several flashes that looked like flashbulbs going off.

A minute passed, two. A figure came into view, rounding the base of the hill: the Crown

Vic's driver. Not running, not even jogging, he walked briskly to the guard rail, stepped over it, and got in his car. The emergency flashers were switched off. The car drove up the slope, went down the other side, and continued at a moderate pace eastward across the park.

Steve hopped back in his car and drove deeper into the park, not bothering to put on his lights. Zooming to the foot of the hill, he skidded to a stop on the shoulder, threw the car into park, and hopped out, hurdling the guard rail and scrambling around the hillside.

The service road had been built for the use of maintenance vehicles doing their park cleanup chores. The underpass was designed for their convenience. Its rounded archway and shaft were large enough to accommodate the passage of a two-and-a-half-ton truck.

Only, it wasn't a truck that stood in the tunnel, it was a Cadillac. Its headlights were dark, its motor was off. The driver's side door was ajar, causing the dome light to glow.

Durwood Quentin III and Ginger were tumbled in the backseat, dead. She'd been shot twice in the left breast, both heart shots, either one of which would have been fatal. Quentin's pants and underpants were pulled down around his knees. A bullet hole punctured the center of his forehead. Clutched in his hand was a small-caliber pistol, all shiny and with mother-of-pearl handles. A .32 probably.

In a glance, Steve could see how it was supposed to read: Quentin hooks up with a hooker. Instead of giving up the booty, she tries to rob him. The pistol was the kind of piece a street hustler might pack. They struggle; during the fight, he shoots her dead. Overcome with shock and remorse, he kills himself.

Except that guys who commit suicide by gun usually don't shoot themselves in the middle of the forehead. But the cops wouldn't let a little detail like that stop them from closing the case.

Steve didn't just stand there scratching his head, puzzling it out. As soon as he saw that Quentin and Ginger were both dead, he was in motion, making himself scarce from the scene.

Outside the tunnel, he saw the lights of the Crown Vic, nearing the far side of the park. Running back to his car, he threw it into gear, switched on the lights, and drove off, taking off after the Crown Vic.

He didn't peel out of there like a bat out of hell. He wasn't a damned fool. That was all he needed, to look like he was fleeing the scene of a crime and attract the attention of some passing police car. That would be all he needed, to get tagged for a double kill he was innocent of!

He drove at a brisk pace, ten miles or so above the limit, but not like some frantic getaway car. The Crown Vic was behaving in the same fashion, proceeding at a moderate clip as he exited the east end of the park. He turned right, southbound.

Not seeing any other cars in the park, Steve took a chance and punched some more speed out of the sedan, zooming it up to sixty to cut the distance, slowing as he neared the east exit.

It opened on to a street that met it at right

angles. He was in luck. The street ran parallel to a highway that was elevated about twenty feet above ground level, supported on sets of stone pillars. Between the pillars could be seen the river, all tarry black smeared and spangled with rainbows of reflected light. The pillars were fenced in by a waist-high concrete median, an impassable barrier. Opposite it, on the other side of the street, was the park. The street was a trough hemmed in at both sides. Vehicles could progress only two ways on it, north or south.

The Crown Vic had turned south out of the park. Steve went the same way. About fifty yards ahead in his lane was a set of taillights. One set of taillights looks pretty much the same as another, but Steve reckoned that it was the Crown Vic. There was no other place for it to turn off.

Steve took off after it, hoping it was his quarry. He had to tread a fine line between going fast enough to overhaul it, yet not so fast that he'd alert the driver to his presence. If it was the Crown Vic, that is. He also had to watch out for police cars looking for speeders.

The vehicle ahead reached the end of the park, where the first cross street opened on the right. The traffic light blinked amber at the intersection. The vehicle slowed at the cross street, but kept on going southbound.

Steve got a good look at it. It was the Crown Vic, all right. He let out the breath he'd been unaware he'd been holding.

He slowed going through a traffic square, letting some space open between him and the Crown Vic. The other, in no particular hurry,

traveled a few miles below the legal speed limit.
Steve did the same. He was still in the game.
But what game was it?

The Crown Vic's driver was no mere tail man;
he was a killer. A double killer, since he'd killed
Ginger along with Quentin.

In hindsight now, Steve could see how his opposite number had worked the play. This was
no cowboy job; it was a carefully planned setup.
The killer knew about Quentin, knew that he
was a compulsive horndog with a risky kink for
down-and-dirty street hustlers, knew that The
Booby Hatch was one of his regular spots.

Steve had been dogging Quentin for the last
two nights, picking up the target's pattern to
work out his best angle of approach. He'd seen
no sign of the man in the Crown Vic on either
night, and no other suspicious persons either. If
they'd have been there, he'd have known it. He
had the hunter's instinct for such things. He'd
been out of action for over six months and had
only recently resumed field operations, but he
wasn't that rusty. The medics had certified him
as fit for duty and dammit, he knew he was fit.

Which meant that some other interested
party had also been planning to X out Quentin.
Who? Some fellow accomplices, afraid that he'd
put the finger on them? Or maybe some other
government agency had its own reasons for
wanting Quentin out of the way?

Whoever it was played rough. Ginger was the
bait, the decoy. The killer must have had her
lined up in advance. In his mind's eye, Steve
visualized how it all went down:

The killer meets with Ginger outside The Booby Hatch to finalize arrangements—she having no idea of just how final those arrangements are going to be. Most likely, he sold it to her as a simple blackmail operation. Lure some rich jerk into a compromising situation and put the squeeze on him for hush money.

The killer's careful not to be seen with her at the club. She's not the type to be easily forgotten, and any guy escorting her would have been noticed by envious gawkers. She goes in first, he following later. Somehow, he puts the finger on Quentin, giving her the high sign that here's the mark. She moves in on Quentin, doing what comes naturally. Satisfied that contact has been made and the acquaintanceship is progressing, the killer exits, going back to his car.

Ginger leaves the club with Quentin; they get in his car and drive away, the killer following. Ginger steers Quentin to nearby Claghorn Park, probably by telling him she knows a nice private spot where they can trick without fear of interruption. Quentin, more than half drunk, doesn't need much persuasion; he's a novelty-seeker, so that aspect would appeal to him, too.

Of course the locale had been chosen by the killer, who'd made sure in advance that Ginger would know the site. Once he sees the Cadillac enter the park service road and disappear into the brush, he drives to the park's west side entrance. Ginger has Quentin pull into the tunnel underpass; they climb into the backseat and start getting it on.

She's waiting for her hidden partner to show

up; he'll flash a phony badge and play cop, or maybe he'll play the outraged husband or some similar version of the old badger game, throw a big scare into Quentin and shake him down for some big dough—

Only, the shakedown artist is really a killer and puts the blast on Quentin and Ginger both.

Some of the details were subject to change, but Steve figured that's pretty much how it was worked. The killer was an artist in his way, too; he'd framed it so that it'd look like an open-and-shut case to the police. A hooker's botched holdup, a struggle for the gun, she's shot, in a fit of remorse Quentin kills himself.

That closes the file. Neat, no loose ends.

Except that the killer was unaware that another killer was dogging Quentin and knew the real deal about how the scene had gone down.

After going south for a quarter mile, the Crown Vic changed lanes, entering a ramp that sloped up to the highway. Steve yielded long enough to let another car enter the ramp before him, then followed.

The highway was split by a median, leaving two southbound lanes and two northbound lanes. There was a fair amount of traffic in both directions; light to moderate, and zipping along.

No matter the lateness of the hour, there was always plenty of movement in the city. Once again, Steve was struck by how many people did their errands by night. It all worked in his favor, however, supplying him with plenty of cover while he kept on tailing the Crown Vic.

He was reminded of that corny old gag about the guy who had mixed feelings: His mother-in-law drove his new car off a cliff. Steve had mixed feelings, too. His mission was to neutralize Durwood Quentin III, but some stranger had beaten him to the punch. Now Quentin was dead, but Steve was left holding the loose ends.

The higher-ups in the Dog Team disliked loose ends. Quentin had been duly marked for demolition and then suddenly, from out of nowhere, some unknown third party horns in and does the job. The higher-ups would want to know more about this unknown.

Dog Team members are granted a good deal of freedom of movement when out in the field. The peculiar nature of their service and assignments demands it. The higher-ups tend to view with disfavor operatives who have to continually check back with headquarters for instructions. Initiative is prized. Steve Ireland was determined to find out all he could about the Crown Vic killer.

Traffic was moving along at a nice, brisk clip of about fifty-five miles per hour. The breeze from the open window felt good; Steve hadn't realized how much he'd been sweating. It was a muggy night.

The highway stretched southward into a funky part of town, a slum district. The ribbon of road was elevated so travelers could zip along their way, above the hazardous inner city.

The Crown Vic, several car lengths ahead,

signalled a right turn, making for the Tyburn Street exit. Thanks, chum, very considerate of you, Steve said to himself. The Crown Vic killer was a cautious driver, obedient to the rules of the road. Of course if he was really cautious, he'd have stayed the hell away from Tyburn Street; that was a rough neighborhood night or day. Plenty of drug dealing, prostitution, and gang activity.

Steve would have liked to have had another car between him and the Crown Vic, but nobody else seemed minded to take that exit. Slowing, he hung back until the other had dropped out of sight on the exit ramp before sliding into the approach lane.

Headlights flashed in his rearview mirror as another vehicle swung in behind him toward the exit. Typical, Steve thought, a cynical twist on his tight-lipped mouth; if the guy behind him had been in front of him, he could have used him for cover to tail the Crown Vic.

Steve eased into the exit ramp, slowing as he started the descent toward street level.

Harsh, blazing glare filled the sedan's interior. The car behind him had its high beams on. Only it wasn't a car at all, it was some kind of truck. A tow truck, looked like—

Down below at the bottom of the ramp, the Crown Vic was halted, standing diagonally so that it blocked access to the street. The driver got out of the car and started shooting at Steve. A bullet starred the windshield on the passenger side, frosting the glass as it tore through the car, burying itself somewhere in a right rear support for the roof.

A tremendous impact struck the car as the tow truck butted it from behind. Glass shattered, metal crumpled.

Steve had his seat belt on, but even so, he received a hell of a jolt, a real bone-jarring thud. For an instant, he saw the world in triple images before his eyesight came back into focus.

Another slug from the gun wielded by the Crown Vic's driver tagged the sedan's windshield, disintegrating it. A hail of crystal cubes of safety glass pelted Steve, as if a couple of shovelfuls of rock salt had been flung into the front seat.

He was bent forward, almost doubled over from the force of the rear-end collision, so most of the glass hit the back of his neck, shoulders, and upper back, stabbing them with dozens of needles of stinging pain.

His car was moving now, sliding forward as the tow truck pushed it, shoving it with its massive oversized reinforced-steel front bumper. The tow truck driver must have been stomping the gas pedal because Steve could hear the engine whining higher and louder in a steady, rhythmic rise and fall.

More bullets tore through the sedan, this time coming from behind, from the tow truck.

The tow truck's front met the sedan's rear at an angle. Instead of pushing the car straight forward, it pushed it at an angle. Tortured metal yowled as the sedan's right front fender ground against the ramp's outer stone retaining wall. It caught in place, arresting its forward motion.

Steve hit the seat belt release. For an awful, heart-stopping instant, nothing happened, and he was seized by the fear that it had locked up; then there was a click and the belt came undone and he was shucking it open and off himself as he rose, springing up from his seat.

The Crown Vic killer had done him a favor by shooting out the windshield, because there was nothing in Steve's way to stop him as he scrambled over the top of the steering wheel and dashboard and through the big gaping slot where the windshield had been. Slithering like a snake across a hot rock, he lunged across the buckling car hood, dropping down on the driver's side of the pavement.

The rib of a vertical abutment stood out from the inner side of the ramp wall a few feet away. Steve rolled toward it. Oil and gas were leaking from the underside of his wounded car. A fusillade of bullets from the tow truck ripped harmlessly overhead.

More rounds came came his way from the Crown Vic's driver. Steve caught a glimpse of him standing with his gun hand braced against the car roof, muzzle flashes spearing from the tip of the weapon.

Bullets thunked into the driver's side of the sedan as the killer tried to get a bead on Steve. One tore out a palm-sized chunk of pavement near Steve's head, spraying his neck and shoulder with rock chips.

Then Steve reached the shelter of the abutment, crouching, getting his back against the square-edged side of the pillar. Taking him out of the Crown Vic driver's line of fire. He reached for his hip, and the gun was out of his waistband and in his hand fast. He was facing the tow truck. It was white and painted on the front in big red letters was the legend BELTWAY TOWING.

It held a two-man crew, a driver and a shooter. The shooter was hanging out of the passenger side of the cab, way out, holding on with his left hand and wielding a big-caliber gun in his right. A skinny ferret face showed beneath a flat, narrow-brimmed forager's cap. He was angling for a shot at Steve, but the sedan was in his way. He kept leaning further and further out, trying to find the range.

The sedan worked both ways, blocking Steve from getting a clear shot at the gunman. He had a nice clean firing line on the driver, though. He squeezed off a couple of rounds, putting them in a tight group through the windshield and into the silhouetted outline of the figure hunched above the top of the steering wheel.

The driver slumped forward. His foot must have come down hard on the gas pedal because the tow truck gave a sudden lurch forward into the side of the sedan. The frame snapped and the car folded into a V-shape, arresting the tow truck's forward motion so that it jerked to a halt, stalling out.

The shooter lost his grip and, with a cry, fell out of the cab to the pavement. He fell hard, dropping his gun. It skittered across the asphalt, sliding under the sedan. He crouched on hands and knees beside the tow truck. Steve could see him beneath the vehicle's undercarriage; at least, his hands and arms, and his folded legs.

Steve shot him in the leg. The shooter flopped facedown, writhing on the pavement. Steve put another shot into his side, under his arm. He stopped thrashing and lay still. His forager's cap was still jammed tight on his head.

Smoke rose from the crumpled sedan; unseen flames crackled. Steve turned his attention to the Crown Vic's driver and threw some slugs his way. The guy jumped behind the wheel and sped off.

Steve fired a few more rounds at the vehicle's rear, but scored no hits. The Crown Vic rounded a corner, out of sight.

Steve now knew that there'd been a flaw in his calculations. Apparently, the killer had been aware that Steve was tailing him after all. No doubt he'd used his cell phone to contact his buddies in the tow truck to help prepare a surprise party for Steve. Turned out the surprise was on them, though.

Steve ejected the empty clip and slammed home a full one. On foot in this neighborhood, he'd need it.

He wanted to put some distance between himself and the sedan before the fire really got going. He reached the bottom of the ramp and was a half block away before the gas tank blew up.

FOUR

Doc Wenzle said, "What about that car you wrecked last night?"

Steve Ireland said, "What about it?"

"They don't exactly grow on trees, you know," Doc Wenzle said. "Any time I have to requisition a new one, I have to bust my butt. All that red tape kills the better part of a day."

Steve could well imagine. It was a big deal to procure any piece of Army equipment from the appropriate provider, even something as basic as a replacement fork for a mess kit. Documents had to be processed through channels; that was the Army way. The difficulties were multiplied a hundredfold when the Dog Team was involved. The Dog Team wasn't even supposed to exist. Officially, it didn't. To all but a relative handful of insiders within an ultra-restricted, near-phantom chain of command, there was no such animal.

The Team were attack dogs. Killer attack dogs. The fact of a supersecret, last-resort assassination capability of the U.S. Army was political dynamite. That that unit's bailiwick covered not only foreign but also domestic operations was even more explosive. Should incontrovertible proof of its existence ever fall into the hands of the media or the politicians, the results would be beyond cataclysmic, not only for the military but for national—global— security as well.

Of course, one of the benefits of having such an enforcement arm was the ability to plug leaks by any means necessary . . . speaking of last resorts.

The Army wasn't the only branch of the U.S. military in possession of such a capability. Steve Ireland knew for a fact, from bumping into their operatives once or twice in various hot spots and war zones around the planet, that the Navy maintained a similar, shadowy counterpart of the Dog Team.

Other government agencies also ran their own hit squads. The CIA, for one. Steve had the idea that if, say, the FBI or NSA needed to have the button pushed on somebody, they wouldn't have to look too far or too hard to find somebody else to do the job. Because that's the way the world is built.

Like other organizations requiring a degree of clandestinity to operate properly, the Army had a secret, annual "black" budget to draw on to finance said operations. Information about the size and scope of the black budget was Above Top Secret, to prevent the politicians and bureaucrats from sticking their long noses into it. A piece of the black budget, a small piece really, a fractional percentage of it, paid for the Dog Team and its ops.

An elaborate and elusive in-house infrastructure of subdivisions of departments, shadow bureaus, third-party cutouts, adjunct offices, and a host of similar bureaucratic shell games and dodges was in place to fund and supply the Dog Team, a unit that, again, had no official existence.

That was the beauty part of the Army, a bureaucratic organism so big, complex, intricate, and far-reaching that it provided any number of nooks and crannies to hide things in. Steve often wondered what other mind-staggering secret projects and divisions were concealed within its leviathan bulk.

He realized that his mind had been wandering while Doc Wenzle continued to grouse about the laborious paper-shuffling chores Steve's caper last night with the Crown Vic killer and company would entail.

When Wenzle paused in his complaint to take a breath, Steve said, "Don't blame me, blame Beltway Towing. They're the ones who wrecked the car."

"We checked on that," Doc Wenzle said, switching gears. "Beltway Towing is a legitimate outfit. They've got a contract with the city to haul away stalled cars, illegally parked cars, vehicles with too many unpaid traffic tickets—"

"And you call that 'legitimate'?" Steve said, scoffing.

"They reported a stolen tow truck last night,"

Wenzle went on, ignoring Steve's remark. "It was boosted out of one of their garage lots. The police dispatch record shows that the call came in not long before you had your little run-in with the wrecker. The company looks clean, as far as that goes. No tie-in with your playmates that we can find."

Steve shrugged, then winced. He was a mass of aches and pains from the roughing up he'd gotten last night when the tow truck had played bumper cars with his sedan. Nothing was broken or sprained—he'd been checked out by a medic earlier today—but he was bruised and tenderized from head to toe.

The back of his neck, his shoulders, and upper back were scored with so many minor cuts and abrasions from being showered with a spray of broken glass when the windshield was shot out, that they looked like somebody been using them for a tic-tac-toe board.

It was early afternoon of the day following his night with the Crown Vic killer. Steve was in the inner office of a modest-sized suite on the fifth floor of the Gall Building, an office building in a commercial business section in Washington, D.C. A brass nameplate on the outside of the door accessing the hall corridor identified the office suite as the locale for "Holloman Research Associates."

The suite consisted of a small waiting room and beyond that, a larger inner office with a storeroom and a bathroom branching off it. The waiting room featured two singularly uninviting straight-backed, armless wooden chairs, a coatrack tree, and a potted plant. The plant was artificial, but it still looked droopy and wilted. There was no reception area and no receptionist.

The inner office was where Wenzle held court. Opposite the door, a window with a southern exposure was set in the wall from a point waist-height to the ceiling. A desk the size of a compact car was parked in front of the window. Behind the desk sat Doc Wenzle, his back to the window.

The desktop sprouted a keyboard and several flat-screen monitors. Piled high on it were several stacks of files and documents. A side table held a printer and two computers. The hardware was all linked and interconnected with a web of cables.

An oversized brown leather couch stood against one of the side walls. An armchair stood facing the desk at an angle. Steve Ireland sat in it, perched on the edge of the seat. He looked fidgety because the seat cushion had a broken spring in the middle of it and it was damned near impossible to get comfortable on.

The office was a Dog Team front. Secrecy, insulation, and compartmentalization, that was the Dog Team way.

For example, Steve Ireland had been in the Pentagon any number of times on various service-related tasks, but never once on Dog Team business. As far as he knew, the outfit had no connections inside that building, not an office or a desk or even a scrambler phone in a broom closet. As far as he knew—which didn't go very far. The Team could be run out of the Secretary of the Army's office and he wouldn't have an inkling of it. Hell, maybe it was. But that was a matter way above his pay grade. Besides, the higher-ups, whoever they might be, reportedly took a dim view indeed of overinquisitive Team members. And that could be hazardous to your career. Not to mention your health.

Even working through cutouts and assumed identities, the outfit tried to minimize direct contact with military bases on U.S. soil. Overseas, especially in hot spots and hostile environments, the restrictions were a bit more flexible, but still tight.

Here in the Capital, the Gall Building was just one of hundreds of civilian, commercial office buildings. Its anonymity suited Team purposes. Holloman Research Associates was more than a front; it was a real business. It was legally incorporated, registered with the appropriate financial regulatory agencies, and duly paid all federal, state, and city taxes.

It published a monthly newsletter, "J.D. Holloman's Information Alert Bulletin," an investor's tip sheet specializing in precious metals and currency trades. It had several hundred paying subscribers.

There was no J.D. Hollomon, or rather, Doc Wenzle was J.D. Hollomon, at least as far as purported authorship of the newsletter went. Most of the computers and filing cabinets were used for collecting, collating, and analyzing data about the worldwide precious metals and currency trading business.

Wenzle had a feel for the market, and managed to crank out fairly creditable forecasts, thanks in no small part to information supplied by Army Intelligence sources and specialists.

It was a front that was nearly impossible to crack because it was for real. But it was still just a front for Dog Team business.

Here in Washington, Wenzle was Steve Ireland's handler, his case officer. Steve assumed that Wenzle had a stable of other Team members that he also ran; in any case, Steve kept his assumptions to himself.

The office site was fixed with hardened security precautions. The windows, made of bullet-proof glass, were tinted on the two-way-mirror principle; those inside could look out, but those outside couldn't see past the reflective exterior. Hair-thin wires embedded in the glass generated inaudible interference patterns that prevented outside snoopers from beaming the panes with lasers that would otherwise turn them into listening posts, allowing those with the proper hardware to eavesdrop on any conversations taking place inside the rooms.

Most of the computers on display in the office were store-bought civilian hardware with no more than the ordinary security features. What seemed to be a storeroom annex off the main office was the real nerve center of the outpost. Built into a wall panel was a cunningly concealed, ultra-secure communications console that served as Wenzle's link to the Dog Team's datalink net for sending and receiving encrypted messages. Any unauthorized personnel tampering with the wall panel or console would trigger an auto-destruct mechanism that within seconds would turn the hardware innards into lumps of fused metal.

Doc Wenzle was a big man running to fat. Thin, stringy strands of dark gray hair were plastered down in a comb-over across the top of a shiny, mostly bald scalp. Watery pale blue eyes in baggy pouches peered out from behind round-lensed, wire-rimmed spectacles. He had a bushy, iron-gray walrus mustache. He wore a sleeveless blue sweater vest over a long-sleeved shirt and tie. His collar was sweat-stained, his tie knot loosened, and his sleeves rolled up over his elbows.

Wenzle looked as unmilitary as they come, another mark of the effectiveness of his cover. The Dog Team was strictly an Army op all the way, and to be holding down Wenzle's post here in the Capital called for an outstanding service record. Steve figured him to be probably a colonel, but the trappings of rank were just one more potential giveaway to be shedded by a veteran Team player.

Was "Doc Wenzle" his real name? Steve doubted it. There was no need for Steve to know his handler's true identity and every reason for him not to know. Security. Steve said, "As long as you're doing the paperwork, you could put in for another gun for me, too."

Wenzle said, "What happened to yours?"

"The one I used last night? Lying in pieces scattered around the bottom of the Potomac."

"Good."

It was a good gun and Steve hated getting rid of it, but that was standard operating procedure. Ballistics could have tied the gun to the two guys in the tow truck that he'd killed. He wasn't going to take a chance on having it in his possession and then, by some quirk of ill luck, getting picked up by the police on some trivial beef like a traffic violation.

Like all the hardware he used on an assignment, it was "sterile," its past history of ownership a dead trail. Somewhere along the way, it had been acquired so that there was no way of tracing it back to him or the Army.

The same went for the car he'd used on the job. He'd picked it up at a prearranged site, a midtown parking garage. The license and registration were legal enough, made out to an assumed identity he'd also been supplied with for the mission. But a trace run on the vehicle identification numbers and the plates would only lead the authorities up another blind alley.

Doc Wenzle said, "You didn't come here unarmed." It was not a question.

The office door opening on the corridor was fitted with sensors that would detect the presence of weapons or explosive devices on any visitor standing outside it. All doors in the office were made of armor plate covered with a wood-finish veneer.

Under his sporty blue blazer jacket, Steve was heeled with a small, snouty blue black semiautomatic pistol worn in a clip-on rig that held it flat against the small of his back. It was one of his own pieces, legally registered to him under his real name of Steve Ireland. He had a permit to carry it, too, no small feat in the antigun environment of Washington, D.C., where the crooks all had guns but law-abiding citizens were disarmed to the fullest extent possible by a squalid, cynical, and infinitely corrupt city government.

The permit was another example of the long reach of the Dog Team's phantom arm. It was part of Steve Ireland's cover identity. That is, the artificially crafted persona, the legend, that he went under using his real name of Steve Ireland.

In that guise, he was a salaried civilian employee of the Department of Defense, a postal inspector attached to ECOMCON, a courier system used solely by and for the Pentagon. The post allowed him to carry firearms while on duty, and since he was potentially on call twenty-four hours a day, technically, he was always on duty and authorized to be armed night and day, around the clock. The courier system covered both foreign and domestic routes, providing him with a pretext to operate anywhere the Pentagon had interests, meaning pretty much anywhere around the world. His cover job came with a civil service rating and matching pay grade; he used his real Social Security number and duly paid his yearly federal and state income taxes.

Yes, Steve was armed, and if he'd had his druthers, he'd be packing a heavier-caliber gun and a knife up his sleeve, too. But that would have been overdoing it for going about his routine chores on a hot June weekday.

He said, "I'd be afraid to set foot in this town without something I could lay my hand on fast if needed. Don't you read the papers? Washington's the murder capital of the nation."

Doc Wenzle nodded. "I know. Makes you kind of proud, doesn't it? At least we're first in something. Speaking of the papers, last night's little escapade got a pretty decent splash in the morning editions."

Steve nodded. "Quentin and his lady friend made the front page of the *Post* and the *Washington Times.*"

Steve had made a point of picking up both papers earlier to read their accounts of the double kill. Reading his press clippings was one of his guilty pleasures. Though he could claim only a peripheral involvement with this one.

"Looks like the cops and the press both bought the murder-suicide angle," he said.

"Which ties up the Quentin sanction nice and neatly," Doc Wenzle said. "No thanks to you."

Steve held out his hands palms-up in a what-are-you-gonna-do? kind of gesture. "Maybe if I had a little better advance intelligence, I wouldn't have gotten beaten to the punch."

Wenzle said, "Consider yourself lucky you didn't wind up as a page one headline yourself."

"That's not luck, that's skill," Steve said.

Wenzle looked dubious.

Steve actually figured he'd been lucky, damned lucky, to come out of the ambush alive, so he didn't press the point. "Those two guys I bagged didn't make page one. They were in a little squib buried in the back of the metro section."

"A gang killing, the papers called it," said Wenzle, chuckling.

"On Tyburn Street, that barely qualifies as crime news. More of a social event," Steve said. "That's one tough neighborhood. I was glad to get out of there in one piece."

"Too bad. Won't make much of an entry in your scrapbook."

Steve shook his head. "No scrapbooks for me, Doc."

Wenzle's bushy eyebrows rose over the tops of his glasses in mock surprise. "No? I thought all you top-ranked trigger-pullers keep scrapbooks of your exploits. A passel of elite prima donnas, the whole lot of you—killer elite. Always checking up on your stats to see where you rate among the competition. More ego than a theaterful of ham actors."

"Not me. I'm the modest type." Steve assumed a righteous expression. "Humility is my greatest virtue. I take great pride in it."

"Bah."

Steve went on. "The papers said the two bodies were unidentified. Any leads on them?"

"Ah, now you come to the point of our little kaffeeklatsch," Doc Wenzle said, smiling. It was not a particularly nice smile. "As a matter of fact, we do.

"The shooter was one Gavrilo Sandor. The driver was burned too badly when the tow truck caught fire to make a definitive ID, but based on Sandor's modus operandi and known associates, it's a pretty sure bet that he was one Dimity Vane."

Steve said, "Sandor? Vane? Never heard of them."

"No reason why you should have," Wenzle said. "We wouldn't have either, except that we got a line on them through their bossman, Quentin's executioner."

Steve leaned farther forward in his chair, and not just to get some relief from the broken springs in the seat cushion. "The man in the Crown Vic . . ."

"That's right."

"And who might that be?" Steve's expression was mild, almost dreamy.

Wenzle grinned, showing yellowed buck teeth. He knew he had Steve's full attention now. He made a show of shuffling around some files on his desk, making room on the blotter for his folded hands, savoring the moment, making it last.

He said, "Those cell phone photos you snapped of him going into the club were no great shakes, but they were adequate enough for us to run them into the Netlink facial identification software."

"And?" Steve prompted.

"We identified him," Wenzle said, smug and relishing it.

"What is this, a quiz game show? Who is he?"

"Donny Piersall."

"Who?"

"Donny Piersall," Wenzle repeated. "Odds are

that he's the one that did the job on Colonel Sterling and made it look like suicide."

"Ah," Steve said.

"An interesting local character, is our Donny. A real personality. He used to be a city cop in the Detective Bureau, working vice and narcotics. For a while there, he cut quite a swathe through the ranks of the big-time pimps and drug dealers, busting them left and right without fear or favor of how well connected they were with City Hall, racking up a string of high-profile convictions. He wasn't too particular about how he did it either, leaving behind a trail of broken bones and busted heads as well as a half-a-dozen kills. Justified kills, all in the line of duty, mind you, and considering the character of the deceased, nobody was too broken up about it. The media ate it up, calling him 'the Hero Cop,' a one-man anticrime crusade."

Steve said, "Sounds like a candidate for Officer of the Year so far, but I sense a 'but' coming up."

Wenzle nodded, all outward affability. "Donny the Dick's motives weren't entirely selfless. Seems like all his crusading was being done to wipe out the competition of the drug and vice lords who'd been paying him off for just that."

"In that case, I'm surprised he wasn't made Chief of Police."

"Luck is all," Wenzle said. "His turned sour when he shot the wrong man by mistake. He was supposed to hit an independent dealer who'd been operating on protected turf without permission. The spotter who pointed him out to Piersall messed up and fingered the wrong guy. Donny shot him in the line of 'resisting arrest.' He must've put about twelve bullet holes in him. Then it turned out that he'd gotten the wrong man, some innocent citizen who'd been out enjoying a night on the town. He was clean, with no police record, which made it even more suspicious when he was found in possession of a handgun, a cheap Saturday night special. Donny claimed he'd been reaching for it, causing him to shoot in self-defense. Of course it was a throw-down gun, a plant which Donny'd brought along for just that purpose.

"Even so, he might have been able to wriggle out of it, but the kid was the son of a ward boss whose district was instrumental in getting the mayor elected and keeping him in office. So Piersall had to go. Rumors and allegations about his extracurricular activities were flying, but nothing was ever proved for two good reasons. One, any potential witnesses turned up dead, and two, Donny had plenty of dirt on the city government, from the cop on the beat all the way to the up to the mayor's office. He was kicked off the force, but skated clear of all criminal charges."

Steve said, "So how does a rogue ex-cop tie in with Durwood Quentin III and the Brinker scam?"

"I'm coming to that," Wenzle said. "Want some coffee?"

"No, thanks."

"I do. Mind getting me a cup? I'm a fat old man with trick knees and it's an effort for me to get out of my chair." Wenzle lifted his coffee mug, proffering it.

Steve rose, toting the empty mug over to the coffee urn. In truth, he was glad for the exercise; his rear was getting numb from perching on the edge of the chair. A couple of inches of blackish brown liquid lay in the bottom of the pot. It smelled burned. The smell of it made his stomach churn.

Wenzle said, "Put some of that creamer in it, will you."

A container of nondairy creamer stood beside the hot plate. Nondairy? Nonorganic was more like it, off-white powder that looked like drain cleaner. Steve shook some into the bottom of the mug.

Wenzle said, "More, please."

Steve added some more of the stuff. Wenzle said, "Don't be stingy, it's not like it's costing you anything."

Steve filled the mug half full of the powder before Wenzle said, "Okay, that's enough."

Steve said, "Sure you want some coffee with your creamer?"

"Sarcasm ill becomes you, soldier."

Steve poured in the coffee, the resultant goop turning grayish brown. Holding the mug at arm's length to avoid getting a whiff of the contents, he crossed to Wenzle and set it down on his desktop.

Wenzle reached greedily for the mug, pulling it toward him. He used a pen as a stirrer. He held the mug under his nose, savoring the vapors rising off the brew. Raising the mug, he quaffed a long pull, then smacked his lips. "Ahh . . ."

Steve sat down, starting as a wire from a sprung spring jabbed him in the rear. "Ouch!" he said, quickly shifting position. "Damn! Why don't you get some decent chairs in here?"

"Because that'd only encourage visitors to waste time sitting around here all day," Wenzle said, looking smug again.

"Yours looks comfortable enough."

"I have to sit around here all day, but I'm not wasting time. You, you've got business elsewhere."

Steve brightened at that; it meant that Wenzle was ready to get to the crux of the matter. Wenzle drank some more coffee. "This talking is thirsty work."

That never seemed to inhibit him otherwise, Steve thought, keeping the observation unvoiced. "You were saying something about Pearsall," he said aloud.

Wenzle set down the mug and rested his folded hands on the desk. "After being bounced from the force, Donny went into business for himself. Same line of work, strong-arm stuff, violence, hijacking, extortion, and murder. Without a badge to hide behind, he had to operate more circumspectly, but it didn't cramp his style that much. He gathered a gang of like-minded associates around him. The Black Glove Crew, they call themselves. That's the kind of work they do, black-glove stuff where you don't want to leave behind any fingerprints."

Steve said, "Are they mobbed up?"

Wenzle shook his head. "Independent

contractors. Seems like the Mob can't bring themselves to trust an ex-cop, no matter how dirty he is. A dirty cop, sure, that's a horse of a different color, because he's got the straight front and fears exposure and that gives them something to hold against him. But an ex-cop like Piersall with nothing to lose, that's different.

"Piersall's been working more of the corporate side of the street. As you may have heard, Big Business has plenty of dirty work that needs doing. Industrial espionage, sabotage, harrassment and intimidation of the competition, not to mention the suppression of squeamish in-house personnel and potential whistleblowers—"

Steve said, "I read the papers."

Wenzle said, "Lately, Donny's been working hand-in-black-glove with an outfit called ISS. Internal Security Services."

Steve frowned, thoughtful. "Sounds familiar."

"Their name came up during the Brinker investigation," said Wenzle. "They're a Washington-based organization that styles itself as a corporate expeditor, combining security operations and confidential investigations. What they are is fixers, hired to solve problems and get results, by any means necessary.

"They've been under contract to Brinker for the last two years. Durwood Quentin had a close working relationship with this man."

Wenzle opened a folder, removed a photograph, and handed it across the desk to Steve Ireland. It was a glossy eight-by-ten head shot of a man who'd been unaware that his picture was being taken.

The subject was about seventy, a well-preserved seventy, white-haired, clean-shaven, with a long, oblong-shaped face. His eyes were dark and alert. Walnut-sized knots of muscle showed at the hinges of his jaws; his mouth was a short horizontal line, the lips thin to the point of being virtually nonexistent.

Steve knew that Wenzle must have a very good reason for showing him the photo. He studied it carefully, committing the image to memory.

"That's Greg Mayhew," Wenzle said. "Lieutenant Greg Mayhew, to give him his full title. He used to be number two in the capital police's old Political Intelligence Unit. There's not a dirty little secret about the movers and shakers in this town that he doesn't know about. After reaching retirement age, he left the department with a full pension and founded ISS."

He handed Steve a second photo, this one depicting a woman, fortyish, with shoulder-length blond hair, oval-faced, her attractiveness slightly offset by a too-sharp, pointy chin. Steve eyed it, then looked over the top of the photo at Wenzle.

"Elise Danner, a CIA analyst for twenty years before retiring to become Mayhew's co-principal in ISS," Wenzle said.

Steve put one photo on top of the other and set them both down on Wenzle's desk. Wenzle said, "Quentin and Mayhew were tight. Quentin went to Mayhew to handle Colonel Sterling when he started blowing the whistle about the Chinese arms scandal. Sterling couldn't be bought, bluffed, or bullied, so Mayhew farmed the problem out to Donny Piersall. Mayhew's been using the Black Glove Crew for the rough stuff.

"Piersall himself personally filled the Sterling contract. Recently, Mayhew began harboring doubts about Quentin's reliability. What with all his drinking and compulsive whoremongering and other erratic behavior, Quentin looked like he was coming unglued, cracking up. And he could tie Mayhew to Sterling's murder.

"Mayhew contracted Piersall to get rid of Quentin. Piersall put his plan into motion. The girl—Virginia Alden was her name, if you're interested—was a hooker known to Piersall from his vice squad days. She had a record for blackmail and extortion. She was expendable from the start. She was the honey trap, the sex lure designed to get Quentin where Piersall could give him the chop. Her, too. It would look like a classic case of murder-suicide and that would be the end of it."

Steve said, "And then I happened along."

Wenzle nodded. "When Donny realized that someone else was tailing Quentin, it must've given him quite a start."

"What I'd like to do is give him a finish—a big finish."

Wenzle looked owlish. "I daresay that might be arranged."

"I'm all ears," said Steve.

"But don't get too cocky. He's no pushover, as you found out last night. He came pretty close to finishing off you."

"Go ahead, rub it in," Steve said bitterly. "I

notice you've got all the answers today. I could have used some of that intel last night."

"I'll admit we were a little bit behind the learning curve."

"That's big of you." Steve tried hard not to sneer.

"Thanks to the some of the information you provided, especially those photos of Piersall, we were able to piece the rest of it together," Wenzle said.

Not for the first time in their association, Steve wondered if when Wenzle said something like "We pieced it together," he was using the royal "we," that is, "I," meaning, "I, Wenzle did the thinking," or if his "we" meant he, Wenzle, and some of the higher-ups had done the deducing. Much of the inner workings of the Dog Team was a mystery to Steve. As usual, he kept his conjectures to himself. It was no mystery at all that it was considered bad form to be openly inquisitive about the outfit.

Instead, he said, "Glad the night wasn't a total loss."

"Not at all, not at all," Wenzle said, making an expansive hand gesture. "Quentin was neutralized and in a way that doesn't track back to us. The press and the police are both satisfied with the story that Quentin and the hooker fought over the gun, he shot her during the struggle, and then killed himself."

After a pause, he added, "Donny framed it up very neatly. He does nice work."

Steve Ireland made a disgusted face. "Christ! Why don't you recruit him then?"

Wenzle, unruffled, said, "Because he killed Colonel Sterling and he's not going to be allowed to get away with it."

"That's more like it," Steve said, some of the tension easing up inside him.

Wenzle looked him straight in the eye. "A Team member, especially a field operative like yourself, is like any other kind of performer: no good without a certain amount of temperment. It's part of the pride and professionalism. But too much can be dangerous.

"Just a cautionary note of advice, Steve. Take it as you like, or not."

Steve nodded, accepting the justice of the rebuke. "I'll take it. My apologies, Doc."

"None needed."

"I've been a little short-fused lately anyhow, and Piersall's making me for the tail and nearly boxing me in stung me to the quick."

"Perfectly understandable."

"I needed a reminder to lighten up. Thanks, Coach."

Wenzle held up a hand palm-outward, signifying the matter was closed. "'Nuff said."

Truth was, Steve had been on the sour side for a while, and not just since getting back into harness in the last few weeks. It dated back to Dagaari, more than a half year ago.

Dagaari was a town in Somalia, a bleak, barren, sun-blasted hell of a country on the Horn of Africa's East Coast. When most Americans thought of Somalia, if they thought of it at all, they remembered it as the site of the notorious "Blackhawk Down" incident. The U.S. had been playing Uncle Sugar, sending in troops as part of an international famine relief operation. As usual, no good deed goes unpunished. A local warlord shot down a U.S. Army Blackhawk helicopter; the surviving crewmen were massacred and their bodies dragged through the streets by some of the grateful citizenry. U.S. forces pulled out a short time later.

That had been close to two decades ago, and if the average American Joe today was asked about Somalia, assuming he even knew what and where it was, he'd most likely opine that the U.S. was well out of that benighted land.

Unfortunately, things weren't that simple. Somalia was located in a strategically important site along vital Red Sea and Indian Ocean shipping lanes. Dagaari was an important regional center where a militia leader had exploited an Al Qaeda connection for guns and money to make himself a powerful warlord.

Steve Ireland had been part of a Dog Team mission to neutralize said warlord. His squad was working with a unit of Ethiopian commandoes operating in the area. Troublesome neighbor Somalia was a perennial hotbed of banditry, terrorism, and lately, even piracy; Ethiopian forces periodically made incursions across the border, cracking down on the most blatant offenders.

The sanction came off smoothly, without a hitch, the warlord's career coming to a close as his skull disintegrated under the impact of a high-velocity round fired from a sniper rifle in Steve Ireland's hands. It was the exfiltration where the mission went sour. Steve's squad was en route toward a rendezvous with the helicopter that was going to take them out of the country when the vehicle they were riding in came to a Dagaari crossroads and was ambushed by a roadside bomb. IED, Improvised Explosive Device, in official parlance. Most of the passengers were killed outright; Steve was thrown clear of the blast, but he caught some shrapnel in his guts and some bad burns, too.

A couple of the Ethiopians had survived, too, and they were able to patch him up enough to keep him alive long enough to deliver him to the pickup site. He was airlifted out and turned over to a team of Army medics. It was touch and go for a while, but after long hours of heroic surgery, they were able to stabilize his condition and pull him through.

So he was told; the last thing he remembered was the transport vehicle slowing down at the crossroads to let a donkey cart pass by. The cart was being driven by an oldster so wrinkled and withered that he looked like a living mummy. Seated next to him on the front seat was a boy who couldn't have been more than eight years old. The boy was slight, with spindly limbs and a big head that looked like it was mostly all eyes. Steve recalled thinking that the kid must be the oldster's grandson; that was the last coherent thought he had before the world blew up.

It wasn't the world that had blown up, of course, just the donkey cart, or rather, the explosives concealed in the cart's hopper. The oldster and the boy had been instantly obliterated, crashing the gates of Paradise on the wings of glorious martyrdom. Steve often wondered if the kid was in on the plan, or merely an unwitting pawn sacrificed on the game board . . .

So it turned out that he and his teammates hadn't been done in by a car bomb, but a donkey cart bomb. A sneaky bit of improvisation, that explosive device. To this day, Steve was unsure if the blast had been retaliation for expunging the warlord, or a random strike by some zealous enthusiasts taking the opportunity to rid the world of a handful of devilish infidels. If anybody in authority knew, they weren't telling Steve.

But such speculation came later, much later. Steve's first conscious memories after the blast were of waking up in a stateside hospital. After that came a series of operations, followed by periods of recovery, which were inevitably followed by still more operations. Much of that time was a surreal montage of images and scraps of memory, due to the fog of the painkillers he was continuously pumped full of.

His treatment was first-rate; it was some time before he realized that he was not in a military hospital per se, but instead in a private facility, a clandestine clinic maintained for the treatment of wounded, sick, or otherwise impaired personnel with access to classified information. All the staffers, from doctors and nurses down to the orderlies and even the janitors, had cosmic-level security clearances. After all, there was no telling what kind of secrets a patient might babble or cry out when out of his—or her—head with pain or on drugs. It made sense; for covert operatives, a black clinic.

A lot of time and trouble had been involved in putting Steve Ireland back together, but that made sense, too; a lot of time and trouble had gone into making him the precision instrument that he was, namely, a Dog Team assassin.

Months of agonizing rehab had followed before the medics had certified him physically and mentally fit for duty.

Parts of his face had been badly burned; skin grafts made him look good as new, though imparting a certain stiffness to his features, a kind of masklike immobility. This outwardly imposed poker face could be something of an asset in the assassin's trade, he supposed, once he got used to it. For now, though, when he gazed in the mirror, the face looked much the same as it had always been, but it felt like that of a stranger.

When he found himself thinking that way, all he had to do was think of the other members of his Dagaari squad, all as dead as Carthage. That put things into perspective. Still, he was hungry for a win, and the thought of last night's encounter with Donny Piersall was as irksome as grains of hot sand under the eyelids. Emotionally speaking, that is.

So Doc Wenzle's heads-up was a timely reminder not to let emotion cloud his professionalism. Wenzle was saying, "It's the tie-up between Piersall and Mayhew that we find interesting."

That "we" again.

"Mayhew's ISS played a vital hidden hand in the

Brinker affair. There've been other indications that Mayhew's been digging into things that are none of his concern. Not with Quentin; the Brinker deal was only one of Mayhew's sidelines. ISS has apparently been serving as a clearing-house for all sorts of classified intel to all sorts of buyers," Wenzle said. "We'd like to know more." He paused, seemingly waiting for a reply.

"Meaning?" Steve said.

"Meaning that we'd like Mayhew to be taken alive if possible," Wenzle said. "Your run-in with Piersall seems to have had a positive aspect. It's got Mayhew worried. He's gone to ground. He's forted up at his Maryland estate, with Piersall and his Black Glove Crew playing watchdog."

Steve said, "Convenient."

"Very," Wenzle agreed. "It's a fairly isolated locale, with the nearest neighbors a half mile away."

"When do I go?"

"Tonight. The estate's on the water, and Mayhew has his own private boat. He may be thinking of running. Again, we'd like him to be taken alive, but what's more important is that no unfriendly interests gain access to the se-crets locked inside his head. Better he should lose that head than get away, if it comes to that."

"Understood."

"We have reason to believe that the Danner woman is with him. The same applies to her. We'd like her taken alive, too, but . . ." Wenzle didn't finish the sentence. He didn't have to.

Steve said, "And Piersall?"

"Law enforcement as such is a job for the

police, not for us," Wenzle said. "On the other hand, the Black Glove Crew has proved itself a nuisance and more. Time to close the files on them permanently."

"With pleasure," said Steve.

FIVE

In a second-floor bedroom of Greg Mayhew's manor house at Arnot's Acres on Chesapeake Bay, a woman stood in the center of the floor, her body rigid, trembling, her eyes wild, her hands closed into fists that were held pressed to the sides of her head.

Fear is a physical thing.

Elise Danner knew that now, tonight, knew it for a fact, a reality that vibrated every fiber of her being. She'd thought she'd known what fear was when the Brinker deal had first started to go sour, when the FBI had started poking around in the case—when it stopped being a matter of interest and inquiry and officially became an investigation: the Brinker Defense Systems case.

There had been inquiries into Brinker before, starting when that officious little Colonel Sterling in the Pentagon's Procurement Division finally managed to convince the Inspector General's office that there might actually be something after all to the allegations he'd been making for months to anyone who'd give him a hearing, that Brinker's arms deal to supply weapons and ammunition to police forces in Iraq and Afghanistan was rotten clear through.

He was right, of course; as the chief analyst and second in command of Internal Security Systems, she knew just how rotten it was. She and her ISS boss and partner, Greg Mayhew, had worked closely with Brinker head Durwood Quentin III to put the whole deal together.

It had been no easy task. Wheels had to be greased, a small army of politicians and bureaucrats bribed, not just in Washington, but in Beijing, Kabul, Baghdad, and even in Tirana, Albania. The Balkan connection was key because that was the cutout, the front, necessary to procure the arms and ammo from the People's Republic of China, U.S. corporations being forbidden to do weapons deals with the PRC.

The PRC armaments were worse than useless, so old and outdated that they were more dangerous to the users than anyone else, but so what? The arms had to come from somewhere, they had to be delivered to the end users to fulfill the terms of the contract, and the price was right.

Such subterranean transactions were ISS's stock in trade, and a very lucrative trade it was. Both Danner and her principal, Mayhew, each had a not so small fortune tucked away in offshore bank accounts, and their share of the Brinker deal had substantially fattened those golden nest eggs.

A great deal of time, money, and effort had

gone into building an international web of corruption to make the Brinker deal happen. And then that magnificent edifice of dirty money and sticky-fingered conspirators had been jeopardized, all because some nitpicking Army bean counter in the Pentagon wouldn't stop kicking up a fuss.

Sure, the deal stank to high heaven. What of it? It wasn't like there weren't dozens of other deals just as dirty going down daily throughout the federal government. Who wouldn't enrich themselves by hook or crook on the taxpayers' money if they had the chance? That was the system, the facts of life.

But the little colonel refused to see it that way. He was persistent, and even a horsefly can drive a bull moose half crazy if it keeps annoying it long enough. When Sterling had his fatal rendezvous with a shotgun in his garage, it had been a relief to all concerned, except for the dead man's grieving family and friends, but who were they? Nobodies.

Elise Danner had her suspicions about the true nature of the colonel's death; more than suspicions, because she knew ISS boss Greg Mayhew, knew him intimately, and part of that knowing was the certainty that when rough stuff was required, he knew who to go to, to get it done. But that part of the business was none of her business and she steered clear of it; what she didn't know couldn't hurt her.

Sterling's demise made her happy, as it did all the others involved in the Brinker deal, because it meant that a boat-rocker would rock the boat no more. Official interest in the contract melted away, and the conspirators went back to grabbing all they could of the dirty money that kept rolling in.

The hell of it was, though, that everything was connected to everything else. The Department of Justice became curious about how a well-connected senior congressman had come by several vacation homes and a brand-new, half-million-dollar yacht. When he was unable to reconcile these acquisitions with his tax returns, DOJ and the Treasury Department really went to work on him. Threatened with a twenty-year prison sentence, the legislator broke and spilled his guts, revealing the details of a vast criminal conspiracy involving government contracts and private contractors. Naming names, he told who did what and how much they got paid for it.

One of the names that came up was Brinker Defense Systems. Probers started digging, and the whole business about its shady arms deal was reactivated. Congressional subcommittees held hearings, whose investigatory results were just about nil.

But when the FBI got involved in the case, Elise Danner got worried. The Bureau wasn't as easily hoodwinked as a bunch of headline-hunting officeholders. It wasn't so much the Brinker arms deal that worried her; ISS, as always, had covered its tracks with a veritable labyrinth of shell companies, false fronts, and phantom figureheads. But ISS had many interests and operations, some of which might not hold up so well when exposed to the spotlight. A few of them might well be labeled treasonous by those less-than-broad-minded G-men.

That's when Elise Danner first began to know fear, the stirrings of a gnawing anxiety that loomed ever larger as the investigation intensified. Up to now, it had been all fun and games at ISS, brushing aside the rules like cobwebs, running intricate rings around the legalities to make things happen and generate cash flow. Everybody was doing it, all the wised-up insiders were riding the government gravy train, and ISS happened to be doing it better than most. She reveled in the intrigue, in her cleverness in constructing elaborate ploys and ruses to outwit the law.

But with the FBI bloodhounds nosing around trying to pick up the scent, suddenly it wasn't fun anymore. She and Mayhew were certain that their defenses were armor-plated and in-dictment-proof, as they kept telling each other more and more often as the pace of the probes quickened.

Durwood Quentin III loomed ever larger as a matter of concern. His dealings with ISS were not such as should be brought to light in open court. Of course, he couldn't very well reveal the machinations without incriminating himself. But if he should get tagged for something else, some unrelated scam, he might well give up ISS to cut himself a better deal with prosecutors.

Worse, his behavior was growing steadily more erratic with each passing day. He dealt with the pressure with ever more intense bouts of drinking, drugging, and whoring. Elise Danner found herself wishing and hoping that something would make him go away and stop being a problem. Like Colonel Sterling and the problem he'd presented had gone away. Only, the feeling was infinitely more intense in Quentin's case. Sterling had threatened profits, but Quentin carried the menace of prison bars for his associates.

Recently, on more than one occasion, she had expressed to Greg Mayhew her desire that Quentin should just . . . go away. Mayhew had indicated that such, too, were his thoughts on the subject. No more had been said about it between the two; no more needed to be said.

Rather than allaying her fears, the realization of her wish had only multiplied them, rocketing them into hyper-drive.

The first she learned of the last of Quentin had come early this morning, around dawn, as she was taking her daily jog in the affluent neighborhood of Alexandria, Virginia, where she lived. She had a good body and worked hard to keep it fit, her breasts high and firm, belly flat, and buttocks taut.

In recent weeks, the workouts had become even more important to her as a way of coping with the stress and anxieties generated by the Bureau's investigation. They had helped her burn off some of the tensions.

She'd been outfitted in her usual jogging regalia of sports bra, T-shirt, gym shorts, white socks, and running shoes. And the one accessory she was never without, her cell phone.

Now more than ever, when she needed to be apprised of fast-breaking information, which could come at any hour of the day or night. The cell was worn in a little holder that was clipped to the top of her gym shorts over one hip.

Her neighborhood featured houses that were elegant, expensive, and sited on spacious tracts well separated from each other. The area was conveniently close to CIA headquarters in Langley, but only the highest-ranking officials, those officed on the building's seventh floor, the level occupied by the Agency's key power brokers and intelligence mandarins, could afford to live in the neighborhood.

During the years she had worked as an analyst at Langley, the prospects of her living here had seemed as remote as her scaling Mount Everest. Only after leaving the CIA, and taking her extensive network of contacts and connections with her to partner up with Greg Mayhew at ISS, had her fortunes taken the sudden and dramatic upturn that allowed her to buy her dream home in the neighborhood.

The area didn't have any sidewalks, so she jogged in the street, following a mile-long course along picturesque, winding lanes. She ran in the middle of the road, her sneakered feet beating out a percussive rhythm on the asphalt.

The sun had come up, but was so low that its heat had not yet begun to be felt; she cast a weirdly elongated giant shadow before her. Dew sparkled on well-manicured lawns. Lights still burned in lamps mounted over the front doors of grand homes. Most of the houses showed dark windows, with only a few lights shining behind curtains to indicate the presence of early risers.

Elise Danner was deep into her jogging rhythm, her ponytailed hair flailing back and forth across her shoulders, her breathing deep and regular, arms working, long legs flashing, as she ran on the balls of her feet.

Her cell phone rang. Not so much of a ring tone as an electronic bleeping, fast and urgent.

She was deep into her concentration and the intrusion jarred her, throwing her off stride. Instantly and instinctively, she knew that this could not be good news.

She pulled up short, slowing to a walk. The cell bleeped again. Unholstering it, flipping it open, she recognized the caller's number as that of Greg Mayhew. Answering, she said, "What?"

Mayhew said, "Where are you?"

"Out jogging."

"Go home. I'll meet you there."

"What's up?"

"Not on the phone. I'll be right over," he said, cutting off the connection.

She realized that her heartbeat and pulse were racing faster now than when she had been jogging. Her hands shook as she put away the cell. She turned, retracing her route, going back the way she came. Not jogging, walking. She had trouble catching her breath.

Mayhew reached her house before she did. His Hummer stood at the curbside, idling. It was the largest model of the brand available; it looked like a square-sided omnibus.

Mayhew stood beside it, hands on hips, waiting impatiently as he watched her approach. Seventy, he looked a well-preserved fifty, lean, spare, and fit. He had a full head of hair, snow-white, but all of it his. His eyebrows were white inverted Vs, his skin was bright, shiny pink. He wore a lightweight, navy blue nylon wind-breaker, open and unzipped; a green sport shirt; khaki slacks; and blue boating shoes with white rubber soles.

He was not alone, Elise Danner saw to her dismay. With him were Donny Piersall and an-other man unknown to her.

She knew that Piersall was Mayhew's go-to guy for the rough stuff. He sat in the driver's seat of the Hummer. The window was rolled down and he rested a folded arm so that it was half hanging out the window.

The other man sat behind the front seat. He had short sandy hair, a gingery goatee, and dark, watchful eyes in a chiseled, well-featured face. He looked tough; Elise Danner immedi-ately tagged him as one of Piersall's people.

She halted a few paces away from Mayhew, studying his face. He looked vaguely irked, but that was pretty much his habitual expression, so there wasn't much to be gotten there. Low-voiced, pitched for Mayhew's ears alone, she said, "Greg, what's wrong?"

"Nothing," he said flatly. That was contra-verted by his being here now. Indicating her house, he said, "We'll talk inside."

Donny Piersall thrust his head out of the open Hummer window, looking like he hadn't a care in the world. Flashing a big, cocky grin, he said, "Hi, Elise." Like they were big buddies.

For most of her adult years, it had been a guiding principle to keep the Donny Piersalls of the world out of her life. She'd known others like him, mostly action men from the Agency's covert ops branch. Violence was what they were about, they liked it, and the need for it hung around them like the electric charge of an aura.

Now, here he was, with another sideman who was no different, parked out in front of her house in the early morning light of a June weekday. She felt slightly nauseated, but she nodded to him in acknowledgment of his greeting. No sense in antagonizing him with the cold shoulder, not now.

Mayhew was already starting up the flagged walkway toward her front door; she started after him, conscious of Piersall's gaze following her. She didn't have to look to know he was eyeballing her; she knew him well enough to know what he would do.

She punched in the access code on the numerical keypad set to one side of the front door, deactivating the alarm system. Then she and Mayhew were inside, in a central hall where a beige-carpeted staircase spiraled up along the curve of the well to the second-floor landing. The space was thick with gloom, still deeply shadowed, hushed.

Mayhew's arm dropped to his side, causing the flap of his jacket to fall open. A snub-nosed revolver was holstered on his hip.

Elise Danner gasped. "My God, Greg! A gun?!"

She'd been worried that they were going to be served some papers or, at worst, arrested. But a gun was pointless against those possibilities. That's what lawyers were for. Mayhew wasn't going to shoot it out with the G-men.

He said, "Don't get excited. It's simply a precautionary measure."

"Against what?"

"Trouble. We'll talk about it later."

She planted herself flat-footed, determined not to move until she got some answers. "We'll talk about it now, now that you've thrown a scare into me. Are we in danger?" With some of the clients they serviced, that was always a possibility.

He was quick to say, "No, no."

Her eyes flashed, hard and intent in the dimness. Skeptical. An eyebrow arched. "That gun, those two gorillas outside . . ."

Mayhew took a deep breath, exhaled. "All right," he said. "Someone might be making a move on us."

She said, "Who? What kind of a move?"

"I don't know who, not just yet. Don't even know if they are making a move, if their intentions are hostile. They could be, though. Best that we go to the Acres for a while until we sort things out."

She said, "Now?"

"Right now. Get changed and pack an overnight bag and do it quick."

"Greg—"

"You know I'm not the type to hit the panic button. I wouldn't be doing this if I didn't think it was necessary. Like I said, it's strictly precautionary. But necessary."

"Can't you tell me anything more?"

"I'll tell you all I know along the way. But let's get moving. Now."

"I'll have to shower first—"

"Fine," Mayhew said, his tone indicating it was anything but. "Hop to it, girl."

Elise Danner took a shower in the second-floor bathroom. Standing naked under the hot steaming spray, she shivered. The moist heat failed to take the chill out of her bones.

When she was done, she toweled dry, not even bothering to blow-dry her hair, a key indicator of the disruption of her normal routine, because she was a woman who always took great care of her appearance at all times. Mayhew had once opined in his sour fashion that she was the type who'd put on makeup before taking out the garbage. It was an exaggeration, but only a slight one.

He stood around waiting in her bedroom while she got dressed. They'd been intimate for a time, early in the start of their partnership. Not lovers, but intimate. Despite his age, he was still able to perform in bed, after a fashion. Minimally. But she had ways to excite him and get him off. With Mayhew, it wasn't about the sex; it was about the power, about his being in control. It wasn't very nice, but she'd done far more distasteful activities in the past to advance herself, and she'd have done a lot more if that had been needed to secure her place in and piece of ISS.

But that aspect of their relationship was long passed. If Mayhew was still sexually active, and she suspected he was, in his way, he was getting his kicks elsewhere, which was fine with her. Once they'd gotten the sex bit over and done with, they could concentrate on their one real, abiding common interest: making money.

Now, dressed in a bra and slacks, she padded barefoot about the bedroom, packing an overnight bag.

Mayhew said, "You'll hear about it sooner rather than later, so you might as well know now. Quentin is dead."

She pulled her head out of the closet where she'd been grabbing some clothes and looked at him. "Is that what this is all about?"

"Partly."

"I take it he didn't die of natural causes," she said dryly.

"One of those chippies he liked to chase pulled a gun, or something," Mayhew said. "They're both dead."

Elise Danner was puzzled. "That's good, right? So what's the problem?"

"Some character's been following Quentin around. Not one of ours. A stranger. Donny spotted him. A couple of his boys tried to question him, find out who he is, who sent him. He killed them," Mayhew said.

"Killed them?!"

He nodded, a short, curt gesture. "Snuffed them out without so much as a by-your-leave. Whoever he is, he's a professional. A professional killer. It's a pretty sure bet that he killed Quentin and the chippie, too."

She said, "But why?"

Mayhew shrugged. "Who knows? Quentin had his thumb in a lot of pies and not just our deal. A lot of folks might have reasons to want him dead. The point is, the killer knows about us, about ISS. And we don't know anything about him, or who he's working for.

"So under the circumstances, you can see why it's best that you and I drop out of the limelight for a while instead of walking around with big fat targets on our backs, not knowing where or when our unknown friend might decide to pay us a visit."

Elise Danner pulled on a blouse and finished packing fast. Without consciously thinking about it, she picked out a pair of sensible, low-heeled loafers from her shoe tree, shoes that were good for running in.

Built into a secret compartment in the floor of her walk-in closet was a concealed safe containing important documents—important to her—bank books, personal ID, that sort of thing, along with ten thousand dollars in cash, getaway money.

She said, "Should I bring my passport?"

Mayhew snorted. "We're just laying low for a few days, not taking it on the lam. I never ran away from a fight in my life. If it is a fight. That's the hell of it, I just don't know what it's all about.

"But I will," he added grimly.

Elise Danner said, "But the killer took out two of Piersall's men—"

"That doesn't mean a thing," Mayhew said, waving it off. "Donny's boys come on strong. He came on stronger. That doesn't mean he's gunning for us. But we're not going to sit around wondering and waiting for him to move on us."

Selecting a handbag with shoulder straps, she opened it and dumped the contents of her purse into it.

Her laptop was hardened with top-level encryptors and fail-safes, but she decided to take it with her anyway. A mountain of confidential data was locked into its hard drive. Valuable information that might serve later as a bargaining chip.

She tucked the laptop into its carrying case, slinging the strap over her shoulder. She slung the handbag over her other shoulder. Mayhew didn't offer to help carry her overnight bag and she knew better than to ask. She grabbed the handle and picked it up. "Let's go," she said.

She and Mayhew went downstairs. She reached for the front door, but Mayhew intercepted her, saying, "Wait a minute."

He went to one of the windows, lifting the edge of the drapes and peering outside. Piersall stood leaning against the side of the Hummer, smoking a cigarette. His sideman was still sitting in the backseat. All looked quiet and normal. The most intrusive element was Piersall. He didn't look like he belonged in the neighborhood.

Letting the curtain fall away from his hand, Mayhew said, "Okay."

Elise Danner used the indoor keypad to reset

the alarm system; then she and Mayhew exited via the front door.

Piersall took a last drag on his cigarette and flipped it away, into the street. Opening the rear hatch of the vehicle, he said, "You can stow your gear in the back. Here, let me help."

"Thank you," Elise Danner said.

"We aim to please," he said, his smile oily, flashing a mouthful of movie-star-level dental work. She suspected his teeth were all capped and professionally whitened. When her bags were in place, he opened the right rear door for her, motioning for her to enter. Indicating his sideman, he said, "This's Bennett."

Bennett nodded, saying, "Hi."

She said, "Hello."

Bennett's overall look and well-trimmed, ginger-colored goatee gave him a raffish look, reminding her of picture book illustrations of Robin Hood. Being one of Donny Piersall's associates, he might steal from the rich, but it was a surety that he'd never give any of it to the poor, she thought.

She climbed into the backseat, Piersall closing the door behind her, sealing her in. One good thing about the Hummer; it was roomy, so Bennett didn't intrude on her personal space. Not that he seemed interested in her, not like Piersall.

Mayhew sat in front, on the passenger side. Piersall got behind the wheel, starting up the Hummer and driving away. Elise Danner wondered when and under what circumstances she would return home. She made a point of not looking back.

Arnot's Acres was Mayhew's country estate, a sprawling piece of property in a woodsy area of Maryland by the bay. It had a rustic quality—rich rustic.

Once, it had been prime farmland, hunting and fishing grounds, the private precincts of the old-time landed gentry who had carved out vast tracts for their own domains. It had been discovered and acquired by the new rich, the rising mercantile barons who wanted scenic beauty and privacy away from the big cities, but not too far away. The great estates had been acquired before they could be sold off piecemeal and subdivided into smaller lots. As a result, the county had escaped the blight of overdevelopment and still retained much of its rural charm.

The modern-day gentry now occupying it enjoyed all the benefits of country living without the hassle of operating working farms. Most of the waterfront properties were second homes, exclusive and expensive, used for weekends and vacationing. Jealous of their secluded retreats, the new owners presented a united front against future development, thwarting the encroachments of suburban sprawl.

Arnot's Acres was a prime piece of property on the bay, a spacious clearing of rolling hills and fields and meadows carved out of the woodlands.

Arnot himself had been a pre-Revolutionary

landowner who'd first used the locale for an extensive and lucrative smuggling ring, buying and selling all sorts of contraband luxury goods— wines, brandies, rum, fine silks, and such— evading the King's crippling import duties and excise taxes. The trade had done well by Arnot, allowing him to amass a fortune and establish himself as a rich and respected country squire. A real Tory, loyal to King and Crown.

Came the Revolution, and Arnot's backing the wrong horse caused him to lose all and vanish into obscurity, leaving only his name to mark the site of his onetime domain. Now, centuries later, the proud owner of the property was Greg Mayhew.

Its centerpiece was a modern-day manor house, a multistory mansion set on a rise overlooking the water. Its rich, silver-gray wooden exterior harmonized with the natural beauty of the surroundings, the bay, fields, and sky. Grouped around it were several smaller outbuildings, among them a barn converted into a multivehicle garage, a toolshed, and a kennel for Mayhew's guard dogs.

Jutting out from the shoreline at right angles, a sixty-foot-long wooden pier thrust out into a cove of the bay, a sheltered natural harbor. Moored alongside the pier was a handsome cabin cruiser, sleek and streamlined, built for speed and power.

Mayhew's property had neighbors to the right and left; their houses could be seen, distantly, but they were well out of shouting distance. The mansion was set back an eighth of a mile from the main road, a stretch of two-lane blacktop running parallel to the waterfront.

A gravel road connected the mansion to the strip of farm highway. A shoulder-high white wooden rail fence marked the edge of Mayhew's land; set in it was a triple-barred white metal gate that barred access to the gravel road.

Night fell heavily here. Darkness was omnipresent, lights were few and far between. The manor house and its outbuildings made a patchy yellow glow on the body of the land and the water's edge.

In the main house, on the second floor, Elise Danner occupied a guest room that had been reserved for her use. Suite of rooms really. There was what could be called a drawing room, a bedroom, and a private bathroom. She was in the bedroom, the room that put the most distance between her and the other occupants of the house.

Like the rest of the mansion, her suite was comfortable, well appointed, and furnished with all the impersonality of a hotel room.

What it was, was a cell.

She was under no illusions on that score. She was under confinement. She had the free run of the house, but that was all.

One thing she knew for certain: Durwood Quentin III was dead. That she knew because she'd seen it on the big flat-screen TV that was part of her suite. It had earned almost sixty seconds coverage on the national network news;

no mean feat, considering how little program time was devoted to hard news as opposed to pop culture pap and personality filler. The local news broadcasts had given it a much bigger play. The story was tailor-made for the tube. It had all the elements: politics, big money, sex, and violence. They were treating it as an open-and-shut case. Rich guy kills street hooker and himself.

Whatever the truth about Quentin's demise, it had taken more than that to sting Mayhew into taking cover at Arnot's Acres. And he had made sure that she, Elise Danner, was right there with him. He wasn't leaving her free and at large, and it wasn't because he was worried about her safety. She knew him too well for that. He'd had her picked up because he was worried about his own safety, about what she could tell about the inner workings of ISS if somebody grabbed her and put the squeeze on her.

It wasn't the feds that had thrown a jolt into him either. That was apparent from the way he'd been handling himself since arriving at the estate. Not just because he had Donny Piersall's heavily armed goon squad patrolling the premises, though that was alarming enough in itself.

No, it was in the details. On arrival, he'd ordered his caretakers to close the curtains on all the windows throughout the house. Because of concern that somebody outside might be spying on him? Or because he feared that somebody might take a shot at him when he was outlined behind a clear glass pane?

She'd always found the main house chilly and unwelcoming at best; it was too much structure for too few occupants, grandiose and barnlike, its oversized rooms and high-ceilinged halls dwarfing the individual. The best thing about it was the vistas of countryside and bay visible from the windows. With the curtained windows blocking out the views, the house felt more opressive than ever.

Mayhew was being careful to stay inside, and had told her to do the same, for her own safety. Not that she had any inclination to go wandering about out of doors, with the chance of a run-in with the caretakers and their guard dogs, or Piersall and any of his people. He was bad enough, but his crew seemed a whole lot worse. They were a piratical-looking bunch, and seeing them reminded her that real, historical pirates weren't picturesque characters with eye patches and colorful parrots perched on their shoulders, stumping around on peg legs and going on about fifteen men on a dead man's chest, yo-ho-ho and a bottle of rum. The genuine article were black-hearted brigands who thrived on rapine and brutality and would cut your throat for a doubloon or just for the fun of it. No, she'd hate to be cornered by some of Donny's people if she were alone and out of sight of any other witnesses.

"Don't go taking any strolls," Mayhew had told her. "You make a better target out in the open."

Target? Who'd want to shoot her? Not the FBI or any other DOJ investigatory agency she'd ever heard of, and she thought she knew them all, from her own years as a CIA analyst. She had no idea that presently she was about to be disabused of that notion . . .

There were more than a few ISS clients, active and former, who might fit the bill. Inside intelligence about the workings of Washington was a lucrative commodity, and ISS had been none too fastidious about whom it sold its wares to. Some were Very Bad People indeed, representing countries where torture and murder were standard operating procedure.

Elise Danner had never seriously considered the possibility of blowback from one of their transactions personally affecting her. Now, though, she could think of nothing else.

Not just exterior threats menaced her. Behind these walls lay the most dangerous potential threat of all: Greg Mayhew himself.

Should he think that she might somehow be detrimental to his interests, he'd eliminate her without so much as a second thought or an iota of regret. Again and again, her anxieties fastened on a realization that had struck her almost immediately on arrival today at the Acres: It was a nice spot for a murder.

And with all that wide expanse of bay right at hand, ideal for disposing of a body. Mayhew's boat was moored right at the pier . . .

Elise Danner now knew the meaning of fear. It was a physical thing, a bodily reaction. Nerves stretched to piano-wire tautness. Constant churning in her guts, like she wanted to throw up. The feeling of being about to jump out of one's skin, like she was going to snap under the pressure and lose it, going out of her head.

And she dare not show it. Any sign, any hint that she might be a weak link could be the deciding factor in provoking Mayhew to get rid of her.

This was fear. Or so she thought.

But in the words of the old saying, "You ain't seen nothing yet."

SIX

Moochie had what he considered the best post: gate guard. He was placed way to hell and gone from everybody else, stationed at the estate's front gate, while everybody else was back at the house. He was supposed to keep watch for suspicious activity on the main road and patrol along the fenced-in landward perimeter of the property.

Suspicious activity? That was a laugh. He'd been out here for almost four hours now, since ten P.M., and the only activity he'd seen was three vehicles going by. That, and a possum crossing the road.

The vehicles had been a car, a pickup truck, and a minivan, and they'd all appeared during the first hour of his post. The minivan had been the first, rolling along the eastbound lane of the two-lane blacktop. Doing about thirty miles an hour, neither slowing down nor speeding up, just going on its way. The lone driver was a woman, but he couldn't see her well enough

to tell if she were young or old, good-looking
or homely.

There were no street lamps on this stretch of
road; the only light nearby came from a flood-
light mounted on a metal pole to one side of
the triple-barred gate, illuminating it. The gate
was closed and locked. The lock was one of
those electromechanical devices. It had a built-
in sensor that responded to a preset frequency
from a keying device. Mayhew and the caretakers each had one of the handheld devices allowing them to come and go as they pleased. The
mechanism could also be unlocked by a key
signal from the house. Visitors had to park outside the gate, get out of their vehicles, and speak
into a device that looked like a parking meter
but was actually an intercom connecting with
the house. They'd have to state their name and
business; if they passed muster, a remote would
unlock and open the gate, which would automatically close and relock once they'd entered.

Moochie was inside the fence, on foot, and
not equipped with one of keying devices. He
was equipped with a hunting rifle, a pistol, and
a flashlight; also, with a cell phone, which was
one of a bunch of cells that Piersall had supplied his crew with. They were to be used for
this one job, and when it was done, they would
be collected and disposed of.

Moochie, twenty-five, was the youngest member of the crew. He had a rooster's comb of
stiff, oily black hair and a long, thin, bony face.
He was skinny, with pipe-stem limbs, partly by
nature and partly because he was a meth tweaker.

A city boy, slum-born and bred, he had a total lack of inhibition about the infliction of violence, which had resulted in a successful criminal career, culminating with recruitment into Piersall's crew. He was urban to the core, and country living held no charms for him. This back-to-nature bit, he felt, was strictly for the birds. He'd go nuts if he actually had to live out here in the middle of nowhere.

The floodlit gate was a zone of light, and he generally stuck close to it for most of his stretch of guard duty. A half-moon hung high in a sky mottled by thin, drifting clouds. Moonlight picked out the long, rolling fields stretching toward the house and the ribbon of the blacktop road.

He toted a hunting rifle. He was no hunter, at least not of the field-and-stream variety, but he had a facility with rifles. His weapon of choice was the handgun, and he had one tucked into a hip pocket of the baggy, cargo-pocketed pants he was wearing.

Twenty minutes after the minivan passed, a pickup truck drove by going westbound. The general darkness allowed Moochie to see the vehicle's lights coming from a long way off. It drew abreast of the gate. The driver's-side window was open. The driver was a fat-faced old guy wearing a soft fisherman's hat. He kept right on going. Moochie stood watching for a long time as the pickup's lights dwindled, winking out in the distance. There wasn't much else to do out here.

Around midnight, the sound of a powerful engine winding out somewhere in the distance made him pick up his ears. A car approached from the west, zooming along the straightaway. Man, it was moving, really moving!

For an instant, he thought maybe this was it, action was breaking. He trembled with eagerness, holding the rifle waist-high in both hands.

A car flashed past, a muscle car, a convertible with the top down. It must have been doing seventy, seventy-five miles per hour. A glimpse of the occupants: A guy was driving and a girl sat in the front seat with him, her long hair streaming behind her like the tail of a comet. A big-ass sound system was cranked up loud, blaring some heavy metal music that competed with the engine's roar.

Then it was gone, rocketing down the road and away.

False alarm. What a letdown, Moochie thought. Still, there went one dude who knew what it was all about. No wonder he was going so fast. He was probably racing to get the hell out of these boondocks. And into that bitch's pants.

That happened around midnight. After that, nothing. Not another vehicle came along. Time dragged by. Moochie thought he'd go out of his mind with boredom. Every fifteen minutes or so, he was supposed to phone the house to report in. Mace was handling the calls at that end, like a dispatcher. Other crew members also reported in regularly on their patrol routines.

Tyrone was covering the pier and the cove. The caretakers, Jimmy Mac and Karl, made the rounds circling the house and outbuildings. They were Mayhew's people and they were more than just caretakers. They looked like they could handle themselves pretty good. They wouldn't be working for Mayhew if they couldn't. They both went around armed. Piersall had passed the word to his crew not to give either of them any crap.

Jimmy Mac was the dog handler. He made the rounds with a pair of leashed Rottweilers. Moochie wouldn't want to be around if they ever got unleashed. They were big, mean-looking brutes. They didn't bark much when left to themselves in the kennel, and never made a sound when Jimmy Mac was around. They just stood there glaring with eyes like reddish-brown marbles and breathed hard. Not panting, but just breathing hard, like they were just itching to slip their leashes and get at you and start tearing. They ever came at Moochie, he wouldn't waste any time wondering what to do, he'd blow them away. This he'd decided. Let Donny square things with Mayhew afterward. Karl was the other caretaker, a big shambling hayseed-looking guy who didn't say much. He made the rounds with Jimmy Mac. When it came time to report in, Karl did the talking.

Sal, one of the crew, was on roving patrol in the jeep, circling the grounds. Havoc Renna and Bennett were in what used to be the chauffeur's quarters, back in the day when one of the previous owners had had a chauffeur. The quarters were a couple of rooms on the upper floor of the stable-turned-garage. Renna and Bennett didn't have to make any rounds. They were the two big guns of the crew, especially now that Sandor was defunct. Sandor had been a hot shooter, too, and whoever burned him down must've been pretty good. Moochie was hazy on the details, because Donny hadn't exactly been too forthcoming about how Sandor and Vane had gone down. One thing Donny had made clear to all the crew, though. If they caught sight of a dark-haired, clean-shaven guy, a "stiff-faced guy with dead-looking eyes"— whatever that meant—they were to shoot first and ask questions later.

Back in D.C., that description would fit a couple hundred thousand guys, but out here in the sticks, it was different. Moochie had no problems on that score. If he saw anybody out here, day or night, whose looks he didn't like, he'd shoot first and ask questions never. If it was the wrong guy, tough. That was Mayhew's problem. He was supposed to be a big shot. Let him square it.

Anyway, Renna and Bennett were the hot rods now, and Donny wanted them posted close to the house as a main line of defense. So they could lounge around in the rooms above the garage and watch TV, listen to the radio, play cards, or do anything else they damned well pleased as long as they were on call.

Big, oxlike Mace was in the main house, monitoring the reports. There was a woman in the house, too, but Moochie hadn't caught so much as a glimpse of her. She was Mayhew's bitch, he guessed, if that white-haired old bastard could even get it up. He wondered what she looked like. Bennett said her looks were okay, but didn't elaborate. That was Bennett, though; nothing much interested him except his guns and using them. Donny was spending a lot of time in the main house. Maybe Donny was getting some off the bitch. Donny was a real chaser; he'd go after anything in skirts.

Moochie wondered what all the fuss was about to bring the whole crew out here in the middle of nowhere. Shouldn't they be back in D.C., looking for the guy who burned down Sandor and Vane? But it looked like Mayhew was the target. That's who they were protecting. Moochie had only the sketchiest of ideas of who Mayhew was and what he did. He was rich, going by the size of the estate, the big house, and the fancy boat. He must be into something dirty, or he wouldn't be hooked up with Donny. He was supposed to be an ex-cop. Moochie hated cops, ex- or otherwise. Donny was an ex-cop, too, but that was different because he hadn't been a real cop, but a crook with a badge, which was okay.

Around one A.M., Moochie had gotten a start when he heard something moving about in the underbrush close to the wooden rail fence. The fields fronting the road were knee-high in weeds. Moochie leveled his rifle, dropping into a crouch.

Something scurried around nearby. It sounded close, real close, like within a dozen yards or so, but Moochie couldn't see a damned thing. He was ready to start blasting. The rustling continued, like whoever was making it didn't give a damn if Moochie heard it or not. Nobody could have sneaked up on Moochie, he was sure of that, but what—

An animal the size of a small dog suddenly broke cover, wriggling out from under the fence and into view on the blacktop. Moochie had to fight hard to keep from shooting.

He had a clear view of it in the light of the gate's lamppost. The creature had a long, pointy snout and a long, skinny hairless tail like a rat. It half waddled, half scrambled across the road, dropping into a ditch on the other side and out of sight.

He was a city boy, but he realized it was a possum. The little bastard had given him a jolt, startling him. He wished now he had shot it, the little prick! But then Donny would have been all over his ass if he'd pulled a stunt like that, so it was just as well that he hadn't. Christ, he'd never hear the end of it from the crew if a possum had panicked him into popping off!

All the same, though, he pointed the rifle at the spot where the possum had dropped into the ditch and said, "Bang!"

He laughed out loud, but it had a hollow sound, and he choked it off almost as soon as it had gotten started.

Finally, two A.M. rolled around, the end of his shift. Hell, his relief should have been here already. He reached for his cell to sound off about it, but then he saw a pair of headlights round a corner of the main house and appear at the far end of the gravel road. Sal, in the jeep. "About fucking time," Moochie muttered, pocketing the cell. Something he'd never have dared to say to Sal's face.

The headlights neared, closing the distance, resolving into the outline of the jeep. The vehicle raised a pale cloud of dust in its wake, churned up from the gravel road. The glare bothered Moochie, and he put a hand over his eyes to shield them. He was damn glad to see the jeep, though. He was looking forward to some human company back at the main house—get some hot coffee and maybe a sandwich. What he really wanted was a couple of lines of meth, but the summons from Donny for the Mayhew gig had come suddenly, and he'd been caught short without a reserve of his favorite drug. Maybe it was just as well; if he'd had some, doing it out here in hickland would have had him running in circles like a hamster in one of those wire wheels they put in their cages.

Nearing the gate, Sal slowed, slewing the jeep around in a half circle that put it sideways facing Moochie as it jerked to a halt. The maneuver kicked up a lot of dust, plumes of it wafting through the twin beams of the headlights. Moochie got some in his lungs and started coughing.

Sal got out of the jeep and rounded the front of it, crossing toward Moochie. He left the motor running. Sal had a spade-shaped face and was short and chunky. He laughed when he saw Moochie coughing. Moochie forced himself to stifle it. Sal said, "Having fun?"

Moochie hawked up a glob of phlegm and spat, clearing his throat. Some of it got on his mouth and he wiped it off with the back of his hand. "It's fucking dead out here. Not even a car going by for hours. This is worse than being in solitary."

"How would you know?" Sal said, sneering. "You ain't never been in solitary."

Which was true. Moochie had spent some time in reformatories and done a few short stretches in the county jail, but he'd never served time in a real penetentiary, as had Sal. Sal had done a two-year bid for theft and a separate, five-and-a-half-year term for manslaughter. He was known as a stand-up guy who'd never ratted anyone out, as he continually liked to remind anyone within listening distance.

Moochie fired back, "That's because I'm too smart to get caught."

Sal smirked. "Keep on thinking like that and you'll be inside in no time."

"Yeah, I'll be inside the house while you're out here pulling gate guard. In fact, I'll be on my way right now, thank you very much."

"Hold on, lemme call in first," Sal said. He flipped open his cell and talked into it. "Hello, Mace? It's me, Sal. I'm at the front gate now . . . Hold on, I'll ask him." He moved the cell away from his mouth. "Anything happening out here, kid?"

Moochie said, "Not a fucking thing."

"All quiet," Sal said into the cell. "What else would you expect? Okay, Mooch's coming in now. I'll report in in a half hour. Another thing, Mace. I ain't staying out here no four hours. Two hours, tops . . . Don't tell me your problems.

I don't care who you get, but send somebody to relieve me at four. How should I know? Tyrone can pull a stretch out here, or Karl the care-taker. Tell you what. You come out here and I'll sit in the big house fielding the phone calls . . . I am not fucking kidding. Two hours tops. Talk to you later."

Sal closed the cell and dropped it into the right breast pocket of his gaudy sport shirt. "Fucking Mace. How come he gets all the soft jobs?"

Moochie shrugged. "Donny likes to have him around."

"Yeah, like a pet dog."

"I'll tell him you said that."

"No, you won't, kid. You got more sense than that."

Moochie decided to change the subject. "Anything going on back at the house?"

Sal shook his head. "Donny and Mayhew are thick as thieves, Renna and Bennett are playing grab-ass in the garage, and Jimmy Mac is doing it doggie-style with one of his Rotties. He's the one taking it up the ass."

"I'll be heading in then."

"Can't wait to get some of that Jimmy Mac action, huh? You'll have to wait your turn, though. Karl's on line ahead of you. So's the other Rottie, for that matter."

"Have fun out here, Sal."

"It's nothing to me, kid. I like the peace and quiet. Especially since I'm getting paid for it."

Something rustled in the weeds nearby, and for an instant Moochie thought the possum had returned. His back was toward the source of the noise. Sal was facing it.

Sal pulled a face, eyes popping, jaw dropping. His reaction was so comically exaggerated that Moochie had to caution himself to keep his own face straight. This was priceless, a tough guy like Sal being spooked by a possum.

Uttering a wordless cry, Sal clawed for the gun at his side. A black blot the size of a half-dollar appeared in the center of his forehead. Simultaneous with it came a metallic chunking thud, like the sound of an engine slipping a piston rod.

Sal's head snapped back on its neck with a recoil comparable to its connecting with a swung baseball bat. He followed it, tumbling backward, hand still clutching the butt of the gun he hadn't been quick enough to draw from its holster.

Barely had all this registered on Moochie's brain when the back of his head exploded, ending all awareness. It, too, was accompanied by that metallic thunking sound.

He was flung forward, sprawling partly across Sal's body, which already lay flattened on the gravel road.

Steve Ireland knelt on one knee in the weeds inside the fence, about a half-dozen paces east of the gate. His right hand held a pistol with a metal cylinder attached to the muzzle. The attachment was about the size and shape of a canned energy drink, longer and thinner than a beer can. A wisp of smoke curled from bore in the center of the cylinder.

The cylindrical attachment was a suppressor, what Sal and Moochie would have called a silencer. It had reduced the report of the two gunshots to a pair of metallic clunking thuds, and eliminated almost all of the muzzle flare.

Steve was bareheaded, except for a pencil-thin communicator worn on the left side of his face, a headset transceiver that was a curved tube with one end terminating in an earpiece and the opposite end in a small knob near his mouth. A sleeveless utility vest was worn over a protective Kevlar bullet-proof vest, which was worn over a dark T-shirt. He needed the utility vest, its multi-pockets holding mostly spare magazine clips and shotgun shells. The clips were for his guns and the shells for the sawed-off, twelve-gauge riot pump shotgun worn slung by a strap across his back. Baggy dark pants and hiking boots completed the outfit.

Out here in the country by the bay, it was cooler and less humid than it had been in the city, but between the utility vest and the flak jacket and the hardwear, it was still hot as hell. Comfort is often the first sacrifice to efficiency.

He'd been inside the fence for some time, an hour if not more. He'd low-crawled through the weeds with exacting slowness, worming his way toward Moochie. Moochie had preferred loitering under the gate lamppost to walking the fence line. The few times he'd walked the fence, he'd been mightily unobservant, unknowingly passing close to Steve each time.

These seemingly open fields provided plenty of cover if you knew how to exploit it, rocks and shrubs, ditches and swells and hollows. And that's not even taking into account the abundance of knee-high weeds blanketing the ground.

Steve had made his final approach when the jeep drove out to the gate. Its noise had obscured what few small sounds were made by his passage, while its lights helped totally obliterate whatever night vision Moochie had managed to acquire during his vigil. Sal was even more clueless.

Once Sal had finished reporting in, that had spelled his end and Moochie's, too. Steve could have made the kills from the prone position, but he'd felt a little more secure making them from the kneeling position, so he'd knelt on one knee, using that position to steady his gun hand.

Generally, he was a headhunter. The torso shot is the safest option according to the rule books; the bigger the target, the easier it is to hit. True enough, but in this day and age, you never knew who might be wearing a bullet-proof vest under their garments, even a pair of hoods like these two he had just eliminated. Never underestimate the enemy. Besides, at this close range, making the head shots required no great feat of marksmanship on his part. Even with the suppressor. He was no great fan of suppressors. They could be tricky at times, tempermental. But he'd tried this one out earlier today and it met his specifications, so he felt comfortable enough using it to make the double kill. Silence and stealth were assets on this mission for as long as they could reasonably be maintained.

Rising partly up out of the weeds, he'd tagged Sal first, drilling him square in the center of the forehead, then putting the second shot in the back of Moochie's cranium. Kill the brain and instant death ensues, shutting down even any reflex muscular reactions.

Steve reached for his headset communicator, switching it on. He'd had it switched off since beginning his final approach, not wanting any distractions while he was getting set to deliver the deathstroke.

A tingling throb in the tube running along his jawline and a faint, tinny buzzing in his earpiece told him the device was functional.

"Eye here," he said. "The gate is secured. Over."

He spoke no louder than a whisper. The transceiver components were microminiaturized, the tiny beadlike condenser microphone as remarkably sensitive to transmit the softest sounds as the earbud audio pickup was to receive them. A thin flexiplastic earpiece circled the base of his left ear where it met the skull, anchoring the headset in place.

The replies followed:

"Oh here. Acknowledged."

"Bee here. Acknowledged."

"Enn here. Acknowledged."

"Emm here. Acknowledged."

The mission had drawn a five-man unit. For the sake of verbal shorthand, each member had taken the first letter of his last name for a call sign. None of them shared the same last initial.

Steve was "Eye" for Ireland.

"Oh" was Osgood, the driver.

"Bee" was Bryce, like Steve a member of the assault squad going in.

"Enn" was Nevins, also an assault squad member.

"Emm" was Mantee, the boat-handler covering the cove.

The jeep was parked parallel to the road, facing west, its headlights throwing long twin cones of radiance in that direction.

A patch of woods about fifty yards away inside the fence and east of the gate yielded two figures. Bent almost double to minimize their profile in the open field, they hustled over toward the gate, joining Steve. Like him, they crouched behind the jeep, keeping it between them and the house.

They were Bryce and Nevins. Bryce, a black man with a shiny, clean-shaven scalp, had a heavyweight fighter's build. Nevins had short wavy hair with a widow's peak and a long-muscled swimmer's build. They were similarly outfitted like Steve, except that Bryce was armed with an assault rifle and Nevins with a Swedish knockoff of an M-4 machine gun.

That was part of the cover story, the legend, going in. The Dog Team higher-ups didn't want this to look like a military operation, didn't want any hardware used that could be traced back to the military in general and the Army in particular. Not even weapons that were officially listed as having been lost, stolen, or strayed from arsenals or National Guard armories, of which there was no shortage. They wanted it to look like gang-related activity. That would play right into Piersall's crew's background. They were home-grown thugs with no international connections.

Considering the state of crime today, a lot of gangs were armed with heavy firepower. Bryce's weapon was a foreign-made knockoff of an M-16. Ditto for Nevins's piece, a Scandinavian arms company's clone of an M-4. Steve's riot gun actually was American made, but there were plenty of them in circulation and the weapon had no particular military connotation. More of a police connection really. That would jibe with Mayhew and Piersall's ex-cop background.

All the hardware was sterile; that is, their histories tracked back to a dead end with nothing to incriminate their actual source—namely, the Dog Team's munitions supplier. That went for the handguns with which the squad was supplied; the ammunition, too. Just in case the operation went sour and weapons were left behind with their dead wielders and not secured by the survivors, if any.

The only really high-tech equipment they carried consisted of the transceiver communicators. Costly and sophisticated though they were, they were commercially available. A trace on the serial numbers would reveal only that they were part of a lot stolen from the inventory of a Chicago "spy store," one of those outlets where the public can buy all kinds of electronic eavesdropping equipment to snoop on errant spouses, business rivals, and so on.

Steve spoke into the communicator. "Eye to Oh, Eye to Oh. Come in, please. Over."

"Oh here, over," replied Osgood.

"You can move up here now, over."

"Roger, over."

"Eye, over and out."

Osgood was the driver. Four of the five-man squad had arrived by land. Their vehicle was a Klondike, one of the largest of all SUVs. The model had been discontinued by the manufacturer because it was such a gas guzzler that none but the extremely well heeled could afford to keep it fueled, but that wasn't a concern to the Dog Team. The Klondike was on the far side of a rise on the road to the east, about a quarter mile away, standing in an off-road glade. Earlier, Steve, Bryce, and Nevins had disembarked from it to make their way through the woods to the front fields inside the fence at Arnot's Acres. Osgood had stayed behind with the vehicle.

The fifth member of the squad, Mantee, had come in by water. He was skippering a small, low-slung open speedboat, which now lurked on the other side of the western arm of the Acres' cove. His mission was to ensure that nobody escaped on Mayhew's cabin cruiser. To that end, his craft was mounted with a .50-caliber machine gun. Military hardware, sure, but it sourced back to the military of a South American country, so there was no tie-in to the U.S. Besides, if it came to that, Mantee could always dump it overboard, sinking it in the depths of the bay.

Steve contacted Mantee, alerting him that they were about to make their move. Mantee acknowledged.

Steve unscrewed the suppressor from the gun

barrel and pocketed it. No need for silencers from this point on. He had two pistols, this one and another, which he wore in a belt holster on his right hip. He preferred a shoulder rig, but between the vest and the flak jacket and the sawed-off riot gun on a strap, it would have been too damned complicated. He dropped the pistol in a wide, deep hip pocket. These cargo-pocketed type pants sure were handy.

The Klondike rolled downhill, gliding to a stop near the front gate. Its lights were dark, Osgood driving by the light of the moon. None of the squad had been equipped with night-vision goggles in order to lower the military profile of the mission and maintain the gang-land cover legend.

The Klondike was a big brute, dwarfing a Hummer. It was the kind of SUV that if you wanted to go on a fishing trip, you could fit a canoe inside the rear compartment with the hatchway closed. There was plenty of room for the four men and their gear, with space left for a couple of prisoners if they managed to take any.

The machine came with a V-12 engine, but there had been some customizations: bullet-proof glass, armor plating, and a reinforced frame, shocks, and suspension. The special heavy-duty tires were solid rubber; they would have to be literally shot to pieces to stop working. A special option was the installation under the headlights of a pair of secret compartments, each fitted with a mounted automatic shotgun. The weapons had drum-shaped rotating magazines filled with shells. A set of switches on the dashboard would open twin panel lids and bring the weapons into play. The modification originated with big-time south-of-the-border drug lords, again buttressing the gang-related legend should the vehicle somehow fall into the hands of the authorities.

Osgood's assignment during the assault was the on-land equivalent of Mantee's on the water: to intercept any potential escapees. He'd lay back and cover the landward avenues of retreat.

Steve indicated the jeep with a tilt of his head, saying, "Why walk when you can ride?"

He, Bryce, and Nevins got in the vehicle; Nevins behind the wheel, Bryce on the passenger side, and Steve in the rear. Steve and Bryce unslung their weapons, holding them at the ready.

Nevins swung the jeep around in a curve, putting it on the gravel road pointing toward the house. He started for it, driving at a moderate pace, not wanting to alarm any of the occupants by signs of undue haste.

SEVEN

Mayhew and Piersall were in the big hall of the main house, brainstorming.

A wide, high-ceilinged space, too grand and overbearing to be called a living room, it suggested the banquet hall of a manor house, minus the long table and high-backed chairs. The fireplace was as big as a walk-in closet. No fire burned there now. Opposite it was an L-shaped, three-piece sectional sofa open on the side facing the hearth. Its plush leather upholstery was cocoa-colored. The coffee table was a highly polished mahogany slab the size of a life raft. Sectional and slab sat on a rectangle of ornately patterned red and brown rug.

Its south wall fronted on a pavilion overlooking the bay. The west wall featured a built-in wet bar, lined with bar stools and complete with an old-fashioned brass foot rail. That's where Mayhew and Piersall were, perched on two stools, leaning on the bar facing each other.

Mayhew was drinking rye whiskey. That gave

Piersall a laugh. Just like Mayhew somehow to drink rye. Whoever drinks rye anymore? It was an old man's drink. Piersall was drinking fine black-label Tennessee sipping whiskey and chain-smoking.

A big-screen TV was tuned into a baseball game. Piersall didn't know who was playing and didn't give a damn. It was just on for background noise, the volume low, but loud enough to mask his and Mayhew's talk from the underlings, the crew members or caretakers who wandered by from time to time. A radio would have served the purpose just as well.

Piersall drained his glass and poured another. He was drinking it straight up, without so much as an ice cube added. This was prime stuff, why dilute it? The fact that he was drinking Mayhew's private stock made it taste all the better. He was drinking it on Mayhew's dime, too, since Mayhew was paying for his time, and the time of all the rest of the Black Glove Crew. Mayhew had already run up a pretty hefty tab, but that was okay, he could afford it. With Piersall, the meter was always running. This was business, not pleasure. Of course, if he could mix the two by working up a nice glow on Mayhew's expensive booze while getting paid for it, why, that was a double dividend. Mayhew gave him a dirty look. "Go easy on that stuff. I don't need you getting sloshed."

Piersall said, "I can handle it."

"Like you handled that red-hot who gunned down two of your best boys?"

Piersall refused to rise to the bait. He was

used to Mayhew's sharp tongue; it didn't cut any ice with him. Mayhew needed him or he and the crew wouldn't be here now. That was the bottom line.

He took a taste of the whiskey, savoring its sweet-spicy burn on his tongue before swallowing. "They were a long way off from being my best boys, Greg."

"Vane maybe, but that Sandor was pretty sharp. He was no pushover."

"The shooter got lucky," Piersall said. "That won't happen again now that we're ready for him. Anyway, that's your fault."

Mayhew's smooth pink face reddened, his white tufted eyebrows lifting. "My fault? How do you get that?"

"You didn't tell me that somebody else had designs on Quentin. If I'd known, I'd have planned accordingly. I can only operate on the information you give me, Greg."

"It's your job to be ready for unexpected contingencies."

"I was ready," Piersall said. "The job got done. I moved on the stranger, too. That he got away was just a bad break, that's all." He drank some more whiskey. "Anyway, there's been no comeback on the Quentin kill. Everybody bought the story."

"Except for the stranger. He knows better," Mayhew said. "Him, and whoever he works for."

Piersall tilted his head in agreement. "Which brings us back to the Big Question." He put special emphasis on the words "Big Question." He said, "Who does he work for?"

"Christ! If I knew the answer to that, you wouldn't be sitting around here swilling my best booze. You'd be out collecting scalps," said Mayhew.

"Unh-unh," Piersall said, shaking his head. "Somewhere inside, you do know the answer. There's some clue, some tell, some piece of information that points back at the sender. It's just a matter of sorting through the pieces and putting them together to make them all add up."

Mayhew got a little redder in the face, accenting the whiteness of his tufted eyebrows and the bright blue of his eyes. With his head of thick white hair, those brows, and the sharp beak of his nose, he reminded Piersall of a white owl. Mayhew said, "I can do without the lecture on investigative work, thank you very much."

In the glow of the whiskey, Piersall felt expansive. "Let's look at the facts. We know that the guy wasn't law. Otherwise, the Quentin kill would have gone down as a hit and the cops would be looking for the hitter, and hasn't happened. Of course, the cops could be pretending to buy into the story to lull the killers—us—into a false sense of security until they lower the boom, but that's not how it reads."

Mayhew shook his head, a flat denial. "My sources in the department, and I've got some damned good ones, say the brass and the homicide boys have bought into the murder-suicide theory."

"Which is one less thing for us to worry about," Piersall said. "So we know the stranger was no lawman, either local or federal. They're not so cooperative about covering up kills."

"Quentin was into a lot of shit. A lot of people had reason to want him dead. Maybe the stranger was working on contract for one of them."

"Maybe," Piersall conceded. "Whoever he is, he's a pro. But he's not Mob. My sources among the wiseguys have told me that. He's not with the local syndicate and he's not from any out-of-town branch either."

Mayhew frowned, unhappy. "You'd better be damned careful pumping those hoodlums for information. Get them interested, and they'll have a handle on you," he said. "On me."

"You know me, Greg, I'm the soul of discretion. I don't tip my hand."

Mayhew was thoughtful. "The stranger's a freelancer then. A hired gun."

"Could be," Piersall said. "He's not underworld, though. Otherwise, I'd've heard of him. There's not that many unaffiliated contract killers out there. Pros, I mean."

Discovering his glass was empty, Piersall refilled it and took another belt, getting a kick out of the dirty looks Mayhew was giving him. He got a kick out of the whiskey, too. Mayhew really was a grumpy old bastard. If he thought Piersall couldn't handle the stuff, he had another think coming.

Prepared to dazzle him with his sagacity, Piersall played his trump card. "Maybe we're looking at this from the wrong end."

"How so?" Mayhew said, snappish.

"Yours," Piersall said. Resting a beefy forearm

on the edge of the bar, he leaned toward Mayhew to make his point. "You're into a lot of shit, too, stuff that I don't know about. Maybe Quentin wasn't the target. Maybe it's you."

Mayhew was all set to get a grudge on, but dropped it as the import of Piersall's words sank in. "Keep talking, Donny," he said, even-toned.

"It's simple," Piersall said. "Maybe this is some kind of comeback from something else you've got going on. The stranger was interested in Quentin not for himself, but as an angle to get to you."

"I've considered it," Mayhew said. He hadn't touched his drink for some time; the ice cubes were all melted, leaving a pale, wheat-colored liquid in his glass. The glass was beaded with condensation; it looked like it was sweating. Gripping it tightly, Mayhew raised it to his lips, drinking deep. When he set it down, the glass was empty. His palm and the insides of his fingers glistened with moisture. He wiped them with a cocktail napkin, crumpling it into a ball and dropping it into an ashtray filled with butts of cigarettes already smoked by Piersall.

Knowing he had scored, Piersall pressed his advantage. "Anybody that you've got a beef with lately, or that's got one with you? A dissatisfied customer maybe. Or a rival. A man can't do business without making some enemies. Maybe that's where the heat is coming from.

"In which case, the solution is simple. Finger the most likely suspect and we'll dig into him. If there's something there, we'll find it. Then we'll take his head and your problems are over."

Rattling sounded as Mayhew reached into the ice bucket, hauled out some cubes, and dropped them into his glass. He poured in a generous splash of rye and took a long, solid pull.

Knowing that he had the other hooked, Piersall slackened up the line, giving him some wriggling room before reeling him in. Coming at Mayhew at an oblique angle, he continued.

"Your business is your business, Greg. I'm not one to pry, you know that. But I can do my job better if I've got something to work with," Piersall said. With elaborate nonchalance, he made a show of interest in his drink, sipping it, swirling it around his tongue, and swallowing it, culminating in a softly satisfied "Ah."

After a pause, Mayhew said, "Well . . ."

Not looking directly at him, Piersall reached for the bottle, refreshing his drink.

"There is somebody," Mayhew said, "somebody who might—just might, mind you—have convinced himself that he's got cause for dissatisfaction with the firm . . ."

Piersall said politely, "Oh?"

"He's a foreigner, and you know how those types can be. Touchy. Quick to take offense where none was meant, slow to forgive."

"Like you," Piersall said, grinning.

"Or you," Mayhew fired back. He took another swallow of rye. "He's an Iranian. Darius, his name is. At least, that's what he calls himself."

"You sure get around, Greg." Piersall made his tone admiring.

"I'm in the information business, in Washington, D.C. You meet all kinds."

"This Darius, he's got a beef with you?"

"He might see it that way," Mayhew admitted. "I sold him a piece of, shall we say, confidential information. He got the idea that I sold the same information to someone else."

"Was he wrong?"

"You know how it is in business," Mayhew said. "Yeah, I sold it twice. To him and some group in the Southwest. Two completely separate interests, totally disconnected from each other. I figured there wasn't a chance in hell of either party finding out the same goods had been retailed twice."

Piersall prompted, "But?"

"There's always some lousy complication," Mayhew said, bitter-mouthed. "A middleman in the same business—information, that is—turns out he knew both parties. Biro Fleck."

"What's that?"

"Biro Fleck," Mayhew repeated, annoyed. "That's the middleman. He sold both groups information about me, that I'd been selling the same secrets to both."

Piersall shook his head, bemused. "Your waters run deep, Greg."

"If I could've gotten a line on Fleck, I'd have sicced you on him, Donny. But he's a smart bastard who knows how and when to make himself scarce. He may not even be in the country, for all I know."

"Never too late."

Mayhew shook his head. "It's not Fleck that concerns me, it's Darius. A hard and unforgiving man. The Southwest group I'm not worried about. They're a bunch of Iraqi humps that are here illegally. I've got enough on them to sink them and they know it, so there's no danger of comebacks from that department."

Piersall said, "Iraqis, Iranians . . . you mix with the damnedest people."

"Business is business, you take it where you find it." Mayhew's features took on a stubborn cast, defensive.

"Hey, I'm not casting stones. I'm no flag-waver. Like I give a shit," Piersall said, snickering.

The tautness in Mayhew's face slackened. "Turns out Iran and Iraq have got no use for each other. In fact, they hate each other's guts. Which was another thing I was counting on when I sold them both the same intelligence. If it wasn't for that damned Fleck . . ."

"Sure, sure, but what about this Darius?"

"Him being Iranian, he didn't take any too well to the knowledge that the Iraqis had the same supposedly exclusive info he did. Neither did the Iraqis, but they're a long way off and in no position to kick about it. But Darius, that's another story." The tension returned to Mayhew's face. "Darius is here, in D.C. And I don't have the hold over him that I do over the Iraqis. He's a secretive bastard and I've never been able to learn much about him: his background, home address, friends, loved ones, associates. I know enough about him to know that he's the type to come looking for some payback. Maybe the stranger is working for him."

Piersall shrugged. "If he's in D.C., we can get

to him. You must have a way of contacting him; after all, you did business with him."

"I only met face-to-face with him once or twice, always in public places," Mayhew said. "He usually worked through other people, cutouts."

"No problem. We get hold of them, squeeze 'em, and find out where Darius is. He winds up on the bottom of the Potomac and all your troubles go away."

Mayhew fretted. "If it is Darius who's putting on the heat . . . I'm not sure. But if I had to pick the one person who might be gunning for me, he's the one."

"If it's not him, no big deal," Piersall said. "You can cross him off your suspect list and you won't have to worry about him in any case."

"I'm not worried," Mayhew said, getting huffy, his neck cords quivering. "I fear no man, and don't you ever forget it. I buried better men than him when I was just a rookie cop in uniform, and I'll put a bullet in his guts without batting an eye if it comes to that."

"Don't get yourself in an uproar. Nobody's casting any aspersions on your manhood," Piersall soothed. "I just meant that whether or not he's the problem, we'll fix him."

"And collect a nice fat fee for yourself in the process, eh, Donny?"

"Like you said, Greg, you take your business where you find it. And if this Darius is the guy, I'll make sure that he gives up the name of the shooter who burned down Sandor and Vane," Piersall said. "I've got a score to settle with that guy."

Mayhew said, "I'll drink to that."

Refilling their glasses, they clinked them together in a kind of toast. Before they could down their drinks, though, the shooting started.

The gravel road forked as it neared the main house, one branch curving to the left to form a driveway that swept up to the front entrance before continuing to the building's northeast corner, then rounding it to continue to the rear of the house. The other branch followed a straight course paralleling the house's west face; at the southwest corner, it forked again, one branch swinging left behind the back of the house into a yard between the outbuildings, the other following its straight course toward the pier on the bay.

No ordinary gray gravel would suffice; no, the pathways were made of white gravel, fine small white stones that made the straightaways and forking branches glimmer pale and ghostly in the moonlight, against the dark body of the ground.

Nearing the first fork, Nevins slowed the jeep to a crawl so Steve could hop out without the vehicle stopping. Steve peeled off to the left, toward the front of the house. The jeep, with Nevins and Bryce, continued straight, gliding past the mansion's west side, then forking left into the yard between the back of the house and the outbuildings.

They'd all switched off their transceivers, folding them up and pocketing them before going into action. In combat, such techno-gimmicks were often more hindrance than help, and could prove a lethal distraction when the utmost concentration was required. Time enough for the communicators when the shooting stopped and the killing was done . . .

Crouched low, almost double, Steve quick-timed it toward the front of the west wing. All the windows had closed curtains, muffling the lights in the rooms behind them. Night gloom was thicker there than at the pillared, porticoed front entrance, which was bathed in brilliance from ground-level floodlights.

Steve got up close to the looming wall, hugging the cool dimness as he made his way toward the front entrance. Before he reached it, gunfire sounded from the rear of the house.

The jeep rolled on into the yard, an open space framed by a toolshed, the barn garage, and some smaller cube-shaped structures scattered toward the right. The yard was well lit by outdoor lamps. In its center were grouped four figures: two men and two dogs. The jeep lurched to a halt, Nevins hitting the high beams to dazzle the opposition with their glare.

The caretakers, Karl and Jimmy Mac, were in the middle of making their rounds. Karl, big and shambling, wore a checkered shirt, work pants, and boots, and carried a rifle. Jimmy Mac was short, scrawny, and bowlegged. In one hand was a brace of leashes, each leash atttached to the neck collar of a Rottweiler. The Rottweilers appeared to be the size of Shetland ponies. In the headlights, their eyes blazed like balls of blood. They bristled, quivering with menace.

Karl leveled his rifle, firing waist-high. A round struck the jeep's front grille; a second shot blew out one of the headlights.

Bryce hated guard dogs. Once, on a stealthy night raid against the headquarters of a Central American drug lord, a guard dog had closed with him unexpectedly as he was crossing a dark patio. Possibly due to its training, possibly because its vocal cords had been surgically severed, it emitted no warning bark or growl. There was the scrape of its paw claws against the flagstones and the impression of something swift and inexorable as it charged, and then it was on him. He just had time enough to instinctively throw up his arms to protect his face and throat. Fangs ripped and tore his flesh; the impact of the lunge knocked him down. At that, he was lucky; some attack dogs are trained to go first for the groin. This one went for his throat. Bryce lay squirming and writhing on his back on the patio stones, muscular forearms ripped and torn by a fanged muzzle that sought his neck. Somehow, he got one forearm wedged deep between the beast's jaws, freeing his other arm to wrap around its neck. A big, powerful man, he got the devil dog into a headlock and, bringing his weight to bear, succeeded in breaking its neck. Pain and loss of blood nearly finished him, but he managed to survive. The doctors did what they could, but he still bore the scars to this day, and in cold or damp weather, could still feel their phantom bite deep in his flesh.

Now, when Bryce saw the Rottweilers, he opened fire on them. His weapon's selector was set on auto-fire and he triggered a three-round burst into the nearer of the two animals, downing it.

Jimmy Mac screamed, "No!"

Startled by the gunfire, Karl threw himself to the right, his right. His feet got tangled up with each other and he fell, tumbling sideways.

This saved his life, because Nevins squeezed off a burst of machine gun fire his way, and instead of chopping Karl in the middle, it passed harmlessly over his head. Falling, Karl still kept hold of his rifle. Hitting the ground, he rolled away from the line of fire.

When the first guard dog was shot, Jimmy Mac had unthinkingly released his grip on both leashes. The other dog, the one not shot, launched itself toward Bryce. Bryce let go with a burst, putting a half-dozen rounds into it. The momentum of the Rottweiler's charge carried it all the way to the jeep, even with most of its head shot off and its chest riddled.

Jimmy Mac pulled a handgun out of his pants pocket and fired at Bryce. Bryce and Nevins had both left the jeep, diving out their respective sides. Bullets from Jimmy Mac's gun blew out the windscreen and thunked into the engine block. The engine began jammering in a loud, discordant rhythm, like it was trying to shake itself apart.

Nevins fired from the prone position, stitching Jimmy Mac up the middle. Jimmy Mac fell backward, his gun hand raised straight up, pointing at the sky, reflexively firing off one last blast before he flopped over on his back, dead.

Nevins squirmed to one side, wriggling on his belly, looking for Karl so he could shoot him. But Karl was out of sight, having managed to duck behind a stone pillar at the foot of a short, wide staircase leading up to an extensive pavilion at the rear of the house. Karl stuck his head out for a look-see. Nevins's gun muzzle pointed at him and fired. But Karl had ducked back in time. Nevins's rounds cratered the square-edged pillar, ripping off chunks of stone. It sounded like a jackhammer breaking up pavement.

The jeep's wounded engine continued making an ungodly racket, muffling, but not completely obscuring, the sound of a second-floor sliding door in the front of the barn garage being flung open. The doorway was a relic of the era when the barn had been just that, a barn, and the upper loft had been used for storing hay bales and such that were winched into place.

In the doorway space appeared Havoc Renna, wild-haired, wild-eyed, with a Herculean physique, holding a machine gun pistol in each hand. His weapons were of the Uzi variety; he started firing down into the yard below.

Bryce, who had come tumbling out of the jeep's passenger side, somehow got his feet under him and half stumbled, half fell toward the cover of a toolshed.

Up in the loft, Renna was working his guns like fire hoses, holding the triggers down and spraying lead. A tremendous volley of slugs tore up the ground below. Seeing Bryce in the corner of his eye, he swung the machine gun pistols in the intruder's direction.

Bryce lost his footing and fell, but not before reaching the toolshed, belly-crawling behind it. A fusillade tore through the wooden-walled shed, ventilating planks, richocheting off pieces of equipment inside, spraying clouds of wood chips. Bryce's face was in the dirt as he concentrated on flattening out his body as much as possible. A hand span away from him, the earth shuddered as a line of slugs tore into it.

Renna was firing blind; he couldn't see Bryce, but he knew he was behind the toolshed and kept pumping lead into it, hoping to tag Bryce that way.

Nevins got set to shoot Renna, whose massive form framed in the square of the loft doorway made a ripe target. A round passed so close to Nevins that he could feel the rush of its passage just missing his head.

It came courtesy of Karl, who'd just taken a potshot at him with his hunting rifle from behind the pavilion stairway's banister. Nevins returned fire, but Karl had already ducked safely under cover and Nevins's rounds damaged only the stonework.

Nevins was in a bad position, stretched out prone in the open to the right of the jeep with no cover. He was just lucky that Renna's attention was caught by Bryce, because Renna could have nailed Nevins sure if he'd focused on him first.

Behind and to the left of Nevins was a blocky metal cube, an exterior component of the big house's extensive air-conditioning system.

Some kind of ventilator or heat-exchange unit. It was about four feet high, five feet long, and three feet deep. It stood ten feet away from the house's rear wall.

To Nevins, it looked like a good place to be, anyway a hell of a lot better than where he was. Firing another burst at Karl to keep him pinned down, he rose crouching, pivoted, and made a dash for the blocky cube unit.

The motion registered on Renna, who swung his guns in Nevins's direction. In that instant they came up empty, the clips exhausted.

Nevins dove headfirst over the unit's grilled top, clearing it and landing hard on the other side. Karl popped up from behind the stone banister and shot at Nevins, but missed. Two rounds thwacked into the wall of the house.

The fall partly knocked the wind out of Nevins, but he kept moving, gathering himself, huddling against the side of the cubed unit. Its metal exterior felt cool against the side of his face.

In the loft, Renna ducked back out of sight to reload. In the center of the yard, the shuddering jeep made a hell of a racket. Karl shot at Bryce, missed. Bryce low-crawled around the corner, behind the back of the shed, putting it between himself and Karl. It covered him from Renna, too.

Nevins poked the machine gun muzzle around the edge of the cube, probing for an opening, an opportunity. From the ground floor of the barn, the garage area, came a flicker of movement and a volley of slugs. A third defender had come into play: Bennett. Wielding a big-bore semiautomatic pistol, he tried to take off Nevins's head.

Nevins had seen the newcomer in time to pull his head back out of range. The cube unit vibrated as some slugs tore into it. Its smooth-sided exterior must have contained a mass of machinery, thwarting deep penetration by the rounds, flattening them into lead smears.

Nevins had reason to be doubly grateful for its solidity, as Renna resumed firing, this time at him. The cube unit absorbed bullets, which hammered it like rivets being driven in.

Things were getting hot!

On the other side of the building, when the shooting started, Steve Ireland made his move. He'd planned to go in by the front door, using the riot gun to blow open the locks and clear the way. If he had his druthers, he'd have used a grenade, but grenades had been ruled off-limits for tonight's mission by the higher-ups, in the interest of furthering the nonmilitary, gang-related nature of the assault. Not that some of these gangs lacked grenades and machine guns and whatnot; hell, some of the big-time cartels had their own fleet of aircraft, and even submarines.

Thinking twice, Steve decided to change tactics. For all he knew, the front double doors might be reinforced and crossbarred.

Beside him loomed the façade of the mansion's west wing, with its array of high, curtained bay windows. Their sills were about chest-high. The curtains were thick, opaque, blocking off all view of what lay inside. Mayhew was certainly a man who valued his privacy. Impossible to tell from the outside whether the room within was occupied or not. Not that it mattered much either way.

Standing a few paces back, Steve loosed a blast into the nearest window, immediately following it up with another.

Glass panes exploded inward, disintegrating in a mass of shards, bringing down drapes and curtain rods with him. The tall window might just as well have been hit with a wrecking ball. Crystalline fragments cascaded, raining down on the interior. A pall of gun smoke hung in the air.

Within lay a wide, handsomely appointed, well-lit space, seemingly unoccupied. Steve glanced up at the top of the window frame, making sure no glass shards remained to work themselves loose and come down like guillotine blades. That would be a hell of a note, to get decapitated while making his entry!

Some saw-toothed fragments remained sticking up out of the sill like glass fangs. Steve's riot gun had a short, chopped wooden stock; he used the butt end to sweep the shards clear. Grabbing the sill, he chinned himself up and inside.

Broken glass and ragged, shredded drapery made a hell of a mess on plush, deep-pile wall-to-wall carpeting. Steve moved to one side, so as not to be outlined with his back turned toward where the window used to be. He didn't know who might be roaming around out front. Moving out of the potential line of fire, he put himself between two curtained windows, his back to the wall between them.

Standing half-crouched, legs bent at the knees, Steve worked the slide, jacking another shell into the chamber. There was a ringing in his ears from the previous blasts. There was also a wheep-beeping sound, irritatingly persistent, which he realized was no auditory effect but rather an alarm, doubtless triggered by his forced entry.

He faced south, toward the rear of the house. The surroundings were rich, all cream-colored carpeting and pale blue walls lined with engravings of old-time hunting and racing prints.

Sizable though it was, the space he was in was a kind of anteroom to a much larger room that lay beyond, on the far side of an archway gaping in the opposite wall. On his left, a high, square-sided portal accessed the front entrance and main hall. It was ablaze with light, its rose marbled floor shot through with iridescent gold-colored veins. Or maybe they were shot through with real gold, Steve didn't know. From a high ceiling hung a crystal chandelier.

The front hall was all white brightness, while the room beyond the anteroom was dimly lit and thick with the shadows. Steve headed that way; it seemed sneakier. He padded light-footed, unable to avoid stepping on pieces of glass scattered on the floor. The carpet was so plush that he felt like he was practically wading through it. He approached at an oblique angle, not wanting to be outlined by the archway.

The arch opened onto a dining room, its long axis running north-south. In its center was a chair-lined table that could comfortably have seated a dozen guests. Above it, hanging down from the ceiling, was another chandelier; this one was unlit. At the opposite end was a door, outlined in light that shone on its far side. It and the light flooding through the archway from the anteroom were the only sources of illumination; no lights burned in the dining room.

The irritating wheep-beeping continued; the alarm system extended throughout the house, Steve guessed.

He crossed the dining room sideways, side-stepping crabwise, like a basketball player's lateral move. Presented less of a target profile that way. The west wall was lined with curtained windows, the east by tall glass-fronted wooden cabinets containing stacks of plates, cups and saucers, crockery of all kinds. Steve moved his crabbed way between the cabinets and the table.

The far door must have been a swinging door, for suddenly it swung inward and open, continuing with such force that it crashed against the inner wall.

Standing in the doorway, backlit, was a hulking man-mountain, a dark outline of a figure that threatened to overflow the confines of the door frame. His features were hidden in shadow, but light glinted on the outlines of the gun held leveled in his hand. A long-barreled revolver, probably a big-ass .44.

Steve shot first, the muzzle flare from his cut-down riot gun resembling a whisk broom made of red and yellow fire. The blast caught the hulk in midsection, blowing him backward out the door.

The hinged, weighted door reversed position, swinging shut. It failed to close all the way, because the man-mountain's big feet were blocking the doorway.

Steve worked the slide, pumping another shell into the chamber. Flattening his back against the wall beside the door, he dropped into a crouch before easing the door open and peering inside. If someone was there waiting, they wouldn't be expecting him to emerge low and would probably shoot high.

The door opened onto a corridor that met it at right angles; on the right, it continued for a few paces before terminating in a blank wall; on the left, it continued for about twenty feet before opening into a kitchen. Steve figured the passageway was used by the help to deliver food from the kitchen to the dining room.

The man-mountain lay flat on his back, stretched across the hallway. His blasted midsection presented a grotesque anatomy lesson, reminding Steve for a moment of one of those biology textbooks where a succession of transparent colored overlays detailed the inner workings of the inner man.

No kitchen help, not this one. Instantly recognizable from the briefings, he was Mace, oxlike enforcer and premium muscle for the Black Glove Crew.

Outside, behind the back of the house, gunfire popped and rattled. Suddenly, gunshots sounded closer, from somewhere in the house beyond the kitchen.

Stepping over Mace's corpse—a long stride—Steve slipped into the passageway, making for the kitchen.

It looked capable of servicing a modest-sized restaurant. In its center was a massive island of a butcher's block table; surrounding it were stainless-steel sinks, rows of cabinets, convection ovens, refrigerators, pantries, and appliances; from ceiling-mounted racks dangled rows of pots and pans.

A breakfast nook littered with a couple of cell phones and a lot of guns, knives, ammo, and empty beer cans, plus an ashtray filled with cigar butts, showed where Mace had been discharging his dispatcher's duties, receiving and tracking the reports of guard patrol units.

On the far side of the kitchen stood the mouth of a passageway connecting with the house's central structure; from there came the sounds of gunfire. Steve made for it. The alarm system kept wheep-beeping.

Outside, the gun battle raged. Among the casualties was the jeep; with a final, yammering lurch, it made a thunking noise and fell still, the engine silenced at last.

Karl's rifle had been quiet for a while; he remained hidden behind the pillar at the foot of the banister.

Huddled behind the back of the toolshed, Bryce alternated firing positions, sometimes popping out from behind the corner nearest to the barn garage, sometimes on the far side, where he had a better line of fire at Karl down by the stone stairway.

True to his name, Renna had wreaked havoc on the toolshed in his attempts to nail Bryce, raining down so many slugs on it that the vertical uprights had been severed, causing the peaked roof to collapse. The top and side wall of the cubical ventilator block were sieved, but its machinery-packed bulk had prevented Nevins from catching a bullet.

Neater and deadlier was Bennett, with his well-placed shots keeping Nevins and Bryce pinned down. One had grazed Bryce's right shoulder, searing a hot furrow across his flesh. Blood soaked his arm to the elbow. He'd torn his right sleeve into strips, wrapping his upper arm and staunching the blood flow as best he could, but it was a concern. The bullet had passed through, severing no veins or arteries, but the blood loss was a weakener and the wound affected his mobility and dexterity to an extent.

Peering around the corner of the shed nearer the house, Bryce glimpsed motion on the pavilion. It was Karl, who'd made his way east along the pavilion's front edge, sheltering behind the stone staircase pillar to hide his movements. Now he was climbing over the balustrade, rifle in hand, in an attempt to flank Nevins and catch him unaware. Covering fire from Renna and Bennett kept Nevins busy and distracted.

Blocking out all thoughts of pain and discomfort, Bryce assumed the shooting position on one knee, using the top of his bent left leg as a platform to steady his supporting bent left arm as he drew a bead on Karl and squeezed the trigger.

The round tagged Karl as he was stepping over the top of the stone rail. His figure wavered, flopping over the rail onto the pavilion, the rifle clattering on the flagstones as it fell from his hands.

He lay on his side, legs working like those of a dog dreaming that it's running. Bryce put another round into him and he stopped moving.

After a pause, Renna resumed firing at Bryce, streaming lead at him with both machine pistols. All to the same lack of effect as before. His bullets had already turned the toolshed into a wreck, but the ruin plus the machinery and equipment within formed a solid barrier to the slugs he rained down on Bryce.

Nevins bided his time, waiting for Renna's guns to empty. At the rate he was firing, the pieces must be red-hot. Nevins hoped the barrels would melt in the bastard's lap.

Renna's guns fell silent. Nevins popped up, firing bursts not at Renna, but at the place in the garage where he figured Bennett was. Bullets ricocheted off the vehicles parked inside. Bennett would be pinned down under cover.

Renna dodged back behind the loft wall to reload. Nevins stopped shooting at Bennett and fired into the wall at the place where he figured Renna would be. His initial onslaught at Bennett was just a feint to buy him the chance for a try at Renna.

Holding down the trigger, Nevins sprayed the loft wall, ventilating it, emptying his clip. A yowling outcry, wild and wailing, sounded from the upper level.

Nevins ducked down behind the metal cube in time to avoid the slugs Bennett threw his way.

Renna staggered sideways, out from behind the wall and into the black square of the open hatchway. He gripped the door frame with one hand, holding himself upright. His other hand still held a machine pistol. He'd been hit, maybe more than once; his hunched form showed a piebald pattern of bloodstains. He vented a squalling shriek of near-unintelligible obscenities as he repeatedly jerked the trigger of an empty gun.

Bryce popped a good, solid shot at Renna, drilling him through the middle. Renna wavered, shaky as a guttering candle flame. Losing his hold, he pitched forward from the waist, like he was taking a bow. Tumbling headfirst out of the loft, he fell into the yard with a crashing thud.

Renna being out of the picture took a lot of heat off Bryce and Nevins. Taking the initiative, they concentrated their fire on the ground floor of the garage, where Bennett's last shots had come from.

Breaking glass sounded from the house behind Nevins. Before he had time to react, he was ripped through the back by a series of tremendous shattering blasts. He lived just long enough to realize that he was dead.

Inside the house, Donny Piersall crouched

beside the glassless window he had just broken and fired through to shoot Nevins in the back. Nevins had been so busy facing off with Renna and Bennett that he'd forgotten to protect his rear. Piersall had gone to the window nearest the outdoor air-conditioning unit behind which Nevins was sheltering, and put the blast on him at nearly point-blank range with a .357. The handgun was loaded with armor-piercing bullets that punched their way through Nevins's flak jacket and into his spine and vitals.

He pumped four slugs into Nevins, loving the way Nevins's body jerked and spasmed under the impact. He threw the last two rounds at Bryce, but the other was farther away and he missed with both shots.

He dodged back from the window, scrambling on hands and knees a half-dozen paces down the hall before Bryce returned fire, triggering a succession of short, quick bursts through the window from which the fatal shots had been fired. They tore up the hallway, but not where Piersall was. The corridor ran between the kitchen and the grand room with the fireplace and bar where he'd been with Mayhew when the shooting started.

Piersall was using speed loads. Sitting on the floor with his knees bent and his back to the wall, he got rid of the empty cylinder and loaded a fresh one.

Some sixth sense, instinct, caused him to look up just in time to see a stranger standing in a half crouch at the end of hallway nearest the kitchen, holding a chopped-down pump shotgun pointed at him.

Not entirely a stranger. Piersall had seen him before, the man with the stiff, masklike face and the dark, intent, ever alert eyes, the man whose interest in Quentin and deadly skill in doing in Sandor and Vane had prodded Mayhew into forting up here at the Acres.

That spark of recognition was just an aside, a stray thought flashing at the edge of Piersall's awareness. His real attention, the center of his awareness, was focused on the shotgun bore leveled at him. That black hole was the biggest thing in all the world, bigger than life itself, as he discovered an eyeblink later.

The blast pretty much blew apart most of Donny Piersall's head. Tomorrow, a forensics team would be picking those gorgeous capped teeth of which he'd been so proud out of the ceiling.

Bennett struck when Bryce started shooting at the house, trying to nail Nevins's killer. Bennett took advantage of the opportunity to dash out of the barn garage into the yard, a pistol in each hand.

Drawing abreast of the front of what was left of the toolshed, he dove for the ground, like a base runner sliding headfirst into home plate. He skittered across dust and stones on his belly, tearing up his underside but unaware of the pain in a rush of kill-fueled adrenaline.

Bryce caught sight of him and started turning,

swinging his rifle barrel toward the other. But Bennett was there first, sprawled flat on the ground, both arms extended, a gun in each hand, pouring a steady stream of slugs into Bryce.

Reports pop-pop-popped away, muzzle flashes crowning Bennett's gun barrels with rings of fire, underlighting his snarling face as he blasted. Bryce rocked under the impact as slug after slug struck home. His flak jacket protected him against some, but not the ones that struck his head, neck, and arms.

The shooting stopped, followed by the merry little tinkling of the last of ejected brass casings raining down on the ground, sounding somehow like delicate wind chimes.

Bryce sagged, slumping, the weapon slipping from his grip. Bennett triggered a few more blasts into the body, but he needn't have; Bryce was done.

Bennett rose, forearms and elbows scraped raw, shirt bunched up around his chest, belly all red and scratched, knees showing through torn pants. He looked like Robin Hood after a rough night in Sherwood Forest.

In the house, a dull hollow boom sounded. Bennett didn't know it, but that was Steve Ireland blowing Donny Piersall's head off.

A set of French doors crashed open; through them, a figure darted out on to the pavillion. Quick as a striking snake, Bennett swung his guns toward the disruption, nearly triggering them until he saw it was Mayhew running out of the house.

Mayhew moved pretty fast for an old guy in

his hunched, crabbed way. Not really running, but hustling in that quick-time jog that spry oldsters can sometimes generate in short bursts of activity.

Scuttling across the patio to its far end, Mayhew lifted one leg over the stone balustrade, then the other. Hanging by his hands, he lowered himself to the ground, which was about three feet below the edge of the pavilion.

Bennett started toward him, almost immediately stopping when a second figure emerged out the French doors onto the patio. Bennett didn't know it was Steve Ireland, but he knew without conscious thought that this was an enemy. He and Steve caught sight of each other at the same time.

Steve's shotgun being empty, instead of pausing to reload, he had discarded it, drawing his pistol, the 9mm Beretta worn holstered at his side, after spotting Mayhew making his exit. Flashing to the patio, he saw Bennett. On the instant, they both started blasting at each other.

Bennett fired first, a split second before Steve, but Steve's aim was truer. Bennett missed; Steve tagged Bennett in the side, spinning him around. Bennett kept shooting, but his aim was off, wild. Steve put another into him. Bennett sat down hard on the ground, upper body weaving, gun hand at his side. A line of blood spilled out the corner of his mouth.

Steve crossed the patio to the stone stairway on the west and started down the steps. Bennett coughed, his mouth spewing blood. He was still trying to raise his gun to bring it into play when Steve shot him dead center in the torso. Bennett flopped back, dead.

Steve took a quick survey of the scene. Mayhew was nowhere in sight. Nevins was stone dead. Bryce's heart still beat, its pulse slow and feeble as Steve pressed his fingertips to Bryce's neck; even as he did so, the last of life flickered out of him and Bryce was gone.

Shouts from the shoreline roused Steve's attention. Mayhew was down at the pier, being helped across the dock toward the boat by a second figure. The second figure fired a few shots at Steve and missed. He was using a handgun, it was a long way off, and he didn't even come close, missing by a country mile.

Steve snagged Bryce's assault rifle, oblivious to the patches of blood staining it. But the clip was empty; no good. He gave the pockets of Bryce's utility vest a quick rummaaging, coming up with a spare clip.

The boat's engines started up, chortling, sputtering, then catching. It sounded like a power lawn motor being fired up, only louder. Steve locked and loaded the clip, starting down the pathway toward the pier even as the boat began edging out into the bay.

It was up to Mantee now. Steve pulled the communicator from an inside vest pocket, unfolding the transceiver, inserting the earpiece, and switching it on. He didn't know whether it would work or not, these high-tech gizmos were fluky and had a tendency to fail when the party got rough. But it hummed with power, the audio bud buzzing tinnily in his ear.

Mantee's speedboat had been lurking on the far side of the cove's west arm. The moon was high, spilling its radiance though a scattering of thin, wispy clouds. The waters of the bay were as hard and shiny black as anthracite coal, save where it was silvered by moonbeams.

The speedboat swung into view, rounding the tip of the cove's western limb as it moved to intercept Mayhew's cabin cruiser.

Steve spoke into the transceiver. "This is Eye. Our primary's on the boat."

"I've got him," Mantee said.

Steve shut up. Mantee didn't need any distractions now. Inside the house, the alarm system continued its damned wheep-beeping.

On the cabin cruiser, Mayhew took the wheel, piloting the boat. He looked as gaunt as the Ancient Mariner of poetry fame, only with a better haircut and a shave. He felt worse, but he knew in his bones that his time was not yet, that he'd pull through again.

He'd had his doubts only moments ago, during that final frantic scramble down to the dock. Good thing he kept himself in some kind of condition with daily workouts; otherwise, he'd never have made it. Even so, he'd been failing there at the end; he'd have dropped sure if not for the intervention of Tyrone.

Tyrone was one of Piersall's people, part of his Black Glove Crew. He'd been posted down at the dock to keep watch for anybody trying to approach by water. When the shooting started, he'd remained at his post, careful not to mix in any of the shooting. Tyrone was a yellow belly when you came right down to it, but it had all worked out for the best as far as Mayhew was concerned.

By the time he'd reached the pier, Mayhew was played out. It was like the dream where life itself depends on being able to flee some deadly menace, only no matter how hard you try, you're unable to do more than creep along at a snail's pace while the foe swoops down on you with swift wings. But this was no dream, it was all real, horribly real.

His limbs numb, impossibly heavy, barely capable of movement, he'd stumbled to the dock, ready to collapse. He'd feared he was having a heart attack. He had no history of cardiac trouble, but there was always a first time and this looked like it. Old age was hell, but Mayhew was determined to hold on to it with a death grip.

Then Tyrone had been there, getting Mayhew's arm across his shoulder and propping him up. Half carrying, half dragging him, he'd rushed Mayhew across the dock and up the gangway into the boat. By then, Mayhew had recovered enough breath to sob out instructions to Tyrone to free the mooring lines. Tyrone had cast them off while Mayhew fired up the boat's powerful twin engines. They'd been kept in tune for just such a getaway and by God, now they were paying off!

Tyrone was no sailor, and there wasn't much he could do except hover over Mayhew and lend a hand to keep him from falling over while he skippered the craft. Then they were under way, dock and shoreline receding as the black waters of the bay widened and deepened.

It was Tyrone, though, who first noticed the quick, jaunty little speedboat that swung into view, carving a curved white wake as it skipped across the surface, moving to cut them off. He'd pointed it out to Mayhew.

Mayhew, heedess, reckless, was determined to be halted by no man now, not with escape so close. If necessary, he'd run down the smaller craft with his own much larger boat, ramming and sinking it to the bottom.

He didn't know that Mantee's speedboat was armed with a fifty-caliber machine gun mounted over the front coaming, and that even now he was preparing to open fire. First, with a warning volley across the cruiser's bow; if that was ignored, he'd shoot it so full of holes that it'd sink like a stone.

Only Mantee didn't have to fire a shot. For, even as he was racing to intercept it, the cabin cruiser blew up.

One instant, it was there; the next, it disintegrated in a cloud of smoke and fire that raised a waterspout and rained a hail of debris. An occurrence that puzzled the hell out of both Steve Ireland and Mantee.

On shore, in the mansion, now that the guns had fallen silent, Elise Danner finally summoned up enough nerve to crawl out of the closet where she'd been cowering since the shooting started. Creeping down the grand staircase, she eased open the front door and fled into the night, running across the fields toward the distant roadway.

In the Klondike SUV lurking at the edge of the property, on guard for some such eventuality, Osgood caught her.

EIGHT

"You're going on a train ride."

The way Doc Wenzle had said it, with the purr of genially malicious relish in his voice, had tipped Steve Ireland that his next assignment would be no picnic.

Now, Steve knew that his worst apprehensions had fallen far short of the reality. He was on board a train rolling west through the Maryland countryside at midday, a freight train whose cargo was a hell's brew that could wipe out an army, or an entire city. Long, narrow windows on either side of the car let in light and landscape. The view was nice—a rural vista of open fields, rushing streams, and gentle vistas—but he was in no mood to appreciate the scenery. He suspected that Osgood and Mantee shared his feelings.

The three of them shared their own private car, not a passenger car but a crew car, the kind used by freight train personnel on long-distance, cross-country runs. It was a combination living quarters, working area, and storage space. Its stripped-down styling reminded Steve of a mobile home or a recreational vehicle. It had the same spare, stark efficiency of design, everything pared down to its essentials.

The forward part of the long, tubelike car held the living area. There was a communal work space, a kind of galley or mini-kitchen, some sets of fold-out bunks built into the walls, even a lavatory, all built around an open central aisle. A bulkhead separated it from the rear, storage area.

Steve, Osgood, and Mantee now occupied the common work space. Hinge-mounted seats and a desktop made of lightweight, composite materials folded out from berths in the walls. The desktop was equipped with safety catches and clips to secure laptops and other movable gear from the hazards of train travel, from vibrations to sudden stops. Steve sure hoped that the train would make no sudden stops. He wasn't too thrilled about its making any scheduled stops either.

Radio was the voice of the train, both for on-board and outside communication. A built-in radio/scanner was switched on at a moderate volume, allowing the Dog Team trio to monitor the extensive signal traffic between the crew and the railroad's extensive traffic control network that kept the train on course through all its myriad junctions and switching points. Not to mention the numerous auxiliary units involved in assisting the transport's smooth and uninterrupted progress, including the forward scout vehicles, helicopters, and spotter planes, and various local, county, and state police agencies watching for trouble along the line.

Steve, Osgood, and Mantee had also each been issued radio handsets identical with those used by the train crew and its defenders. In addition, they each had their own individual cells for Team commo, among themselves or with handlers such as Doc Wenzle. Of course, Wenzle was safe back in his office in D.C., not riding the rails with a toxic cargo, Steve thought sourly.

The trio also had several transceiver headsets similar to those used on the raid two days ago on Arnot's Acres, but those comm units were currently stowed away with much of the rest of their gear.

They were all dressed in civilian clothes, casual clothes and workboots to conform with their cover. Under his utility vest, Steve wore a shoulder harness with his pistol facing butt-outward under his left arm. A neat, flat little .32 was clipped to a holster at the small of his back. The weather was warm, summery; under the vest he wore a short-sleeved shirt, with a long, thin, flat-bladed stiletto-type knife worn in a sheath behind the back of his neck, hanging down between his shoulder blades.

Osgood and Mantee were similarly armed with handguns and whatever additional equalizers they favored. Neither of them had Steve's facility with a blade. Osgood carried a set of brass knuckles while Mantee toted a sap, a leather mini-truncheon whose interior was filled with ball bearings.

The heavier firepower, and there was plenty

of it, was secured in an arms locker in the separate, baggage area in the after part of the car. The arsenal included assault rifles, lightweight machine guns, and grenades, plus some specialty items. Each man had a key to the locked bulkhead door connecting with the after area. At the rear of the car was a locked, solid metal door that gave onto a metal apron platform.

Behind the Team car was a troop car, carrying the train's official defenders, a squad of military policemen and a few officers. They were all Army, but they, too, wore civilian clothes. There was nothing civilian about the M-16s and sidearms they were equipped with, though. The Army was minimizing its official presence on this run, due to its quasi-covert nature.

The next two cars in line were flatcars carrying a couple of Humvees and the customized Klondike, as well as side ramps for quick loading and off-loading. Behind them were nineteen boxcars. Placed in the middle of them was a second locomotive for added power. It was crewless, being guided via computerized remote control by the engineer in the locomotive at the head of the train. Bringing up the rear was a tool car, filled with a variety of equipment, everything from sledgehammers, picks, and spikes to steel rails, cross ties, hoists, jacks, winches, even a forklift. If emergency repairs were needed, the train crew was equipped to remedy all but the most drastic fixes on the spot, without having to wait for the arrival of a special repair train.

Ahead of the Team car was another crew car, this one housing both train personnel and a handful of civilians associated with the transport. Forward of that was the vanguard, the locomotive, the head of this mechanized snake that was gliding west through the green and pleasant precincts of rural Maryland.

No snake ever carried deadlier and more potent venom in its poison sacs than the train was hauling in those boxcars. The quiet, peaceful towns through which the train periodically rolled wouldn't have been so quiet and peaceful had their occupants known the true nature of the cargo borne by it.

The locomotive was a diesel-electric job, the diesel engine powering a monster alternator that powered its steel wheels and not so incidentally supplied the current for the sophisticated computerized controls for the long trail of cars in its wake.

Like the other crew cars, the one ferrying the three Dogs had lights, air-conditioning, and power outlets for the radio/scanner, computers, even the mini-refrigerator and microwave oven in the galley.

Steve Ireland would have been happier if the boxcars were airtight and pressurized to help prevent leakage of their lethal contents, but apparently that was not the case. The cars depended solely on stacked and secured sealed hazardous material containers, HMCs, to contain the cargo's contents. He thought that was pretty damned casual. Not that he'd ever given the matter much thought until a day ago, when he'd reported to the Holloman Research Associates office in the Gall Building to receive his orders from Doc Wenzle.

He and the other two survivors of the mission, Osgood and Mantee, had been extensively debriefed the day after the raid by a three-man fact-finding panel in another anonymous, tightly secured covert Team facility secreted in plain sight in a civilian, commercial office building in D.C.

Steve was plenty steamed, and he didn't mind sounding off about it to Doc Wenzle when he was alone with him at the office. He said, "We lost two good men on that mission, Bryce and Nevins, and for what? Because we were handcuffed by red tape! If we'd have gone in their with heavier firepower, even some grenades, we might not have taken any casualties—"

The corners of Wenzle's mouth were turned so far down that the creases practically reached his chin. "No one's sorrier about their loss than I am, Steve—"

"Sorry doesn't cut it!"

"Neither does getting sore about it," Wenzle said, his tone and expression unchanged, unflappable. "That's the nature of the beast. This peculiar service of ours can only operate under tightly restricted circumstances. Secrecy is paramount, never more so than on domestic operations. If it ever became public knowledge that the Army was running what amounts to its own death squad, it'd blow the lid off this country. A lid that, due to political, economic, and cultural conditions at this particular time, is fastened none too securely in the first place.

"You can imagine the stink the world press would raise about it, starting right here with our own homegrown mainstream media, including certain papers and TV news channels whose names we both know. By the time they got done, the Pentagon, by God, would have to hold a bake sale to fund what's left of the military."

Steve said, "I know, I know . . ."

"I'm an old man, Steve; I don't fancy being raked over the coals by congressional subcommittees for doing what I consider my duty, my proud duty and my privilege, and maybe spending my retirement years in Leavenworth or some federal prison. You, you're still a young man, you could do a twenty-year stretch and still have something of a life yet, but I don't have the luxury. And if you think that's an exaggeration, you must not be keeping up with current affairs."

"I'm not arguing," Steve said. Easing up, he settled back in the chair, only to be painfully jabbed by one of the busted springs in the seat cushion. Irked, he said, sneering, "You're laying it on pretty thick, Doc. What comes next, the violins playing 'Hearts and Flowers'?"

Wenzle, pious, said, "I prefer the 'Star-Spangled Banner.'"

Steve couldn't top that. "All right, you've made your point."

Wenzle drank some coffee. "The planners wanted it to look like a gangland kill so that's how we played it. It worked; the media bought it and that's how they're featuring it.

"Mayhew's boat blowing up was the crowning touch. It made it look like a real Mob hit," he added.

Steve said, "When it blew, I thought for a second maybe you had fixed up Mantee with some torpedoes or an antiship missile."

"Mantee was just as surprised as you, from what he tells me."

"I guess the only one more surprised than either of us was Mayhew."

Wenzle said, "It all worked out for the best. Better that the boat be blown to bits than for it to be sent to the bottom of the bay riddled with fifty-caliber machine gun bullets, for somebody to haul up for examination later."

Steve scratched his head. "Hell, maybe it was a Mob hit. Who knows?"

"We do," Wenzle said, "thanks to the Danner woman. Taking her alive was a real bonus."

"She talked?"

"Try and stop her. She's still talking. Mayhew and Piersall may have frozen her out of the wet work, but she still knows plenty. A real gold mine of information."

"What's going to happen to her?"

"We've got her salted away in a nice secure location free from outside interference. The interrogators will squeeze her dry of everything she knows, including things she doesn't even know she knows," Wenzle said. "After that, if there's anything left of her, maybe we'll turn her, double her, and use her to plant disinformation on her former clients. Or park her in an institution and keep her on ice until her final dispensation is decided. Out of sight, out of mind."

Steve shrugged, indicating it was no matter to him. He turned to a subject of greater interest: "So who killed Mayhew?"

For reply, Wenzle opened a folder, took out a photo, and handed it across the desk to Steve. "This man, we think."

The photo was a candid shot obviously taken without the subject's knowledge, a surveillance photo depicting a tall man with wavy silver hair and a long, rectangular-shaped face. He was well groomed, in a well-tailored suit. Steve studied it, but came up blank. "Don't know him."

Wenzle said, "Danner and Mayhew, too, knew him as 'Darius.'"

Steve shook his head. "Doesn't ring any bells."

"Darius is just a nom de guerre; that's 'war name' to you."

"I know what it means," Steve said curtly.

"His real name is Khalid Khan. He's a top international agent of the Pasdaran, Iran's most deep-black spy service. Ultra-black," Wenzle said. "A lot of Western intelligence agencies have been trying to get a line on him for a long time. We didn't even know he was operating in this country, no less than right here in Washington, D.C. Turns out he was an ISS client, doing business with Mayhew. A dissatisfied client apparently."

Steve said, "Must be if he blew up Mayhew. Can't get more dissatisfied than that."

Wenzle said, "ISS was in the information business, among other things—information as commodity. Mayhew always had his hooks out for whatever sources of intelligence he could develop. Then he sold it to interested parties, primarily agents of foreign powers either unfriendly or actively hostile to Uncle Sam.

"Apparently, he wasn't above selling the same secrets twice, or more than that, if he could find the right buyers. Unfortunately for him, he ultimately found the wrong buyer. He sold something to Darius and then to a second party, and Darius found out about it. Not being the sharing type, Darius got sore. Mayhew was worried about him, about comeback.

"All this is according to Danner, but it seems to check out so far."

Steve rubbed his chin. "So Darius bombed Mayhew for a double cross?"

Wenzle nodded. "Looks like."

"He must have had a bomb planted somewhere on the boat," Steve went on. "But it couldn't have been rigged to blow up the first time the boat went out, because he couldn't have known for sure that Mayhew would be on the boat. Unless he didn't care who was on the boat when it blew and he just wanted to throw a scare into Mayhew."

"Our profile of Darius shows he's not the type for scaring people. He's results-oriented, lethal results."

"Meaning that he or one of his men triggered the bomb with a remote detonator in real time. The bomber would have had to have been onsite at the Acres or thereabouts when we hit the place."

"I'd say that's a logical conclusion."

"I didn't see anybody, no outsiders. Neither

did the rest of the squad. If we had, we'd have moved to intercept them," Steve said. He frowned, thinking. "No, wait a minute. Mantee did mention something about seeing a light out on the bay and thinking it might be a buoy or marker. That was before the blast. Afterward, the light was gone. It could have been a boat.

"In which case, Darius might have seen something of the raid. Hmm, I don't like that part so well."

Wenzle said, "Neither do we." He rested his elbows on the desktop, pressing his palms together so that his hands made a steeple. "Darius was already on our list to be taken or terminated, whichever is more feasible. But this moves him a few notches higher up on the roster."

Steve said, "Have you got a line on him?"

Wenzle smiled, a slow, gentle smile. "Possibly. Which brings us to the point of this whole discussion."

Leaning forward, he delivered the punch line. "You're going on a train ride, Steve."

Steve Ireland hadn't liked the sound of that. The fact of it he liked a whole lot less. The same went for Osgood and Mantee, who'd also drawn the assignment. Wenzle or the planners or both had deliberately slotted the surviving personnel from the Acres raid for the train trek. They'd already crossed paths with Darius, unknowingly at the time. Well, they knew it now. And maybe Darius knew them, at least to the extent of having seen one, two, or all of them during the

Mayhew action. If so, no other Dog Team personnel would have to risk being tagged or typed during the imminent train ride.

Because that was the secret that Mayhew had sold to Darius, the route and timetable of this cross-country train trip. And what a trip it was.

"You might call it a matter of waste management," Wenzle had said, gloating from behind his desk as he described the mission to Steve.

Which was true in its way. The Army stockpile of chemical weapons needed thinning. Originally, they had been developed as a deterrent factor. Official U.S. government policy was that, like nuclear weapons, chemical weapons would never be used for a first strike. Other nations had CW capability; we had to have it, too. In the Cold War, the Soviet Red Army military doctrine had gamed the possible use of chemical and biological warfare should war ever break out in then-divided Germany against U.S.-led NATO forces. Poison gas had been used by Iraq in its war with Iran, and to brutally suppress a Kurdish revolt at home. The Syrian dictator Assad had used CWs to quell a rebellion on his home turf.

More recently, it had become a truism that chemical-and-biological-weapons (CBW) capacity was the poor man's version of nukes, being far less costly and labor-intensive to develop than atomic weapons. These were the famous weapons of mass destruction that had been a prime mover in the preemptive war against Saddam Hussein's Iraq regime. The WMDs in question proved as elusive as a desert mirage, but that's another story.

The fact is that any number of regimes in developed nations and the Third World have CBWs. The U.S. has them, too. We wouldn't use them first, but if an opponent does, we're not going to sit on our hands without retaliating in kind.

Stores of CW weapons, some dating back to the First Gulf War, some even farther back, to the Cold War, had outlived their usefulness and were on the way to becoming active threats. Poison gas and toxic nerve agents designed for battle-field use had sat on the storehouse shelves for too long. Years, decades in some cases. During that time, the canisters and containers of the stuff didn't just sit there inert and intact. Like all substances, they were subject to corrosion, oxidation, and decay induced by the toxic materials they carried.

Like any other business, the business of war periodically requires that the old inventory be cleared off the shelves to make way for new, improved stock. Especially since some of the old stuff was becoming a clear and present danger due to aged and corroding containers.

CWs present a massive disposal problem. You can't just throw them away, buried underground or dumped at sea, because eventually those containers would rust and rot away and begin releasing their contents. No, they had to be neutralized first. This requires expensive, specially constructed incinerators. The high cost of building this ultra-specialized equipment, coupled with the fact that nobody wants to live in the vicinity of a CW incinerator, means that only a handful of such sites exists in the continental United States.

Newest and most impressive of these facilities is the incinerator buried in the hollowed-out guts of a mountain in the Nevada wasteland, a site known as Mesa Rojo, Red Mesa. That's not its real name, but for the purposes of national security, it will do.

It's a long way off from Maryland, but it was the final destination, the terminus, of the train. The toxic train, as Steve Ireland had come to think of it. A load of some of the oldest and potentially most dangerous CW stores would be cleared out of a warehouse arsenal in a facility associated with Aberdeen Proving Ground in Maryland, where such weapons were developed and refined. Hermetically sealed within hazardous material containers, HMCs, they would be loaded into boxcars—twenty in all—and transported by train across the country to Red Mesa for incineration.

It was a most delicate undertaking for a number of reasons. Other incinerator sites were closer to the CWs' point of origin, but lacked the capacity to process such a sizable load in the requisite amount of time. This was a bad lot, its canisters the oldest and most corroded, requiring immediate disposal. Red Mesa's big brute of a burner could handle the job fastest and best.

Another consideration was the route. There wasn't a big city, town, suburb, village, or hamlet that would welcome the passage through its environs of a train hauling twenty boxcars of a hell-brew of overaged poison gas and nerve agents in corroded canisters sealed in HMCs.

No public relations firm, no matter how good, could sell that to the citizenry along the route. Yet there was no other alternative. The stuff had to be gotten to the incinerator at Red Mesa damned quick. The stalling and delays had gone on for years until now time had almost run out. The military and political bureaucracies had reached the crisis point where doing nothing was no longer a viable option.

It was a matter of national security because if nothing was done, sooner rather than later, one or some of those storehoused canisters would spring a leak and then there would be hell to pay. Officialdom reached the inescapable conclusion that what the public doesn't know won't hurt them. The transport venture was classified and wrapped in secrecy, with knowledge of the train's cargo restricted on a need-to-know basis. That would still entail a large number of individuals being in the know, but various Patriot Act clauses and antiterror strictures were invoked to intimidate the loose-lipped and smooth the way for the cross-country run.

People being what they are, though, word of the imminent transport got around, reaching the ears of an ISS informant, who passed it along to Greg Mayhew. With the instinct of a born pimp, Mayhew knew where to peddle the info where it would do him the most good. His first client of choice had been Darius. U.S. relations with Iran, always shaky, were aggravated by Tehran's development of a nuclear weapons program. The threat of a U.S. preemptive strike against an atom-armed Iran was omnipresent. Iranian agent Darius would be interested in knowledge of the toxic train's run, it being powerful knowledge indeed. It was an equalizer, the threat of sabotage presenting an opportunity to blackmail Washington into easing up on Tehran. Or, if it came to it, it had the potential for a terror strike against the U.S. that would make 9/11 look puny.

So reasoned Mayhew, and he reasoned right. Darius bought in, paying big money for details of the planned run. But Mayhew's calculations did not stop there. He knew another possible client, a bunch of Iraqis who were actually holed up in Nevada, of all places. They'd been big shots in Saddam Hussein's regime and they just might be looking for some big-time payback.

Again, he figured right. The Nevada crowd bought in, too. Here was where Mayhew's plans went sour. He didn't deal directly with the Iraqis; he worked through a middleman, a Washington, D.C.-based secrets broker named Biro Fleck. By pure happenstance, Fleck was also a colleague of sorts with Darius. Being the mirror image of Mayhew, Fleck sold Darius the knowledge that Mayhew had sold the toxic train secret twice.

"So there you have it," Doc Wenzle had said, summing up after giving Steve Ireland the briefing in his office at the Gall Building. "Will Darius make a try for the train? Given what we know of the man, it seems possible, maybe even likely. The route's been mapped to avoid cities and towns wherever possible, but it's a big country and a good part of the line goes through populated areas. A lot of opportunities for Darius to do mischief.

"You're going along for the ride. Osgood and Mantee, too. You'll be in charge, Osgood is second."

"Great," Steve said. "The three of us have to ride shotgun on a freight train filled with poison gas from here to Nevada. Is that all?"

Wenzle said, "The train'll be guarded by a squad of military policeman, elite trigger-pullers. They'll be on board, like you three. There'll also be support all along the way, including helicopters and spotter planes scouting the route. Local and state police to clear and protect the line."

"With all that coverage, what do you need us for?"

"This is a covert op. As far as the public is concerned, the transport is just one more freight train passing through. Those boxcars could be hauling cars or auto parts for all they know. The Army's keeping a low profile on this. The M.P.s on the train'll be in civvies. They're more for defensive purposes. You boys will take a more aggressive role. If anybody has to be shot along the way, we'd prefer it to be done by professionals who have handled similar tasks stateside and know how to cover their tracks."

"Yeah, and if it works the other way and we get killed, there's nothing to tie us to the Army."

"That's right. That's the name of the game. Look on the bright side, Steve. You get out of

D.C. just when the weather starts getting muggy and you get to enjoy the fresh air and sunshine of a cross-country trip."

"Unless one of those canisters rips open."

Wenzle made an airily dismissive gesture with his hands, as if brushing away the thought. "Oh, there's little worry of that. Those HMCs are built pretty solid, I understand. They can take quite a pounding with no danger of rupturing, even in case of a derailment."

Steve said, "Unless somebody throws a grenade into them or something."

"There's that," Wenzle agreed, "but that's why you'll be on board. Anyway, if that should happen, you won't have long to worry about it. A whiff of the stuff, or the touch of it on your skin, and you'll be gone like that!" Wenzle snapped his fingers to illustrate the quickness of the "like that" he'd just mentioned.

Steve said, "That's quite a consolation."

Wenzle said, "At the end of your run, you'll be right near Las Vegas. You can blow off some steam there."

"That'll be a real treat."

"Plus, you might get to kill some bad guys along the way."

"Just so the trip isn't a total loss," Steve said.

The legend the planners had worked out for Steve, Osgood, and Mantee was a real doozy. They were given cover identities as investigators for the Federal Railroad Association, with a Department of Homeland Security tie-in that carried major clout. Technically, Steve had the authority to call upon the M.P. squad on board for whatever assistance he might need. They were commanded by a Lieutenant Webber and his topkick, Sergeant Collins, neither of whom seemed overly enthusiastic about taking orders from someone they thought was a civilian.

Tough, Steve said to himself. He had the authority and he'd play it to the hilt if that's what it took to get the job done.

The railroad personnel were mighty accommodating, reserving a private car for Steve and his teammates. They were shown to it by Wes Dudley, civilian foreman and crew chief for the transport. Barely had the last of their gear and armaments been stowed into the rear half of the car than, with a lurch, the train began moving away from the storehouse loading platform and into the Maryland countryside.

Time passed, hilly country rising up around the right-of-way as the train entered West Virginia. Steve Ireland found himself recalling a last scrap of conversation he'd had back at the office with Doc Wenzle.

"You said that Mayhew fingered the train not only to Darius, but to some Iraqis at the other end of the line in Nevada," he'd said.

Doc Wenzle said, "That's right."

"What about them?"

"They'll be taken care of. Our man out there's on the case."

NINE

The man called Kilroy arrived in Adobe Flats on the day of Choey Maldonado's funeral.

Earlier, Hard Tack Brady had been thrown out of the Doghouse Bar by its owner, Nigel Sharkey. The Doghouse was a dive, a gin mill on the southern edge of the Anglo part of town. It was a place of last resort for Brady; most of the other bars in that part of town wouldn't let him in to throw him out. Nigel Sharkey was more tolerant than most, but he'd warned Brady off the last time the weathered desert rat had been in the bar, when he'd caught Brady stealing a shot of whiskey that had been set up for a paying customer. Brady had downed the shot when the patron wasn't looking, tossing it back and sidling away fast. Sharkey, tending bar, had been looking, though. He'd tagged Brady for it, read him the riot act, and bounced him out of the dive.

The Doghouse was a flat-roofed, one-story, whitewashed wooden frame building that fronted Fremont Street, which ran east-west through town and marked the line of demarcation between New Town and Old Town. New Town was where the Anglos, the English-speaking element, resided; Old Town, which had been settled first, was where the Hispanic folks made their homes.

It had been early afternoon when Hard Tack Brady went into the Doghouse Bar. The Doghouse made no pretense of being anything than what it was, a gin mill. A real rummy bar, it made the average honky-tonk look like a gilded pleasure palace. No hot food was served, no live entertainment offered, no dancing allowed. That last was an unnecessary prohibition because what few couples patronized the joint were there for the same reason as the other customers: to get a load on as quickly and cheaply as possible. Hustlers, the oldest and most slatternly mattress-backs in town, frequented the bar in the wee hours, not to drum up business but to spend the night's meager earnings on drink. Mindful of the needs of its alcoholic clientele, it was the first bar to open up in the morning and one of the last to close at night.

Brady eased open the door and eased inside. The space was dim and cool, especially after coming in out of the naked sun. An air conditioner wheezed fitfully, wafting out puffs of moist, clammy lukewarm air. Even a dive like the Doghouse had to have air-conditioning, to cope with the desert heat.

The building's long side fronted the street. Opposite the entrance, on the far side of the floor, a wooden bar ran parallel to the street. It was lined with stools that supported about a half dozen of the town's most confirmed drunks. A TV was mounted on the wall at one end of the bar, tuned to a ball game. Between the bar and the front door were a handful of tables and chairs. In the daytime, they were for thirsty workers who ducked in during their lunch hour for a quick shot and a beer or two, but the rush was long over and the tables and chairs were unoccupied now. There was sawdust on the floor, and the space smelled of stale beer and raw whiskey fumes.

Brady stood motionless, accustoming his eyes to the gloom after the sunbaked glare outside. Behind the bar, Nigel Sharkey needed no such interlude, his eyes already acclimated to the bar's cavelike interior. Recognizing Brady, he came out from behind the bar and started toward him.

Sharkey, about five-seven, was wiry and energetic, balding and bony-skulled, with thick black eyebrows and sideburns that came down to mid-cheek. He rolled up his sleeves as he crossed to Brady.

Brady began, "Now, Nigel—"

That was as far as he got before Sharkey laid hands on him, grabbing the collar at the back of Brady's neck and the belt at the small of his back. Lifting him up bodily so that Brady was up on his toes, he hustled him toward the door, a swinging door with a spring mechanism that automatically closed it to keep any of that air-conditioned air from leaking outside.

Using Brady as a battering ram to open the door, he swept him across the wood-plank sidewalk and pitched him out into the street.

Fremont Street was made of dirt, hardpacked and unyielding except when it rained, and there wasn't a cloud in the sky. Brady sprawled in the dirt, his hat falling off. Sharkey stood there with arms folded across his chest, waiting to see if Brady was minded to contest the issue. Rising on his knees, Brady groped for his hat. Shapeless and sun-bleached, it was the kind of hat that one used to occasionally see adorning the head of a swaybacked old nag pulling the wagon of an old-time junkman. Jamming it on his head, Brady rose shakily to his feet and stumbled off in the opposite direction.

"And stay out!" was Sharkey's parting salute, followed by the spring-mounted door slamming shut behind him after he went back into the bar.

Brady shuffled away, brushing the dust from his palms. He'd been pretty shaky before going into the bar, and the bone-jarring thud of measuring his length in the street had done him no good.

He'd expected no less a welcome at the Doghouse, but there always a chance that Sharkey would be away from the bar on some errand, leaving it to be tended by his nephew, Neal, who might have let Brady try to cadge a drink from one of the barflies. So ended his immediate prospects of getting a drink.

He stood swaying, facing the beginnings of Old Town across the street. No use trying his luck there, at least for the present. Most if not all of the businesses there were closed now, out of respect for the Maldonado funeral. Not out of respect for Choey, who'd be missed by few if any.

The cantinas wouldn't reopen until the last rites had been delivered. Brady decided to have a look at the funeral himself. At least that way, he'd know when the services ended and business resumed. Maybe one of the family would buy the house a drink in memory of the late lamented. The late unlamented, he mentally corrected himself. Plenty of folks would be happy to celebrate Choey's passing, but they dared not show it, not in Old Town, which was run by the Maldonados.

In New Town, it'd be different. There'd be plenty of celebrating going on there later, especially in Sime Simmonds's joints. Simmonds ran New Town, its vice district anyway, and there was no love lost between him and Clan Maldonado. Of course, Sime's people knew to bounce a penniless booze hound like Brady on sight, but once the joints got crowded and the festivities started rolling, there might be a way for Brady to insinuate himself into the mix and hustle some free drinks.

There had to be. Sobriety was not an option. Too long without a drink and he'd crack up. It had already been a long time since his last, and he was feeling mighty poorly. So the funeral it was. Pointing himself west, he started toward the end of Fremont Street. There were other, more direct ways to the graveyard, but not for him. He might not be welcome, and in any case had no desire to call attention to himself with the Maldonados and their hirelings. Not to mention the local law.

Hard Tack Brady was a local character of a type that had existed since silver had first been discovered in the mountains to the west some centuries ago. He was a desert rat, a prospector. Or at least he used to be. Every year, for nigh onto four decades now, he'd spent the winter months doing odd jobs between drinking binges, building up a small stake to outfit himself with some tools and supplies to go prospecting in the warm-weather months. He'd never hit the mother lode, nor even made a modest strike, but from time to time, he managed to hit some minor veins of silver and eke out a minimal living.

In recent years, though, the binges had lasted longer and the odd jobs declined from few to virtually nil. This year, he'd failed to raise a stake with which to outfit himself. He should've hit for the high country when spring first broke. Now, here it was late in June and he lacked the price of a single shot of rotgut, no less the wherewithal to outfit himself with a sleeping bag, pick, shovel, panning tray, canteen, and supplies of canned beans, bacon, salt pork, and other minimal necessities.

Too much to think about now; he'd better concentrate on something simpler and more immediate, like making his way to the graveyard. Trudging west along Fremont Street, he cut an odd, shambling figure. In his early sixties, rawboned and hollow-cheeked, he had long, unkempt hair and a ragged beard. Where the skin of his face showed, long exposure to the elements had left it as brown and seamed as old saddle leather. Outdoor living had partially offset the ravages of booze, leaving him in surprisingly fit condition. The hot, searing sun in a cloudless sky affected him not at all. He was a desert rat. Heat was the least of his troubles.

It didn't take long for him to reach the western edge of town; Adobe Flats was a small town, numbering a population of several thousand souls. Beyond lay a flat, and then the foothills of the Tres Hermanos Mountains. He turned left, going south. It didn't take long to get to the southern edge of Old Town either.

Running parallel with the mountain range, Highway 61 ran north-south through the center of town, cutting it in two. West of the highway and south of Old Town was a plaza, its southern edge bordered by the Church of San Miguel, a mission church dating back to the days of the conquistadors. It was an imposing structure built in Spanish Colonial style, and its long axis ran east–west, its eastern façade sporting a pair of belfry towers. Its exterior was finished in whitewashed stucco with lots of timbers showing. To the west and rear of the church was the graveyard.

Mirroring it at the north edge of New Town was a Protestant church with a white steeple and its own graveyard, for the use of the Anglos.

Hard Tack Brady was ecumenical in his way, being an object of derision and contempt to a majority of members of both denominations.

The San Miguel graveyard had its own caste

system, with the more modest graves with their simple markers and crosses being arrayed on the flat, while the more expensive tombs and memorials occupied the foot of a gentle, near slope of a ridge at the western end of the cemetery.

Circling the graveyard's northern perimeter, Brady climbed the ridge to a weedy knoll overlooking the scene. Its top was crowned by a cluster of low, gnarly shade trees. Brady paused, resting, standing with one hand pressing a rough-barked tree trunk. Circling the tree, he moved cautiously among the tall grasses, searching for snakes. Venomous ones, rattlers and sidewinders. This country was thick with them. Finding none, he found himself a good resting place overlooking the cemetery and church. He sat down on the ground with his back against a tree. It felt good to be out of the sun, in the shade. A handful of small birds perched in the branches, panting in the heat.

Choey Maldonado was getting a first-class finish. The service must still be going on; periodically, organ music sounded from inside the church. The west side of the church was lined with big, black shiny cars for the grieving family and friends.

In the graveyard, at the foot of the ridge, a tentlike canopy open at the sides stood beside a freshly dug grave. Grouped around it was a riot of color, caused by big, bushy masses of floral tributes, urns, bouquets, memorial wreaths, and the like. Off to the side, well out of the way of where the mourners would gather, stood a yellow earthmoving machine, the backhoe that had dug the grave out of the hard, clayish soil. The mound of newly excavated dirt was reddish brown, like the sands of Mars.

Brady smacked parched lips, his mouth and throat dusty dry. His craving for drink was a powerful need. Oh, well, nothing for him to do now but endure it and hope for an end to the drought sooner rather than later.

His eyelids felt heavy; he gave them a rest by closing them. He pulled his hat brim down over his eyes, deepening the dimness. The heat of the day had a lulling effect. Around him, the droning hum of insects rose and fell, like surf breaking on shore. Brady drifted off . . .

He came awake with a start, jolted out of sleep. His heart was beating fast. For an instant, he was befuddled, disoriented. How long had he been asleep? For all he knew, it could have been instants, minutes, or hours.

It was still light out, blue sky and masses of sunlight all around, so it couldn't have been too long. He knuckled his eyes with his hands, rubbing the sleep out of them. A shadow fell across his face, causing him to look up.

Beside him stood a man, a stranger. About six feet tall, he had the sloping shoulders of a heavy-weight fighter and a blocky, square-shaped torso. He wore a tan flat-crowned, broad-brimmed hat that was turned up at the sides. Nothing unusual about that. This was the West, where cowboy-style hats were not a costume but a basic item of everyday apparel.

Under the hat, he had short sandy hair and was clean-shaven, with a wide, open, friendly face. His eyes were blue, his thin straight nose looked sharp as a knife blade, and he showed an easy grin. He wore a sleeveless white denim vest over a gray T-shirt, baggy wide-legged brown jeans, and cowboy boots with sharp-pointed toes. He said, "Howdy."

Brady grunted in response, unsure of what to do. Was the newcomer a guard or suchlike, come to roust him? He wore no uniform, badge, insignia, or sidearm. His right hand clutched the rolled top of a brown paper bag that contained a weighty object of some kind.

Seeing the bag, with its seemingly familiar contours and recognizable shape, Brady's heart gave a lurch. Could it be . . . ? No, no, that was too much to hope for. And yet, he found himself daring to do just that.

The stranger said, "Hope I didn't startle you."

"Not at all," Brady said, the words thick and clumsy in his dry mouth.

"Mind if I join you?"

"It's a free country."

The corners of the stranger's mouth quirked upward at that, in what could have been a small smile. He sat down on Brady's right, facing the cemetery, resting his back against a nearby tree.

Whatever was in the brown paper bag, its contents both rattled metallically and made a liquid gurgle, sending Brady's heartbeat hammering. Yes, it must be—!

Indicating the scene below, the stranger said, "Looks like the show's about to start." If by show, he meant burial, he was right. The grave site was packed with black-clad mourners, dozens, scores of them. The immediate family sat in the front row of several rows of folding chairs under the green, open-sided canopy. They sat closest to the open grave. Not a chair under the canopy was unfilled. Many more persons, men, women, and children, stood on the sides, grouped in an arc that curved around the open grave. A complicated, slinglike apparatus held a big black coffin suspended over the grave. Ornate and oversized, it was an ebony oblong box with gleaming bronze handles.

"Nice to be out of the sun," the stranger said. Unrolling the top of the brown paper bag, he reached in and hauled out a six-pack of beer, tallboys, each about the size of a can of tennis balls. Condensation gleamed on their sides like a beadwork of jewels. Twisting one free from the plastic webbing, he offered it to Brady, saying, "Care to join me?"

Brady managed to croak, "Don't mind if I do." He reached for it, his hands shaking. He held it in both hands to keep from dropping it. He popped the top, white foam bubbling out the wide-mouthed opening. Mindful of some obscure shred of dignity, he fought to keep from guzzling it dry in one mighty chug.

The stranger said, "I hate to drink alone."

Brady said, "Mighty kind of you, friend, mighty kind."

"The name's Kilroy," the other said, holding out a hand. Brady gripped it, shaking it.

"Brady, I'm Brady. Folks hereabouts call me Hard Tack."

"Glad to know you, Hard Tack. Well, here's how." Kilroy drank some beer.

Brady did the same. The next thing he knew, there was a tingling wetness in his mouth, throat, and innards, and an empty beer can in his hand. One was too many, and an ocean of beer wouldn't be enough. Hell, he didn't even like beer. The hard stuff, red-eye, was what he preferred.

Beggars can't be choosers, though, and to him that first tall, cool one was as manna raining down from heaven on the desert.

Kilroy said, "Man sure works up a thirst in this heat, and that's a fact." Yet he was still nursing his first. Gesturing toward what was now a four-pack, he said, "Help yourself, Hard Tack."

"If you're sure you can spare it, Mr. Kilroy . . ."

"Kilroy, just plain Kilroy. Be my guest."

"Thank you kindly." Brady forced himself to slow down, to make this one last. To do so was a triumph of willpower, but he succeeded. Dimly aware that Kilroy had just said something, Brady said, "Sorry, I didn't quite catch that last."

"I said, who's that getting planted down there?" Kilroy nodded toward the grave site.

"You must be new to Adobe Flats, Mr. Kilroy."

"Kilroy," the other corrected.

"Kilroy," Brady repeated, nodding. "That is—was—one of our leading citizens, Mr. Choey Maldonado, taken from us all too tragically soon, too young."

"They're sure giving him a hell of a send-off.

There's more flowers down there than at a Mob funeral."

Brady gave him a sharp look. "I thought you said you were new to our town."

"Just got in today," Kilroy said.

"Then you're a good guesser. The Maldonados are the biggest crooks in Adobe Flats."

"You don't say!"

"Pardon me. I misspoke. The Maldonados are not the biggest crooks in town. They're one half of the biggest crooks in town. The other half is Sime Simmonds," Brady said. Somehow, he had started on his third beer. He went on. "The Maldonados run this part of town, the Mexican-American section. Simmonds runs the north, Anglo half."

"I get you," Kilroy said. "It's equal opportunity for crooks."

"That's about the size of it."

Pointing at a couple of police cars parked outside the graveyard's gates, Kilroy said, "And the law?"

Brady said, "Equal-opportunity grafters. They take from both sides."

"Seems fair."

Brady took another mouthful, letting the beer tingle on his tongue before swallowing. A comfortable fullness nestled in his belly, and warmth circulated through his veins. For the first time in some hours—since the last time he'd had a drink—he felt like he could catch his breath again. He had a slight buzz; his head was starting to feel unmoored from the rest of him.

Under the glow, he began to feel expansive.

He started pointing out the various members of the Maldonados seated in the front row under the canopy. "The old gal with the white hair, that's Mama Rita, the matriarch of the clan. Standing next to her, on her right, that's Rio. He runs the family business."

Rio took up a lot of space. Kilroy said, "Big fella, ain't he?"

Brady nodded. "Meaner than a rattlesnake, too."

"Bad man to cross, eh?"

"Poison," Brady said. "The one sitting next to Mama Rita is Leandro. Her firstborn, but Rio runs the outfit, even though he was her second."

Kilroy said, "Leandro doesn't kick about taking a backseat?"

"Nope. Leandro, he ain't much for thinking, while that Rio, he's smart as a whip. Big brother's content to sit back and let Rio do the brainwork while the money rolls in."

"And the woman sitting next to Leandro?"

"Lupe. The sister."

Kilroy's eyes narrowed. "Even from here, looks like she's got a pretty good shape on her."

Brady chuckled wheezily. "That's probably what the male black widow spider says just before mating with the female of the species. You know about black widows?" Kilroy did know, but it was easier to let Brady go on talking. The other warmed to his subject. "The black widow mates with the male, and after she's had her fun, she kills him and eats him," Brady said.

Kilroy said, "Sounds like my ex-wife."

"Not hardly, mister. You're still around."

"This Lupe's a real black widow, huh?"

"She's buried three husbands, and not one of 'em died a natural death. They all had big life insurance policies, too. She only killed one, though, as far as I know. Cut his throat from ear to ear with a bread knife."

"Nice."

"Never went to trial. The grand jury no-billed her. Ruled it was self-defense."

"And the other two?"

"One was killed in a drug gang shootout and the other died in a car wreck," Brady said. He noticed that his beer can was empty. "This talking's thirsty work . . ."

Kilroy handed him another can. "Enjoy."

"Much obliged."

Kilroy gathered up the empties, dropping them in the brown paper bag. "Don't want to go littering up a graveyard." He was still working on his first beer. He must not be very thirsty, Brady guessed, so Brady didn't mind drinking up the lion's share of the brews. Why not, since Kilroy wasn't kicking about it?

A balding man with a shaggy black beard and a barrel torso stood behind and to the side of Rio. He leaned forward to say a few words in Rio's ear.

"That's Hector," Brady said. "He's what you'd call their foreman. Decent enough, so long as you're not in the way of any Maldonado interests. In which case, he'd squash you like a bug."

A small knot of persons came over to Mama Rita to express their condolences. Brady pointed out the ones he knew. "That blond fellow, the Anglo, is Maddox Kent. Handles the family's legal business."

A group of three went to the matriarch: a dark-haired, bearded, middle-aged man; a matronly woman with a chunky physique and a black scarf tied covering most of her orange-colored hair and knotted under her chin; and a young woman with frumpy dark hair, glasses, and no makeup, wearing a shapeless sack dress, knee socks, and clunky shoes.

Brady said, "Bert Sarkesian, runs a big carpet and furniture store in town. A newcomer to Adobe Flats, only been here a couple of years. Legitimate, from what I heard, but it don't hurt even a straight businessman to pay his respects to the Maldonados. You sure don't want to get on their wrong side. The old gal built like a pillowcase full of doorknobs is his sister; the young 'un's his niece."

The Sarkesians moved, making way for a young blond woman, alone and unescorted, who wore dark glasses, a black dress, black wrist-length gloves, and high-heeled shoes. Long hair was done up in a bun at the top of her head. The sunglasses with their oversized lenses covered much of her face, creating a masklike, vaguely insectoid appearance. With the heels, she was about six feet tall, wide-shouldered and slim-waisted, with a full-breasted, long-legged figure that made Kilroy sit up and take notice.

He said, "Well, hello!"

Observing his reaction, Brady said, "Whoa, boy, better simmer down and take it easy."

"Who's she?"

"Vangie Lynn. A dancer, what you might call a kind of local celebrity. Star attraction over to Sime Simmonds' club."

Kilroy cut Brady a quick sidelong glance. "Dancer, you say."

Brady said, "The kind that takes off her clothes."

"She even looks good with them on. Enough to make the dead man sit up and take notice."

"Don't think he didn't try. Choey wanted to make her real bad, but she was way out of his league."

Vangie Lynn stood talking to Rio for some time, he holding her gloved hands in his oversized mitts all the while. Leaning forward, she gave him a hug and kissed him on the cheek before moving on toward the rear of the canopy.

Brady said, "Whew! That's sure gonna stir up some heat."

Kilroy said, "It already has, as far as I'm concerned. And in the right places, too."

Brady shook his head. "That's not the kind of heat I meant."

"I did."

"You young fellows, that's all you got on your mind, ain't it."

"Not exactly on the mind, old-timer."

Brady snorted. "Vangie Lynn's bespoken for. The sheriff's got it bad for her, real bad. Sheriff Boyle, that is. He's the number-one son of a bitch in Adobe Flats, at least in the law enforcement department. He's torching pretty hard for Vangie."

Kilroy said, "Judging by her and Rio, looks like she's capable of bespeaking for herself."

"That's Vangie Lynn for you. She does as she pleases," Brady said, admiration coloring the tone of his voice. "And her working for Sime Simmonds, too. Ol' Sime and Rio are oil and water. They don't mix. There's bad blood between them, and Choey's death ain't helped cool things down any. Quite the contrary. Ol' Sime, he ain't gonna cotton to Vangie Lynn's showing up for the funeral."

Kilroy said, "Speaking of star attractions, what about the dead man? What's his story?"

Brady spat. "Choey? The kid brother, baby of the family. He never was worth much, didn't amount to a bucket of warm piss. Pure mean through and through. No guts, but with his brothers to back him up, he didn't need any."

"Died young, did he?"

"Not soon enough, most folks would say, but not openly. Somebody gunned him and two gang members out in the desert. Nobody knows who done it. Them Maldonados would sure give plenty to know who, so they'd know who to tear apart. As it is, there's too many suspects. Rio and Leandro are so mad, they could spit."

Brady studied Kilroy thoughtfully for a moment over the top of a beer can. "You seem like a man of sense, Kilroy. Things I'm saying, they're not the kinds of things you want to say out loud in Adobe Flats. It ain't healthy."

"You can rely on me, Hard Tack. I never violate a confidence."

"Of that I'm sure, but you know, a person just

can't be too careful. Thought I'd spell it out, you being new in town and all."

"I'm a closed book."

Brady drank some more. "By the way, what line of business did you say you were in?"

"I didn't say, Hard Tack, but I don't mind telling you. I deal in futures."

"What is that, real estate or something?"

"Speculations. I take my opportunities where I find them," Kilroy said.

A stir of motion rippled through the mourners as two priests began to take up positions near the grave site. Kilroy said, "Looks like the service is about to start. You can't say they're not doing it up big. Two priests for the send-off."

Brady said, "The old boy's Father Fitzpatrick, Father Fitz—he's been here forever—and the young 'un's his new assistant, Father Diego, fresh out of seminary school." He chuckled. "Some of the confessions he'll hear will curl his hair soon enough."

Suddenly, Kilroy grabbed Brady by the forearm, the one not holding a beer. "Did you see that?!" He was intent, his voice low, his manner urgent.

Surprised by the other's dramatic change in demeanor, Brady didn't know how to react, except to concentrate on not spilling a single precious drop of beer. He said, "Huh? Wha'?"

Kilroy said, "Act natural. Don't let on that you saw it."

"Saw what?"

"The gun."

"What gun? I didn't see no gun—"

Kilroy said, "Whatever you do, don't tip that we noticed. I don't know what's going on, but we don't want to get caught up in the middle of things. Now, without making it obvious what you're doing, take a look at those two grave diggers down there."

Brady's face expressed his befuddlement. Kilroy said, "Over on the right, down near the bottom of the ridge, where the backhoe is. Don't move your head, just your eyes. See it?"

Brady's bloodshot eyes rolled around in their wrinkled pouches like two ball bearings in oil, finally fixing on the yellow earthmoving backhoe standing idle some distance from the grave site. Sure enough, two men in gray coveralls huddled furtively behind the backhoe. The coveralls were the front-zip type that garage mechanics and factory hands might wear over their clothes jumpsuit-style.

The duo were positioned so the backhoe and a mound of fresh-dug dirt screened them from the view of the mourners assembled at the grave site. They were visible from the top of the knoll where Kilroy and Brady sat, though.

Brady's mouth was dry again. "I see 'em."

Kilroy said, "One of them's got a rifle."

Brady looked for it and couldn't see it, telling Kilroy just that.

"I saw it," Kilroy said. "He must've just put it down under the backhoe, out of sight." His voice was a whisper, urgent, thrilling. "Good thing they didn't see us."

Brady said, "Why—why not?"

"We're witnesses," Kilroy hissed. "Figure it out

for yourself. The Maldonado crime family, all gathered in one place. And a couple of grave diggers, so-called, lurking nearby with a rifle."

Brady got it. "Oh, Lordy!"

"Shh! Not so loud!"

"What're we going to do, Kilroy?"

"Since they didn't see us yet, what's important is they don't see us now. Lucky this brush gives us some cover. Let's get behind these trees first. No, don't get up, crawl on your hands and knees."

Brady did so, one hand still clutching a beer, the liquid sloshing in the can as he crawled between two tree trunks and got behind them. Kilroy snatched up the brown bag with the empties and the last unopened beer before nimbly scrambling through the trees to lie flat on the ground beside Brady.

Kilroy rose on his elbows, peering between the trees and tall grasses. The grave diggers were still hunkered down behind the backhoe, intently watching the grave site. He said, "Looks like we made it without them noticing us. That's a break."

Brady peered blearily through the weeds. One of the grave diggers was cradling a scoped rifle in both hands. "It is a gun!"

Kilroy said, "Remember, they can use it against us as easily as they can anyone else down there."

"What'll we do now?"

"You stay here, Hard Tack."

"What're you gonna do?"

"I'm going to get behind them, set up a yell.

With all those Maldonados down there, there should be plenty of firepower. At least that way, maybe it'll be a fight and not just a turkey shoot."

"You're loco!"

Kilroy grinned. "I told you I deal in futures. Time to start dealing!"

Brady shook his head. "There's no future in being a dead hero. Anyhow, them Maldonados got it coming. Why mix in something that ain't your business?"

"There's women and kids down there. I appreciate your position. Whoever sent those shooters might be sore if their pitch is fouled."

"You're damned right!"

"I don't blame you for not wanting to tie into it. You can get clear of it. Go down the other side of the knoll into that arroyo there that runs into the brush. Follow it till you're clear of the graveyard and be careful nobody sees you coming out in the open."

Brady said, "I'd help you if I could, but I ain't fooling nobody, not even myself. I'm an old rumdown, I got nothing left."

Indicating the brown paper bag and the unopened beer, Kilroy said, "Don't leave any evidence behind that there were watchers here. Somebody might come looking for you."

Brady said solemnly, "I'll take care of it."

"Okay," Kilroy said. "See you later maybe."

He eased down the west side of the knoll, not rising until the hill screened him from skylining.

"Luck," Brady whispered after the other's

retreating form. Kilroy reached the bottom of the hill, where a dry creek bed lay. He followed it south, circling the hill until he was out of sight.

The evidence of their presence was safe with Hard Tack Brady. First, he made the rest of the opened beer he was still clutching in one hand disappear by chugging it down. He gave serious thought to doing the same with the last intact beer, but decided to save it for later, since there was no telling where and when his next drink might be coming from. He dropped the empty can and the full one in the brown paper bag, grabbed it by its rolled-up top, and half slid, half crawled down the side of the knoll to the creek bed, taking it in the opposite direction to that taken by Kilroy. Following its northward windings through the brush, he put some distance between himself and the graveyard.

Kilroy soft-footed it along the dry creek bed, barely disturbing the stones underfoot. It wound south, then east, rounding the knoll. There was an opening in the brush at the top of the creek bed. He climbed the side, taking a look-see through the bushes.

He was behind the two grave diggers, about fifty feet away from where they were hunkered down behind the backhoe and the dirt mound. From the grave site came the droning rise and fall of the voice of one of the priests reciting the burial service.

One of the grave diggers was the shooter; the other, the spotter. The shooter was bareheaded, the spotter wore a khaki-colored, duck-billed baseball cap. The shooter stood with one knee on the ground, giving the scoped rifle a final going over. The spotter squatted on his heels, peeking through a narrow gap between the dirt mound and one of the oversized wheels of the backhoe. He was watching the mourners, the graveyard stretching to the east, the police cars and hearse and black funeral cortege cars lining the ornate, black iron spear fence bordering the cemetery. Watching everywhere but behind him.

Kilroy reached into his right front pants pocket, pulling out a blue-steeled, snub-nosed .38 revolver. The wooden cross-checked grip felt good in his hand. Slipping between the bushes, he stepped out into the open, arm at his side, the gun screened by his body.

He crossed toward the grave diggers, detouring around crosses marking several graves between him and them. The hard-packed ground was covered with dry grass, loose dirt, and pebbles; his passage created no more noise than the shadow of a drifting cloud. On the ground beside the shooter was the toolbox in which he'd smuggled in the dissassembled rifle. He was fitting a silencer on the rifle muzzle; oddly or appropriately enough, the silencer resembled a beer can.

Kilroy knew the plan. The target was Rio. His execution by silenced sniper fire would trigger a wild panic at the grave site, mourners fleeing in a mad rush. The silencer would ensure that the shot's origin was unknown. The shooter would break down the weapon, stowing it away in the toolbox. He and his partner would join the fleeing throng, using the confusion to mask their exit from the cemetery and their getaway.

He even knew the killer duo. The shooter was Tex Barker and the spotter was his partner, Lee Deetz. They were a pair of contract killers operating mainly along the Gulf Coast, through Texas and the Southwest. Barker was a hefty guy with a brown mustache, Deetz was lanky and long-faced, with an upper lip so thin as to be virtually nonexistent. Barker finished screwing on the silencer and got into position to line up his shot. Deetz squatted down beside him, looking like a lean, long-legged toad gathering itself to make a leap.

They never heard him coming. The first they knew of his presence was when he said, "Howdy, boys."

Deetz started like he'd been goosed. Barker's head swung around like it'd been whiplashed as he looked back over his shoulder to see the speaker. Recognizing him, Barker shouted, "You!"

Deetz was fumbling around with a hip pocket of his coveralls, reaching for the handgun tucked inside it, when Kilroy shot him right between the eyes. Barker tried to swing the rifle around to bring it into play, knowing it for a foredoomed effort. Kilroy's bullet drilled through Barker's forehead.

Taking Barker and Deetz was easy. Now came the hard part: not getting shot by any of the excitable gun-toters in the Maldonado entourage.

The melee was already on, shouts, screams, chaos erupting from the grave site.

Kilroy rested his gun on top of a tombstone. It was a good piece and he'd hate to lose it. Stepping several paces away from it, he raised his hands in the air, holding them open and in plain sight to demonstrate they were empty and unarmed.

Angry shouts, pounding footsteps neared. Suddenly, a half-dozen gunmen came crashing into view, darting between tombstones, scrambling over the dirt mound and circling the backhoe.

All wore mourning clothes, black jackets and pants, black ties and white shirts. Some were bareheaded; others wore hats. The hats were black. The gunmen ranged in age from a skinny kid in his teens to a wizened graybeard. They were angry, frightened, and confused. Some shouted at him in Spanish, others in English. Their guns were all pointed at Kilroy and if some hothead pulled the trigger, it would set off a chain reaction that would turn the group into a firing squad.

A very tense moment. Vital details of the scene began impinging on the awareness of the gunmen. One who'd come scrambling over the top of the dirt mound came down practically on top of Barker and Deetz, whose corpses lay sprawling in the dirt. He jumped back like they were red-hot.

A couple of guns swung away from Kilroy to

cover the dead men. Seconds dragged by as thoughts percolated through the brains of the pistoleros that the downed duo were really and truly dead.

Kilroy just stood there motionless, hands raised, outwardly calm, his expression blandly neutral. He dared not smile because sometimes with gun-waving hotheads who think they've just been shot at, a smile is taken as a deadly insult, to be wiped off the offending face by a bullet.

Someone more observant than his fellows discovered the silenced sniper rifle, setting off a fresh round of heated commentary.

The two Maldonado brothers entered the scene, along with Hector. Rio's hair was combed straight back from the forehead, covering his ears and collar. It was chestnut brown with blond highlights; Kilroy wondered if that was its natural coloring or if Rio had had it dyed. He suspected the latter. Rio had inverted V-shaped eyebrows over hazel-colored eyes and was clean-shaven. His shoulders were ax-handle broad and his massive torso hung down from them like a brick wall, presenting a broad front. He wore a black suit with a white shirt and black string tie. His feet were small, narrow, and neat.

Leandro had curly black hair, a broken nose, and a knife scar running slantwise through his left eyebrow, dividing it in two. He had a well-groomed black beard and a bull neck.

A melon-shaped head and thick limbs had been pasted onto Hector's barrel-shaped torso. Balding on top, he had thick tufts of hair on the sides, seemingly of the same consistency as steel-wool scouring pads. His long, thick ragged beard reminded Kilroy of pictures he'd seen of the pirate Blackbeard.

Rio, Leandro, and Hector brandished no guns, nor did they need to, their followers ably carrying out that duty. Scowling, Hector demanded of Kilroy, "Why you try to shoot Rio?"

"Not me," Kilroy said, shaking his head no. Tilting it toward the two corpses, he said, "They wanted to kill Rio." He was speaking not to Hector, but to Rio.

Rio said, "Who are you?"

Kilroy said, "I killed them."

At that moment, the police arrived, the sheriff and a couple of deputies. For an instant, Kilroy feared that the interruption might trigger off a shooting match, but cooler heads prevailed, namely those of Rio and the sheriff.

Rio's gunmen made their weapons disappear, the deputies holstered their sidearms. The encounter ended pretty much as Kilroy had suspected it would, with him seated in the back of the sheriff's car, riding off to jail.

At least, he wasn't in handcuffs. Once the law showed up and started leaning on Kilroy, the Maldonado crowd got the idea that the cops were persecuting the guy who'd just saved their boss Rio from two would-be assassins. Their hostility fastened on the lawmen, the mood getting ugly fast. Sheriff Boyle had to announce that they weren't arresting Kilroy, not yet, but were taking him to the station for questioning as a material witness.

Kilroy climbed in the back of the sheriff's car. There were no handles on the inside of the back doors, and a wire-screen partition separated the front seat from the back seat. As the police car pulled away from where it was parked outside the cemetery's front gates, Kilroy noticed in the forefront of a mass of onlookers a medium-sized man with straight thick black hair hanging down to his jawline, a ruddy complexion, and a wide, high-cheekboned face. He was Brand, a partner in this joint venture with Kilroy. The two made eye contact for an instant, not the slightest sign or flicker of recognition passing between the two to indicate anything other than that they were complete and total strangers.

The police car rolled east, leaving the church behind.

TEN

The police station—sheriff's department really—was located at the north edge of Old Town, just south of Fremont Street, part of a cluster of official buildings grouped around a square. They had all been built around the same time, early in the twentieth century. Mostly big, square gray stone structures, they included a post office, a library, a municipal building that served as City Hall, and a courthouse with a tower clock. The sheriff's department was sited in the courthouse building.

Boyle and two deputies hustled Kilroy into an office on the first floor. The dispatch room was up front, with an officer manning a high, dark brown wooden desk that stood on a dais so it was raised a foot or two above floor level. A radio crackled with police-band calls, the desk officer responding to them by speaking into a handheld mike. A waist-high wooden barrier separated the dispatch area from the squad room and administrative offices.

Sheriff Boyle was big, beefy, with wavy salt-and-pepper-colored hair and a craggy, thick-featured face that might have been considered handsome twenty years and thirty pounds ago. His assistant, Deputy Mort Lane, had short gray hair, a hawklike profile, and wore mirror-finish sunglasses that he kept on indoors. The third lawman was a big, hulking oaf who looked like an overgrown plowboy in uniform. His name was Viller but the other two called him "Sonny Boy."

The interrogation room was a stark, cubelike space with a gunmetal gray table and a couple of wooden chairs. Deputy Viller gave Kilroy a hard palm-heel shove between the shoulder blades, knocking him into the room so hard that he came up just short of bouncing off the wall.

Kilroy spun, facing the three lawmen as they entered the room. Lane closed the door behind him and casually leaned up against it. His eyes were bright, expectant, in an otherwise expressionless face.

Kilroy said, "Tell that ape of yours to keep his paws off of me, Sheriff, or he's going to get knocked flat on his ass." His voice was flat, even-toned.

Boyle's bushy eyebrows rose; Lane smirked. Viller's face flushed, the lower half of it splitting into a sloppy, loose-mouthed grin.

Viller rushed Kilroy, launching a looping roundhouse right at his head. The blow couldn't have been any more telegraphed if it had been sent by Western Union. Kilroy stepped in, blocking the punch with his left forearm, and immediately countering with a short, hard right jab to the deputy's solar plexus.

Kilroy's counterstrike stopped Viller dead in his tracks, causing him to rise up like he was standing on tiptoes. The deputy's eyes bulged; his mouth was a gaping black hole that sought to draw breath but couldn't. The blow to his nerve-net center had a temporary paralyzing effect.

Kilroy could have grabbed the man's gun, too, if he'd wanted. Instead, he stepped back to deliver a curving leg sweep that struck Viller's feet behind the ankles, knocking his legs out from under him and sending him crashing down to the floor on his back.

Boyle's eyebrows were still raised, but Lane's smirk was gone. Lane drew his sidearm; he was fast. He leveled his weapon at Kilroy, who stood in place, hands at his sides.

Kilroy said, "Think fast, Sheriff, as though your career depended on it, 'cause it does. Would I have pulled a move like that if I didn't have an ace in the hole?"

Lane said, "You're begging for a hole in your guts—"

Kilroy said, "Those two gunning for Rio didn't get taken by accident. Things are happening, Sheriff, big things, and if you're smart you'll look before you leap."

Lane said, "Just give me the word, Rance, and I'll cut loose—"

Kilroy said, "Do that, and the ones they send out after me won't be a nice guy like I am."

On the floor, Viller lay doubled up on his side, hugging himself, sucking air. Kilroy said,

"A shit storm's coming to Adobe Flats. Don't get on the wrong side of it. You already dodged a bullet, you and your whole department. Think what the Maldonado gang would've done if Rio got gunned at his brother's funeral. Worse is on the way if you don't get up to speed fast. You've got nothing to lose by listening."

Lane said, "He's bluffing, Rance."

"Call it," Kilroy said. "Hell, you can always burn me down for resisting arrest later."

Lane said, "You'll wish you got off that easy, smart-ass."

Boyle's brows knit in a frown. He made the act of thinking look like a heroic effort. Reaching a decision, he rested his hand lightly on the forearm of Lane's gun hand. He said, "Easy does it, Mort."

Lane, incredulous, darted a quick glance at Boyle, not wanting to take his eyes off Kilroy. "You're not falling for his line of horse puckey?!"

Sighing heavily, Boyle said, "Too much has already happened today that I don't know the whys and wherefores of. Let's not go off half cocked."

Kilroy said, "I'm going to give you a phone number, Sheriff. Call it and tell them Kilroy sent you and see what happens. If it doesn't pan out, you can always turn your wrecking crew on me later."

Lane said, "That's just what's gonna happen, mister, and before I'm done, you'll be begging for a bullet in the belly."

Kilroy said, "Who runs this department, Sheriff, you or him?"

"I do," Boyle said. "Back off, Mort."

"But Rance—"

"That's an order, Deputy."

"Okay," Lane said, "but I'm keeping this bastard covered. Let him try his tricks on me."

Kilroy said, "Ready for that number, Sheriff?"

"Go ahead."

"Better write it down. I'd hate for us all to come to grief because you misdialed."

"Mister, I sure hope you are bluffing, I surely do. Because I'd really like to see you get taken apart." Boyle reached into the breast pocket of his shirt, took out a notepad and a pencil stub, opened the pad to a blank page, and stood poised with pencil to paper, ready to write. "Go ahead."

Kilroy said a telephone number. Boyle wrote it down and repeated it aloud for confirmation. He said, "That's the state capital exchange."

"That's right," Kilroy said. "I suggest you make the call from a secured line and not one that anyone else can listen in on. You'll understand why when the call goes through. The less people who know about it, the better for all of us."

Boyle turned to Lane. "This won't take long. Do nothing until I return."

Lane grunted. Boyle gave him a hard look and said, "I assume that means affirmative."

"Yes, dammit," Lane said.

Viller was showing signs of life, his hand feebly scratching at the safety flap of his holstered sidearm. Boyle said, "Better secure Sonny Boy's gun so he doesn't do anything stupid."

"Affirmative," Lane said. Still covering Kilroy

with his own gun, he hunkered down beside Viller, unholstering Sonny Boy's gun and taking it, holding it in his other hand so that he now had Kilroy covered with two guns.

Boyle opened the door, glancing back over his shoulder at Kilroy. "This better be good," he said. He went out, closing the door behind him.

Kilroy said, "Mind if I sit down?"

Lane said, "Yeah, I do."

Kilroy shrugged. "Suit yourself."

"It'd suit me better if you tried some more of your tricks on me this time, instead of that dumb ox."

Kilroy tsk-tsked. "Is that any way to speak of a brother officer?"

"He ain't no kin of mine," Lane said.

Time passed. After a couple of minutes, Lane got tired of holding both guns leveled at Kilroy. He lowered Viller's gun, letting it rest at his side, but kept his own gun trained on Kilroy, holding his elbow against his hip.

Five minutes passed before Boyle returned. Under his deep tan, he looked almost as pale as Viller, though without the green tinge. There was a worried look in his eyes that hadn't been there before. Lane looked at him expectantly.

"Well," Boyle began. "Well, well. Seems like there's been a little misunderstanding here."

Kilroy said, "I see you got through to that number, Sheriff."

"Yes. Yes, as a matter of fact, I did. Yes, sir!"

Lane looked disgusted. "Don't tell me this bastard's on the level!"

"That's no way to refer to Mr. Kilroy, Mort."

"Aw, for crissakes, Rance—"

"Put up your gun."

Lane holstered his weapon, his expression sulky, almost pouting. "I wish to hell somebody would tell me what's going on here!"

"In due time, Deputy, in due time," Boyle said. He turned to Kilroy. "I want to apologize for the misconduct of Deputy Viller here. He was way out of line. If you'd like to file a complaint, the appropriate action will be taken."

Kilroy said, "I don't file complaints. Just see that he stays out of my way and keeps his mouth shut about anything he's heard in here."

By now, Viller had managed to crawl to a wall, where he sat with his back to it and his legs stretched out on the floor. He was hunched up, cradling his middle with both arms. He was able to breathe now, short shallow panting breaths. His pained face had a greenish tinge.

Boyle bent forward from the waist, bringing his head close to Viller's to speak to him. "You heard the man, Viller. One step out of line and you'll be out of uniform and back on the farm shoveling shit. And keep your damned mouth shut about this, savvy?"

Viller nodded, tight-lipped with pain. Boyle straightened up, crossing to the door, gripping the knob. "This way, Mr. Kilroy. We'll be able to speak plainly in my office."

Kilroy followed. Boyle told Lane, "Keep an eye on Viller until he's able to get around on his feet. And don't let anyone else in here. I don't want any officers seeing him in this condition; it's bad for morale."

Boyle opened the door and went out into the hall, Kilroy trailing him. At the end of the hall was a T-shaped branching; Boyle's office was on the right. They went inside, Boyle closing and locking the door. Opposite the door, windows gave a view of the parking lot behind the courthouse and beyond that, a public park.

"Have a seat, make yourself comfortable," Boyle said. He went behind his desk, plopping heavily into a swivel chair. Switching on an intercom, he said, "Hold all calls, Myra Mae. I've got a visitor and don't want to be disturbed."

A voice replied over the speaker, "Okay, Sheriff."

Boyle bent over, dipping, dropping out of sight below the desktop, opening a drawer, and rummaging through it. He came up with a bottle of whiskey, set it on the desk. It was three-quarters full. "You a drinking man, Mr. Kilroy?"

Kilroy said, "Sure."

Boyle rose, crossing to a filing cabinet. On top of it was a plastic bag filled with Styrofoam cups. He pulled out a couple, set them on the desk, and splashed a generous portion in each. Holding his cup in both hands, he said, "Cheers," and drained it.

"Here's mud in your eye," Kilroy said, taking a hefty belt. It was good whiskey, smooth with a biting burn he liked.

The sheriff refilled his own cup and gulped down some more. Kilroy said, "To save some time, Sheriff, I'll tell you what happened when you called the number I gave you. You reached a special hotline in the governor's office, a line that's monitored twenty-four hours a day for occasions just like this. You were told in no uncertain terms that I was a special investigator and that I was to be extended every coopera-tion requested. Failure to do so would result in Adobe Flats being swamped with more state and federal law enforcement agents than there are flies on a fresh cow pie. I believe that men-tion was made of all kinds of charges and penal-ties being invoked for failure to extend said cooperation."

Boyle's face was covered with a sheen of sweat, like he'd been misted. The booze had put some color back in his complexion, eyes glittering in a flushed, feverish face. He said, "I'm cooperating. What do you want?"

"First, let me tell you what I don't want," Kilroy said. "I'll lay my cards faceup on the table. You've got a dirty little town here, and it can stay that way for all I care. I'm not here to reform Adobe Flats, except where it happens to affect the pa-rameters of my assignment. So you don't have to worry about your dirty laundry coming out in the wash, as long as you do what you're told. And don't bother wasting my time with any denials about how you run a clean department in a clean town, because you don't and it isn't and I just plain don't give a damn.

"I'm sure that the party on the other end of the hotline to the governor's office got across the point that this is a matter of national security, so there's some nice twenty-year prison terms in federal maximum-security facilities waiting for anybody who obstructs the investigation."

Boyle said, "Yes, that was made perfectly clear."

He went to take another gulp of whiskey, only to find the cup was empty, so he filled it and drank deep. He set down the cup, shuddering. "National security—Adobe Flats? Why here, how . . . ?"

Kilroy said, "I'll let you know as needed. And you'd by God better make sure that you keep it tightly held, or I'll come after you myself."

Boyle, craving another refill, reached for the bottle, but Kilroy got there first, moving it out of the other's reach. "You've had enough for now," Kilroy said, "I want you alert and functioning."

Boyle said, "What do you want me to do?"

Kilroy said, "For starters, I want all the information you've got on the death of Bob Moomjian."

Boyle drew a blank, said stupidly, "Who?"

"Bob Moomjian. A visitor from Las Vegas who died here six months ago."

"I remember now. He got killed in a car wreck. But why . . . ?"

"Never mind why, just do it."

Not having been formally arrested, booked, and processed, Kilroy still had all the personal possessions he'd had on him at the time of his apprehension, minus his gun and some extra speed loads he'd been carrying. From an inside pocket of his denim vest he withdrew a manila envelope and opened it. It contained a number of photographs. He took one out and laid it on the desk blotter so Boyle could see it.

It was a formal composition, a head-and-shoulders studio portrait shot of a man in his mid-to-late-thirties. He had short fair hair, close-cropped, was clean-shaven, and had an alert, level, flat-eyed gaze. He was smiling with his mouth, but the smile failed to reach his eyes.

Kilroy said, "His name's Pete Peters, Jr."

Boyle said, "I don't know him from Adam."

"Find him. He's been in Adobe Flats. I want to know everything about him: where he went, where he stayed, where he ate and drank, who his friends and associates were, his enemies if any; whatever you've got."

He laid out a second photo on the desktop, one of a decidedly different sort. It was a candid shot, taken in a casino. It focused on Pete Peters, Jr., and a female companion. You knew she was a companion by the way they were hanging all over each other. He wore a loud print sports shirt and blazer. She was young, about twenty, with platinum blond hair in a page boy cut. She was heavily made up, with wickedly arched eyebrows, thick eyelashes, and a lipstick-painted mouth. She wore a sleeveless white and black polka-dot dress with a plunging V-neckline that accented the deep cleavage of full, melon-shaped breasts. She and Peters were bent over the rail of a craps table; she was shaking the dice prepatory to making a throw.

Kilroy said, "Her name's Tammi, last name unknown. She's Peters' girl. They met in Vegas, but she left some clues that connect her to Adobe Flats."

Boyle unconsciously licked his lips. "A juicy little piece, but she's not from around here."

"My sources say otherwise."

"I'm not likely to forget a cupcake like that. The town's not big enough for her to hide her light under a bushel. If she was from around here, I'd know her."

Kilroy was insistent. "There's a connection. She may not be native to this town, but she's got friends or associates here. A number of phone calls from her hotel room were made to a pay phone in Adobe Flats."

Boyle shrugged. "I'll ask around. What reason do I give for looking for her?"

"Hell, you're the sheriff, aren't you? You don't need a reason. Pete Peters, Jr., Tammi, or both. I want a line on them, the sooner the better. Yesterday," Kilroy said. "I can tell you this: It ties in with the death of Choey Maldonado."

That piqued Boyle's interest. "How about that!"

"Yes, and that's not all. The attempted hit on Rio is part of it, too."

"Damn!"

Kilroy said, "That's enough to get you started." He glanced at the wall clock; it was close to five P.M. "I'll check back at nine tonight to see what you've got."

Boyle groaned. "Have a heart, man! The night life in this town don't get started until nine. Give me some time so I can canvass the honky-tonks, gambling dens, working girls, and whatnot!"

"Fair enough. I'll check back with you at midnight. You'll be here?"

"Hell, no," Boyle said. "Meet me at the Salt Lick Club. Ask any bartender or cab driver, they'll tell you where to find it."

Kilroy said, "Midnight at the Salt Lick then."

"If I need to contact you before then, how'll I reach you?"

"I'll reach you. One thing more," Kilroy said. "I want my gun back, the one I used today."

"That's evidence—"

"Not as far as you're concerned."

"All right, I'll get it released."

Kilroy said, "Here's a tip to save you some time. Those two hitters today were Tex Barker and Lee Deetz. Barker and Deetz, think you can remember that? Run a check on them and you'll find they've each got a rap sheet a mile long."

A short time later, Kilroy was out on the street, gun in his pocket, ready to continue the hunt. He smiled to himself when he thought of how he'd spun the line about being a special investigator out of the governor's office.

It was true as far as it went; he was accredited as a special investigator for the chief executive in the state's capital. But that was only a cover worked up by the higher-ups in Washington, a legend to cloak and facilitate his true mission here in Adobe Flats. Kilroy was the ace of killers, the Lord High Executioner, the Top Dog of the Dog Team.

ELEVEN

It wasn't the sight of the old man getting slapped around that was so rough, though that was bad enough; it was the sobbing of the younger man, the old man's son, that was starting to work on Kilroy's nerves. And what nerves he had had been worked on in the past by experts.

The ugly scene was taking place in a back room at Toro Loco, a club down in Old Town that doubled as a Maldonado headquarters. The club itself was a lively, happening place with a dance floor, live band, plenty of tables and chairs for dining and drinking, and a long bar. It was about ten P.M. of the day Kilroy came to town, and the place was packed.

Its clientele included not only Hispanics, but lots of crossover patronage from the younger, more adventurous Anglo set. The dance band laid down some sinuous Latin rhythms punched up by a horn section whose range varied from bold and brassy to sweetly lyrical. The crowded dance floor vibrated from the movements of the couples swirling and swaying upon it. There wasn't a spare chair or empty table to be found, and the drinkers were lined up three deep at the bar.

That was out on the main floor. Behind the back of the bandstand were some private rooms, off-limits to the public. One of them was the private office of Rio Maldonado, a spacious rectangle whose long walls ran parallel with the front and back of the building.

A window set high in the rear wall had been painted over with pale green paint. There was a back door out of the place; it looked to be made of solid metal. The walls were wood-paneled. They were decorated by a dozen or more framed photographs of beautiful showgirls, provocatively posed in various states of undress.

There was a golden oak desk, a couple of filing cabinets, some armchairs and a couch, and a well-stocked private bar. All the furniture was grouped against the walls, leaving a generous open space in the center. Kilroy suspected it had been arranged that way to facilitate doings like the one that was taking place right now.

The room must have been soundproofed because the music of the dance band and the clamor of the crowd on the main floor was muted here to a dull background of white noise. Of course, the soundproofing worked both ways, not only keeping the outside noise out, but keeping what went on inside the room from getting out.

The uncarpeted floor was covered with linoleum, probably because it was easier to clean the blood off it that way, Kilroy thought. The room was nicely air-conditioned, with good ventilation.

Rio Maldonado sat behind the golden oak desk, a tumbler glass filled with tequila at hand. Leandro sat in an armchair, smoking a king-size cigar, watching the show. Kilroy sat on a bar stool, facing the center of the room, leaning an elbow on top of the bar.

In the open center space, an older man sat tied to a straight-backed, armless wooden chair. "Manuel," Rio had called him. Kilroy reflected that the guy probably wasn't all that old; chronologically he was maybe ten, fifteen years Kilroy's senior, putting him in his mid-fifties. But he was an old fifty-plus, prematurely aged by a lifetime of hard work and hard times. His hair, eyebrows, and mustache were ash gray, his gnarly face seamed and wrinkled, his hands crippled and arthritic.

The treatment he was getting wasn't going to improve the prospects for his longevity any. He was being worked over by a young thug named Tony. Not so much a working over, really, as a slapping around. A real beating would have probably finished him off. But the slapping around he was getting was no picnic. Tony was laying into him with big, wide open-handed slaps that sent Manuel's head reeling each time they connected. He was tied to the chair not so much to forestall any resistance as to keep him from falling down.

His face was swollen, lips smashed, blood trickling from his nostrils and the corners of his mouth. When he wasn't being hit, he slumped forward in the chair, chin resting on his chest. The ropes looped around his arms and torso binding him to the chair cut deep into his flesh.

Tony was into his work, winding up and leaning into each blow, putting his weight into it, even rising on the balls of his feet to deliver his strikes. His open hand was cupped, adding more impact to the blows. The blows made hollow thwacking sounds each time they solidly connected. Tony periodically altered sides, sometimes smacking Manuel on the right side of the face, sometimes on the left. Sometimes, for variety's sake, he backhanded him, just to break up the rhythm and the timing. More often than not, each blow sent some blood droplets flying.

Manuel was hurting, but not like the young guy lying on the floor. Paco, his name was. He was Manuel's son. He was slight, in his early twenties. He'd taken a real beating. His face was a mask of mottled purple bruises, his nose was smashed flat, his pulpy lips were slashed and bleeding from where punches had cut them against his teeth, of which he was missing a few. One eye was so puffed up that it was swollen shut; the other was open a slit, allowing him to see. That was the eye that was leaking tears as he watched the beating of his father continue.

Kilroy had come along in the middle of things. Paco had already had his beating and Manuel's was in progress when Kilroy had first arrived. Earlier tonight, Kilroy had been approached in the lobby of the hotel where he was staying by Maddox Kent, the Maldonados' legal counsel. Kent had suggested that Kilroy might find it worth his while to stop by the Toro Loco for a little chat with Rio Maldonado. Kilroy had allowed to the counselor that he might just do that very thing. What with cleaning his gun, showering, grabbing dinner, and taking care of a few errands, Kilroy had gotten to the club at about a quarter to ten.

People were lined up outside the club waiting to get in. Kilroy cut to the head of the line, telling the doorman that Rio wanted to see him. That gained him immediate entry, but he had to wait around by the coatroom for five minutes or so for the word to be passed to Rio. Presently, a young gun punk who didn't give his name arrived to escort him to the back, delivering him to the closed door of Rio's office. Hector came out, closing the door behind him. He said, "You got to be searched first."

Kilroy's .38 was in a holster clipped to his belt on his right hip. He peeled back the flap of his sport jacket, revealing the rod. Hector relieved him of it, then gave him a quick, efficient patdown frisk anyway. Kilroy came up clean except for a couple of speed loads in his jacket's lefthand side pocket; Hector let him keep those. He opened the door, indicating to Kilroy to enter. Kilroy went in, Hector following and closing the door behind him. The gun punk stayed outside.

Inside, Rio sat behind the desk, Leandro occupied an armchair, Tony was in the process of slapping around Manuel, and Paco lay huddled on the floor, whimpering and moaning. Tony was winding up for another smack, but held his hand when Kilroy and Hector entered. Leandro stopped puffing on his cigar, taking it from his mouth and rolling it in his fingers, his face expressionless, eyeing Kilroy,

Rio smiled at Kilroy, a toothy grin. "Just finishing up some business. After that, we'll get to know each other better."

Kilroy shrugged, indicating it was okay with him. Hector crossed to the desk, going around the tableau in the center made up of Tony and Manuel. He handed Kilroy's gun to Rio, saying, "That's all he had on him."

Rio laid the gun on its side on the desktop, within easy reach of his hand, near the tumbler of tequila. "Make yourself comfortable."

Kilroy went to the bar. He eyed the rows of bottles lined up on glass shelves on the wall behind the bar, but no one offered him a drink and he thought it might be a bit forward to help himself, so he perched on a bar stool to watch the rest of the show.

Gesturing toward the center of the room, Rio said, "An exercise in community relations. You see before you the Guittierezes, Manuel and Paco, father and son. There was a daughter, Dolores. She was a whore, a good one. She had a real talent for the work. She also had a habit for heroin that caught up with her and she died. Young Paco blames me for it."

From the floor, Paco raised himself on an elbow and forced his smashed mouth to form words. "You . . . got her hooked . . . on the stuff."

Rio smiled. Kilroy would have sworn Rio

actually had a twinkle in his eye. Tony went over and kicked Paco in the belly, doubling him up in a spasm of agonized writhing. He went to kick him again, but Rio said, "No more, I want him to see this. Otherwise, he misses the point of the lesson."

Rio turned to Kilroy. "The crazy ideas some people get in their heads! There's no talking sense to them. Paco wouldn't listen to reason. He told everybody he could that I was responsible for his sister's death, blackening her name instead of letting her rest in her grave. He even took his wild story to the police!"

He and Leandro exchanged knowing glances, while Hector allowed himself a little chuckle. How amusing, that one could be so foolish as to repose any confidence in the law! In this town, Kilroy was inclined to agree with them.

Rio said, "A stubborn fellow, that one. Even a beating failed to make him see the light. Not like Manuel. Manuel had sense, he knew better. He tried to convince Paco to drop the matter. But Paco is a bad son, a disrespectful son, who will not heed the wise counsel of his elders. So he keeps on talking.

"In a family, everyone is responsible for everyone else. Paco is too brave, too stupid to be afraid for himself? Very well, he will learn to be afraid for his father. Manuel must suffer for his son's loose tongue."

Rio turned to Tony. "Go ahead, continue the lesson." Tony went back to work on Manuel, slapping him around. Manuel cried out in pain several times, but never for mercy. It was Paco who broke, begging Rio to stop the beating. Tears ran from his open slitted eye, his thin shoulders hunched with sobbing dry heaves.

Tony stopped the beating. Rio looked at him, raising an interrogative eyebrow. Tony said, "He's passed out, Boss."

Leandro said, "I'll fix that." Rising ponderously from his armchair, he stood over Manuel, puffing on his cigar until the tip glowed orange-red. Taking it from his mouth, holding it between thumb and forefinger, he regarded the tip reflectively, blowing on it to make it glow brighter and hotter.

Paco stirred, rousing himself. Crawling forward, he raised a hand palm-out, crying, "No, don't! Don't—!"

Hector stepped on him, pinning him in place with one size-fourteen shoe. Leandro pressed the lit end of the cigar against Manuel's cheek. Manuel went rigid, returning to consciousness with a cry of pain that ended in a choking gurgle, followed by a prolonged, shuddering groan.

Rio leaned forward across the desk so he could see Paco better. He said, "Think maybe you learned your lesson about keeping your mouth shut?" Between sobs, Paco choked out his promise to keep silence. When Rio had heard enough, he motioned to Hector, who stepped harder on Paco. Paco groaned, writhing under the boot.

Rio said, "That's enough for now. Get them out of here."

Hector went into the hall, returning with the gun punk. Tony untied Manuel's ropes, holding him in place to keep him from falling out of the chair. Hector hauled Paco to his feet and held him upright. Hector said, "They can't walk."

Rio said, "Hector, you stay here. Diego, get Roberto to help."

Diego was the gun punk. He went out, returning a few moments later with Roberto, another young gang member. The duo braced Paco, holding him so he stayed on his feet. Tony got under Manuel, hefting him across his back in a fireman's carry. Motioning with his cigar, Leandro said, "Take them out the back way."

Rio said, "Leave them in the plaza by the fountain, so everyone will know what happens to those who can't keep their mouths shut."

Tony, Diego, and Roberto trooped out with their human burdens. Now Rio, Leandro, and Hector were alone in the office with Kilroy.

Rio said, "Somebody else would have just shot them, but not me."

Kilroy said, "That's right friendly of you."

"Not really. Dead, they're buried and forgotten. Alive, they're a reminder to other wagging tongues to keep still."

"That's all very instructive," Kilroy said. "Mind if I have a drink?"

Leandro smiled nastily, said, "Need a little something to steady yourself?"

"I'm thirsty and I hate to see all that expensive booze going to waste."

Rio said, "I forget my duties as host. Help yourself." Kilroy went behind the bar, eyeing the bottles. He picked out a bottle of premium white tequila and picked up a tumbler. When he turned around, he saw that Rio had his .38 in hand and was holding it pointed in Kilroy's general direction.

Coming around the bar, he crossed to the desk, sitting down in an armchair facing Rio. Uncorking the bottle, he poured a generous portion into his glass, setting the bottle down on the desktop.

Rio said, "That's a top brand."

Kilroy said, "I have expensive tastes." He tossed back a solid belt, exulting in the line of liquid fire that plunged down his gullet to explode in his belly, sending heat rushing to his brain. Not waiting for an invitation, he poured himself a second, ignoring Leandro's scowl.

Rio sat across from him, holding Kilroy's .38, resting his hand on the desktop and pointing the rod at Kilroy. He said, "I don't like snitches. Cops, I hate."

Kilroy said, "Me, too."

"That's funny, coming from you."

Kilroy said, "Is that what this is all about? You think I'm a cop?"

"I don't think, I know."

"That gun you're holding burned down two hitmen to save your hide."

"You thought you could gain my confidence that way."

Kilroy said, "You know enough about the law to know what a defense attorney could do to an undercover cop who killed two men in cold blood as a ploy to get in tight with a gang. He'd tear him to shreds on the witness stand. His testimony wouldn't be worth a good damn."

Rio considered that for a moment. "True enough. Okay, a crooked cop then. I don't like them much either, and I've already got too many of them on my payroll as is."

Kilroy sipped some of that premium tequila. It was fine. "You've got cops on the brain. What put that idea into your head? A head which might not be sitting on those shoulders right now if not for me, I might add."

Rio said, "A little bird told me that you're a special investigator for the governor."

"Wrong," Kilroy said. "I've got the title, not the job. I've got some pull at the state capital that I used to get the title. And I guess you know how easily something like that can be done in this state. All it takes is dollars. The title makes it a whole lot easier for me to get my business done, without having dickheads like Sheriff Boyle interfering and gumming up the works."

Rio said, soft-voiced, "And what business might that be, amigo?"

"Persuasion," Kilroy said. "I'm a debt collector. I collect bad debts. I persuade people who owe large sums of money to pay up."

"Who in Adobe Flats owes you money? A large sum of money, you say."

Kilroy said, "Ah, there we come to the heart of the matter. I'm going to lay my cards on the table and tell you what I told the sheriff. Obviously, you've got an in somewhere in the department, so use your source to cross-check on what I'm going to tell you.

"I'm looking for a man named Pete Peters, Jr. An Air Force captain. Not long ago, he went on a wild tear in Vegas. He's a degenerate gambler and he dropped close to fifty thousand dollars at the tables. Naturally, he couldn't get a line of credit like that on a captain's salary, but there's money in the family and he's got an independent source of income—a trust-fund baby—so the casinos were willing to take his markers for fifty grand.

"Then, he disappeared. Dropped out of sight. Well, he's not the first to pull a vanishing act to weasel out of a gambling debt. Finding guys like that and making them pay up is my specialty. I bought up all his markers and I intend to make him pay in full.

"You've got Vegas connections, check it out for yourself," he added.

"I'll do just that," Rio said. He flashed sharklike teeth in a half snarl, half smile. "In either case, though, you're shit out of luck. Because there is no such person as this Peters in Adobe Flats. Believe me, I know. Gambling is one of my business interests."

"With Peters dropping out of sight to stiff the boys in Vegas for fifty big ones, he's not likely to throw a spotlight on himself by taking a rider in a Nevada gaming club, yours or any other," Kilroy said. "Your boy Hector already tossed me, so there won't be any objection if I reach into my jacket pocket and pull out an envelope."

Rio nodded. Kilroy took a manila envelope from the inside breast pocket of his jacket and opened it, shaking out a few photos. He passed the portrait photo of Pete Peters, Jr., to Rio. "That's my pigeon."

Rio eyed it intently, then shook his head. "Don't know him. And I never forget a face."

"Pass it around. Maybe your brother or Hector has caught sight of him."

Leandro and Hector each examined the photo; neither recognized the subject. Rio said, "You're out of luck, my friend."

"I'm just getting warmed up," Kilroy said. From the envelope he extracted another photo, the one of Peters and Tammi at the craps table. "Here's my hot lead. Peters is not only a gambler, he's a chaser. This babe was his constant companion in Vegas. She goes by the name of Tammi. I don't even have a last name. But I do know that while she was in Vegas with Peters, she made a number of phone calls to Adobe Flats. When I ran down the number, I found it was to a pay phone in the town's commercial district."

Kilroy passed around the photo of Tammi, which got a lot more scrutiny than had the photo of Peters alone. Rio said, "I don't know her, I regret to say. Pity. She looks worth knowing."

Leandro and Hector examined the photo and replied in the negative. Kilroy was insistent. "That doesn't mean she's not in town. She could've changed her hair color, makeup, her entire look. The same goes for Peters. They don't have to be in town either. There's lots of ranches outside of town, mobile homes, trailer parks, where a couple could hide out without anyone being the wiser."

He leaned forward. "But here's the clincher, why I know I'm on the right track. You're right about one thing: I didn't stumble into Tex

Barker and Lee Deetz by accident. Peters and Tammi know I'm after them. As soon as my search zeroed in on Adobe Flats, they got scared. Scared enough to hire Barker and Deetz to eliminate me. I've got connections and got word through the grapevine that they were gunning for me. That's why I was ready for them and got the drop on them first."

Rio, no less intent, said, "Here we come to the flaw in your story. It was not you that Barker and Deetz were trying to kill today, it was me. How do you reconcile that with the facts?"

Kilroy, triumphant, played his high card. "That's not a flaw, it's the key to the whole puzzle. Why would Barker and Deetz want you dead? Because Peters and Tammi hired them to do so. Why do Peters and Tammi want you dead? Because you're a danger to them. And why is that?"

Rio said, "You're telling it."

"Barker was a sharpshooter who kills with a high-powered rifle. How was your brother Choey killed? By a marksman with a high-powered rifle."

Kilroy paused to let that sink in. Rio wasn't looking at him anymore; he was staring somewhere off into space, his face utterly blank and emotionless. A pair of veins the size of pencils bulged on either side of his forehead. Leandro was breathing hard, like he'd just been running a race.

Kilroy brought it home. "Don't you get it? Somehow, your brother Choey crossed paths with Peters or Tammi or both. He knew something that made him a danger to them, made him someone that had to be eliminated. So they set Barker and Deetz on him and had him killed.

"But that's not enough, Rio. You're still alive, you and Leandro. Your brother's killers can't rest as long as either of you is around. If you should ever get a lead on them, you'll keep looking for them until you find them and then they'll die hard."

Rio's eyes came back into focus. "That is so."

Kilroy pressed. "Maybe Choey said something to you, some seemingly irrelevant remark until you start trying to fit the pieces together and realize it's a clue. Maybe it's something he left in writing, or a photograph, or who knows what. Maybe he didn't leave behind any clue at all. But Peters and Tammi don't know that. Instead of leaving it to chance, they take the initiative. Hire Barker and Deetz, two proven killers, to strike again, take out you and Leandro both at the same time. Hell, maybe they want to take over the town themselves, or they're working with somebody who does. It's your town; you can answer that part of it far better than I can."

Rio drew himself up behind the desk, as if through sheer willpower he could concentrate his essence into one supremely lethal and single-minded package. He said, "Kilroy, if you can find my brother's killers and prove it, you can write your own ticket."

Kilroy said, "I just want to collect my fifty grand."

"I'll pay ten times that, a hundred times that, to get the bastards who killed Choey."

"Let's keep it within the realm of the possible. Fifty thousand is my price. As for Barker and Deetz, no extra charge. Call it a token of earnest. After all, they were after my hide, too."

Rio's face clouded. "You can do this thing? I want proof—"

"I'm running down a couple of hot leads," Kilroy said. "Give me twenty-four hours, and I'll deliver proof that Peters and Tammi arranged your brother's murder and put the finger on where we can find them. If I don't, you don't pay. What have you got to lose?"

Rio's smile was twisted. "If you don't, it's all about what you've got to lose."

Kilroy smiled back. "That little demonstration you put on earlier was pretty convincing. For now, though, I've got work to do. My gun?"

Rio, no fool, ejected the rounds from the .38 before handing it to Kilroy. Kilroy said, "Trusting soul, aren't you?"

Rio said, "Kilroy, whatever you do, don't try to leave town."

"Leave this garden spot where the green dollars grow? Not until I collect my fifty thousand bucks," Kilroy said.

After Kilroy left, Leandro said, "I don't like him. I don't trust him either."

Rio said, "What he'll collect is a bullet in the head. But not before he fingers Choey's killers."

TWELVE

Kilroy loaded his gun as soon as he could, ducking into an alley down the street from the Toro Loco club. Nobody had followed him out of the club. Were the Brothers Maldonado then so very confident that they had the town so tightly wired that nobody could skip out on them? Kilroy didn't lack for confidence either. He'd never found himself in a situation, no matter how sticky, from which he couldn't extricate himself. He figured he could enter or leave Adobe Flats as he pleased with no one the wiser. It just so happened that for now, it suited his purposes to stay in town.

Rio and Leandro must be pretty sure that he'd stick around for his fifty-thousand-dollar payoff. From what he'd seen of those two, he couldn't see them paying off on fifty cents if they didn't have to. That was okay; he had a few tricks up his sleeve, too, and wasn't exactly dealing on the level with them.

He fitted a round into the last empty chamber,

closed the .38, and slipped it into his hip holster. It felt good to have a loaded gun again. Nevada had some pretty tough towns: Palo Verde, San Gorgonio, and the notorious Lyncastle, but Adobe Flats was right up there with them. All things being equal, he'd no sooner go around in town with a gun than he would without a pair of pants.

He checked his watch. It was about a quarter after eleven. He wasn't due to meet Sheriff Boyle for another forty-five minutes yet. He followed the sidewalk to an intersection and turned, walking north.

The area around the Toro Loco was jammed with bars, clubs, cantinas, and gin mills. He could have a drink or five to wash out the bad taste in his mouth left by the ugly scene of the double beating he'd witnessed in Rio's office, but decided against it, postponing the pleasure until later. If he started drinking now, it'd be tough to stop with just one or two.

At Fremont Street, he turned right and started walking east toward the town square. Along the way, he thought he recognized a familiar face in the gutter, or rather, a familiar figure. He couldn't see the face at first because of the way the body lay, with its upper body stretched across the curb and its lower body on the wooden plank sidewalk.

It looked like Hard Tack Brady. Passersby strolled past it without giving the man much more than a second glance, except to sneer down at him. Brady's limbs thrashed feebly, so at least he wasn't dead.

Dead drunk was more like it. Kilroy hooked his hands under Brady's arms and hauled him up on the sidewalk, holding his breath as best he could because the man smelled pretty ripe. Brady groaned, mumbling what Kilroy took to be an inarticulate protest at being disturbed. He dragged Brady to the storefront of a business that was closed for the night, and propped him up so that his back was against the wall.

Brady wasn't as plastered as Kilroy had initially assumed. He lifted his head, prying open gummy, rheumy eyes to peer blearily at Kilroy hunkered down beside him. Kilroy grabbed Brady's shoulder and gave him a good shaking to bring him around. Brady said, "Leave me alone, leave me alone . . ."

"You okay, Hard Tack?"

"Huh? Who's that?"

"Kilroy. Your buddy from the graveyard earlier today. Remember me?"

"Sure. My pal. What do you think I am, drunk? I wish I was drunk. How's about buying me a drink?"

"Okay."

"You will?" Brady roused himself, exhibiting a surprising amount of force and vigor. "You really are a pal—"

Kilroy pressed down on Brady's shoulder, preventing him from rising up. "I want to ask you something first."

Brady's squirmings subsided. "Figures. Nobody does nothing for nothing. You're no pal."

Kilroy reached into his wallet, pulled out a ten-dollar bill, and held it in the light in front of Brady's face. "That's Andy Jackson's picture on it, in case you don't know your presidents."

"Gimme," Brady said, snatching at the bill. Kilroy pulled it out of his reach, said, "Talk first."

"My throat's too dry for talking."

"Good, you'll give short answers."

Brady, resigned, sighed deeply. "What do you want to know?"

Kilroy said, "You're a prospector."

After a pause, Brady said, "I used to be."

"You must know the Tres Hermanos and Black Sand Desert pretty good."

"Like I know the back of this here left hand of mine."

"That's your right."

"Huh? Why, so it is. Quit quibbling. I'll tell you this. I know the mountains and desert good enough to know that there ain't a trace of silver left to be found in either of 'em."

"But you keep on going back there. Why?"

Brady shrugged. "Gotta do something. Listen, if you want the story of my life, it'll cost you more than ten dollars."

"I don't," Kilroy said. "All I want to know is if there's a place back there that's bad medicine. Dangerous. A place where people don't go if they want to stay healthy."

Brady laughed, the laughter subsiding into a wheezy cough. "Mister, the whole damned area is dangerous, what with the drug dealers and gunrunners and people smugglers and what-not. You could get shot dead just for being in the wrong place at the wrong time, or because somebody thinks you saw something you ain't supposed to see."

"I'm not talking about outlaws and *contrabandistas*. Something more official, like a piece of private property that someone's got staked out for a private claim, a construction site, warehouse, abandoned diggings."

"It's a desert, see? Ain't nobody building nothing out there, nobody working a claim. What silver there was here played out a long time ago. I know."

Kilroy went on. "Maybe someplace that was open but has been fenced off in the last few months, or posted no trespassing, or has guards—"

Brady suddenly looked cagey. "Maybe . . ."

"What?"

"The ten?"

"You've got to sing for your supper, Hard Tack. What the hell, you'd think I'm trying to chisel you out of a lousy ten bucks—"

"Okay, okay, don't get sore. Remember, though, ten bucks ain't lousy to me, it's real dough."

"Then earn it."

"Not far from Wild Horse Pass, west of the mountains, there's an old abandoned gypsum mine," Brady said. "It's played out, too, just like the silver lodes. About a month ago, some outfit took it over. Don't know what they think they're gonna do with it, because the last of whatever gypsum was in there was hauled out of there back in the fifties. They got some private guards up there, real mean sons of bitches that chase everybody off the property. Real bastards. They caught a fellow I know doing a bit of prospecting in the hills back of the mine, and they beat the piss out of him. Turned him over to the law, too. He got tried for trespassing and couldn't pay the fine, so they gave him ninety days on the county road gang."

Kilroy said, "Who owns it?"

"I dunno. What do you think I am, a realtor? I told you what I know, now gimme the ten," Brady said.

Kilroy gave him the ten, Brady's lumpy, over-sized fist closing around the bill in a death grip.

"One more thing," Kilroy said. "I'm not too popular in certain quarters of Adobe Flats—"

"I wonder why," Brady said, sarcastic.

"So if you're smart, you'll keep our conversation private. It's healthier that way."

"For me or for you?"

"Both."

"Mister, it's already forgotten." Brady got his feet under him to rise, and this time Kilroy didn't interfere. Brady said, "I'm gonna get to work and start forgetting it right now."

He staggered away, lurching into the nearest bar, which happened to be the Doghouse. He must have flashed the ten in time to keep from getting bounced, since no one propelled him out the front door and into the street.

That would come later, no doubt, after he'd drunk up the ten, Kilroy thought. He headed off toward the town square.

Sheriff Boyle's hair was slicked down, he was freshly shaved, and he reeked of cologne. Kilroy figured the lawman had a hot date later tonight, and from what he'd picked up earlier from Hard Tack and some other town gossips and busy-bodies, Kilroy guessed that the date was with that stellar dancing attraction Vangie Lynn.

Boyle grumbled, "Sure took your time about getting here." It was only ten minutes after midnight, but he was impatient to get on with his extracurricular activities. He and Kilroy were in Boyle's office. Boyle shoved a folder across his desk. "Here's the material you wanted, though why you're interested in some of this stuff is beyond me. Like that Moomjian case. Hell, that's nothing but a routine traffic accident. I know, I investigated it myself."

"It's all grist for my mill, Sheriff." Kilroy leafed through the folder, scanning the documents. They looked promising, but he'd know better after examining them in detail back at his hotel room.

Gathering up the papers, he put them back in the folder and slipped it into the manila envelope that it had been in when given to him by Boyle. Rising, he tucked it under his arm. "Thanks, Sheriff, I appreciate it."

"Wish to hell I knew what it was all about."

"It's about handling things quietly so the FBI doesn't have to get called into town," Kilroy said. "Keep cooperating and we can avoid that very thing. It would do a lot of folks not much good if the G-men ever start digging into the way this town is run." Boyle was disinclined to reply, being one of those folks who'd prefer not having to account for themselves to federal investigators.

Kilroy said, "Stay available; things might start breaking fast."

Boyle said, "You can always reach me through the dispatcher, day or night."

"I'll be in touch." Kilroy crossed to the door, pausing with his hand on the knob. Glancing back over his shoulder, he said, "Tell me, who bought up that old gypsum mine on the other side of the mountains?"

Boyle snorted his derision. "That hole in the ground? Bert Sarkesian picked up the property a month or two back. He's the fellow that owns that carpet discount house."

"I've heard the name, seen him around."

"Typical city slicker, comes out here to what used to be mining country and thinks he's going to strike it rich. Reckons he can strike some fresh mineral deposits in the mine using some new-fangled geological gadgetry or something."

"Maybe he's on to something," Kilroy suggested.

Boyle shook his head. "That mine's been checked and double-checked by experts and come up empty every time. All he's doing is digging a dry hole." Boyle's forehead scrunched up, indicating thought. "Say—that Moomjian was coming back from visiting Bert when he wrecked his car and got killed. Drunk. What all you so interested in Bert Sarkesian for?"

"I'm looking for a good deal on some new carpeting," Kilroy said. "Don't think too hard, Sheriff. And don't talk about our business, not even a little bit."

"I know how to keep my trap shut," Boyle said resentfully.

"Good," Kilroy said. "That Deputy Lane looks mighty ambitious. I'd hate to see him running this department instead of you." He went out.

Sheriff Boyle would talk, talk plenty, and Kilroy could guess to whom: Vangie Lynn. No doubt he'd already done so. That explained how Rio Maldonado had been able to get a line on Kilroy so fast. Boyle had blabbed to Vangie Lynn, and she'd relayed the info to Rio. From the way she'd been holding hands with Rio at the funeral, it was pretty obvious that they were more than good friends.

Tonight, when Boyle hooked up with her after her last set at the club, she'd worm still more information out of him, getting an update on what he'd talked about with Kilroy and where the latter's interests were focusing. She'd pass that on to Rio, too. In fact, Kilroy was counting on it, because it would add extra credence to the buildup he was feeding Rio.

So thought Kilroy as he walked from the police station to his hotel. He was staying at the Hotel Cleve, a stopping place patronized mostly by traveling salesmen and tourists on their way to someplace else. It was located in New Town, about six blocks north and three traffic squares west of the police station.

He was not so deep in thought that he failed to notice the car that had picked him up when he exited the station and had been tailing him ever since. Kilroy turned right at the fourth street north of the police station. It was a commercial area, lined with stores that had closed for the business day at dusk.

He went west, walking on the north side of the street. The street was quiet, deserted; he had it all to himself. He and the dark car that was poking along about a block behind, following him.

He came to an area where a building had been torn down, leaving a vacant lot in its place. A sign promised that the site was under construction. The sign was weathered, the paint peeling; it had stood there for a long time. The weeds in the lot were waist-high.

This looked like a likely spot. Kilroy eased the .38 out of the holster and palmed it in his right hand, holding it close to his side. He kept on walking as though he hadn't a care in the world.

They worked it cute. The car paused about a half a block behind Kilroy. There was the sound of a door opening. Glancing over his shoulder, Kilroy saw a guy in a dark suit get out of the front passenger seat, stepping down to the pavement and closing the door behind him. Footfalls sounded as he started walking in Kilroy's wake.

Kilroy had thought they might try a drive-by and he was prepared for it, but the guy getting out behind him meant they would try a different approach. The car resumed moving, driving west past Kilroy. Glancing sideways at it, he saw that it was occupied solely by a driver.

The car rolled on several dozen feet ahead of

him before pulling over to the curb. The driver got out, went around the rear of the car and stepped up to the sidewalk, facing Kilroy and starting toward him.

Running feet sounded behind Kilroy. Glancing back over his left shoulder, he saw the guy already had his gun out. Dropping into a half crouch, Kilroy fired under his left arm, putting two slugs into the gunman's middle.

Kilroy sidestepped to the right, swinging the gun toward the driver. A shocked outcry escaped the driver as he drew a gun from a holster under his left arm. But Kilroy's gun was already out. He put two rounds into the driver, who crumpled into a heap on the sidewalk.

Echoes from the shots racketed down the street, fading into inaudibility. Kilroy straightened up, looking around. As far as he could see, he was alone on the street with the two dead guys. The buidings lining the street remained silent, inert. No lights came on; nobody lifted a curtain or stuck their head out of a window to investigate. There wasn't a car in sight.

The driver was nearer, so Kilroy went to him first. He was thirtyish, with black hair and a mustache and two bullet holes in his chest, one that had tagged him in the left breast over the heart. Kilroy pried the gun out of his hand, a semiautomatic pistol, and dropped it in the right side pocket of his jacket.

The car's engine was idling. Kilroy got an idea. If they could play it cute, so could he. Going to the car, he opened the driver's-side door, leaned over, and tripped the trunk release, unlocking it.

Raising the trunk lid, he hooked his hands under the driver's arms, dragged him to the rear of the car, hoisted him up, and tumbled the body into the trunk.

He looked around. The street was still silent, deserted, no oncoming cars or pedestrians in view. He got into the driver's seat and drove in reverse until he was abreast of the other guy, the passenger. He got out and went to him.

The dead man seemed cut from the same cloth as the driver, except that instead of sporting a mustache, this one had a neatly trimmed black beard. One shot had taken him in the middle, the other had hit in the throat. No life was left in him.

He'd dropped his gun during the shooting; it lay on the sidewalk about six feet away from him. It was a short, snouty, foreign-made semi-automatic pistol. Kilroy dropped it in the left side pocket of his jacket.

He hoisted the body into the trunk. He had to move the dead man's limbs around, wedging them at the sides so they wouldn't stick out at odd angles and keep the trunk lid from closing. He closed it.

When he'd made his play, he'd had to let go of the manila envelope holding the files he'd gotten from Sheriff Boyle. It lay on the sidewalk. Retrieving it, he got in the driver's seat and drove away.

Some blocks away from the scene of the crime, he found a quiet side street and pulled over to the curb to make a cell phone call to Brand. Brand was his partner and teammate on the Adobe Flats assignment. Kilroy was working it from the inside, Brand from the outside. He gave Brand a quick summary of what gone down, telling him where he was going and where to meet him.

Kilroy drove south, down into Old Town. He parked the car on a quiet street behind the back of the Toro Loco club, after first checking the traffic signs to make sure that parking was legal there. It was. No restricted zones, not even a parking meter. A couple of other cars were also parked on the street.

Taking out a handkerchief, he wiped down the steering wheel and all the places he'd touched in the car in order to remove his fingerprints. That was the only reason he carried a handkerchief, for wiping away fingerprints. He wiped down the car keys, leaving them under the driver's-side floor mat.

Grabbing his manila envelope, he got out of the car, using the handkerchief to work the door handle. He closed the door, leaving it un-locked. He wiped down the outside of the car, the handle and trunk lid, and anything else he might have touched. It might have seemed odd to go through these precautions when the corpses had bullets from his gun inside them, the same gun that had liquidated Barker and Deetz. But there was method to his madness. If there was any comeback on these kills, he could always claim that the gun had been lifted by the Maldonados and used in an attempt to frame him. He had a strong feeling, not so much an intuition as a certainty, that before too long they wouldn't be around to contradict him.

He walked to the end of the street, made a right, and went to the place where he'd told Brand to meet him. A pickup truck with a camper van attached stood there; behind the wheel sat Brand. Kilroy climbed in the passenger side and Brand drove away.

He filled Brand in on the latest development and the strategy for tomorrow. He passed the .38 to Brand for safekeeping. Kilroy had plenty of other guns to fall back on.

Brand dropped him off at the Hotel Cleve, where Kilroy reached his room without further incident. For about an hour, he poured over the documents given him by the sheriff. Then he went to bed. He was beat!

THIRTEEN

Like last time, Hector frisked Kilroy outside Rio's office in the back of the Toro Loco. It was mid-afternoon and the club was dead quiet. It wouldn't open for business until later, to catch the dinner crowd. Now there were no crowds, no band and no boozers, only a skeleton crew of busboys and custodial types handling clean-up chores. Fewer witnesses to a murder if murder was called for, thought Kilroy. He hoped it wouldn't be his. He'd laid plans to turn that hope into something more concrete.

Hector's search came up blank, taking the man by surprise. "No gun?"

Kilroy said, "Who needs a gun when you're among friends?"

That only made Hector more suspicious, prompting him to repeat the search more thoroughly this time. He even looked inside Kilroy's manila envelope with the dossier, just in case a flat little pistol was stowed inside. There wasn't.

What was in the dossier was dynamite, but not the kind Hector was used to.

Grudgingly, Hector opened the door to let Kilroy into the office, following at his heels. Rio was seated behind his desk, toying with a switch-blade stiletto. Leandro was there, too, filling up an armchair. Thankfully, neither Paco and his father nor their equivalents were present, getting the treatment.

Rio glanced at Hector. Hector said, "He's not carrying a gun, Boss."

Rio's eyebrows lifted at that announcement. He said to Kilroy, "You must be getting reformed."

"Must be the atmosphere in Adobe Flats. So elevating," Kilroy said.

Rio nodded. "It's been known to give people wings. Not that I consider you a candidate for a harp and a heavenly choir. You look like the type who's headed for the other direction."

"Aren't we all? But not too soon, I hope."

"We'll see. So what have you got for me, Kilroy?"

"Your brother's killer. The guy who tried to make it a triple funeral yesterday by doing in you and Leandro. The guy who's trying to move in and take over the town."

"And who might that be?"

"Bert Sarkesian."

Hector barked out a laugh, but choked it off when he saw that neither Rio nor Leandro were particularly amused. Leandro, sitting slumped in the depths of an overstuffed armchair, rolled his eyes.

Rio ostentatiously stifled a yawn. "The only

thing he's bossing is the carpet concession, and welcome to it. That line of work doesn't interest me."

Kilroy said, "I don't expect you to buy a pig in a poke. I've got proof."

"Prove it."

"What do you know about Sarkesian anyway?"

"All right, I'll play along," Rio said. His seeming nonchalance reminded Kilroy of the elaborate disinterest a cat displays when it begins toying with a mouse. Sometimes, it gives the mouse enough leeway to delude it into thinking it might just get away, and then out of nowhere, wham!—Tabby strikes.

Rio said, "He's an Armenian rug merchant with an extended family who moved here a couple of years ago and set up a discount warehouse emporium to peddle his wares."

"Maybe so," Kilroy said, "but whoever he is, he's not Bert Sarkesian."

"Says who?"

"U.S. customs and immigration service. According to them, the real Bert Sarkesian died during a buying trip in Turkey a few years back." Kilroy took the folder out of the manila envelope, opened it, and withdrew the relevant documents, handing them to Rio.

Rio glanced over them. "Documents can be faked."

"They can, but these aren't. Check on them yourself to see if they're the genuine article."

Rio handed the documents to Leandro, who began studying them, moving his lips as he read through them. Kilroy said, "Then there's the matter of Bob Moomjian."

Rio said, "Who?"

"Bob Moomjian. An Armenian-American who knew the real Bert Sarkesian. They worked together on some fund drive to build a monument to Armenian genocide victims of the Turks way back when. Passing through Adobe Flats a year ago, imagine his surprise when he discovered his old pal had a big store right here in town. He went out to Sarkesian's ranch to visit him. That was the last time anyone ever saw him alive—except for Sarkesian, that is. Moomjian drank too much and wrecked his car on the return trip, killing himself."

Kilroy pulled out the police report on the crash, the coroner's report, and the death certificate, passing them to Rio. Rio said, "So what?

Kilroy said, "Moomjian was a member of Alcoholics Anonymous. He'd been clean and sober for over ten years."

"He fell off the wagon. It happens."

"Let's try something that hits a little closer to home. Here are copies of the hotel receipts showing the calls that little Miss Tammi made to Adobe Flats. They're all to the same number, a pay telephone located just down the corner from Sarkesian's carpet warehouse building. Here's a statement from the phone company pinpointing the location."

Leandro leaned out of his chair, reaching. "Let me see that." Kilroy handed it to him. He took out a series of photos, eight-by-ten glossies.

"Here's the casino photo surveillance shot of Peters and Tammi at the craps table."

He laid out a second photo. "Here's a blowup of Tammi alone."

A third photo followed. "Here's one of Sarkesian's niece Terri, taken yesterday at the funeral."

He had their attention now. Rio said, "You're not seriously trying to suggest that that mousy little bitch—"

Kilroy slapped down another photo. Interrupting Rio, he said, "Here's that same photo of Terri Sarkesian, only with the hairdo and eyeglasses airbrushed out. Compare her face with the one of Tammi."

Rio and Leandro were doing some hard looking now. They were both standing, leaning over the desktop, intently eyeing the photos. Rio said, "They look a little like each other maybe. In the face. But you can do anything with cameras and Photoshop . . ."

Kilroy said, "Take it to an expert on facial recognition patterns, and he'll point out a dozen or more matches between the two that prove that this is the same woman in both pictures. I did. Here's the report, including a chart detailing the matching correspondences. But don't take my word for it. Hire your own expert and see what he says."

He laid down another photo. "And while we're on the subject, here's a reconstruction of what Terri Sarkesian would look like with platinum blond hair and the same makeup as Tammi. Take a good look and tell me that's not the same woman."

It was Leandro who spoke first. "It could be, Rio. It could be."

Rio said, "It could be some fancy computer trickery, too. Con men have gone to greater pains than this to put over scams that pay off a lot less than fifity thousand dollars."

Kilroy smiled. The roles were reversed in the game of cat and mouse and now he was the cat, and it felt good. "You're a hard man to convince, Rio. That's why I've saved the best for the last."

Rio said, "I call. Show your hand."

"It's not here, it's outside. Not far, just outside the back."

"Bring it here then. Hector will go with you."

"I suggest we all go. It's not the kind of evidence that travels well."

"If this is some kind of trick—"

"I didn't go to all this trouble just to be slaughtered by you for running a clumsy con game, Rio. Now do you want to see it or not? If you can't be bothered to show your face on the streeet, maybe Leandro won't be so squeamish."

Rio said, "Careful, Kilroy, careful. You come perilously close to insult. Walk soft." His voice was as husky and rustling as a snake slithering through dry grass.

Kilroy said, "No offense meant or implied, Rio. Try to see it from my angle. I've got my neck stuck out a mile here, but I can't deliver my clinching argument unless you give me a fair hearing."

In the end, they all went out, trooping out of Rio's office and going down the hall to the back door. Rio sent Hector out first, to make sure that everything was on the up and up.

Kilroy said, "If I wanted you dead, Rio, all I had to do was sit tight yesterday and let Barker and Deetz do their thing."

Rio said, "Apparently, I have enemies I don't know about. Why take chances?"

Hector went outside for a look-see, returning five minutes later. "All clear, Boss." They trooped outside then, Kilroy, Hector, and the two Maldonado brothers. Kilroy led them to the car he'd parked on the street last night. It was a cul-de-sac, a narrow street between the back of the club and the back of another building. No other cars were parrked there.

After the cool quiet of Rio's office, the street scene was bright and brassy, flooded with hot sunlight. Kilroy took out his handkerchief, using it to open the driver's side door. He tripped the car trunk release; the lid unlocked, opening an inch or two.

He went around to the rear of the car, the others crowding around him. He lifted the lid and let them have a look at what lay inside. The bodies had been in the trunk for hours in the hot sun; Kilroy held his breath as he opened it up. The others were unprepared and got solid lungfuls of the stench, producing rounds of gagging and coughing.

Standing to one side, Kilroy said, "Know them?"

Leandro said, "It's Jim and Ray, Sarkesian's nephews!"

Rio slammed down the lid. Kilroy said, "I didn't know their names, but I recognized them from yesterday. They were part of Sarkesian's entourage at the funeral."

Rio said, "What's it all about?"

"They tried to take me last night, after I left the club. Instead, I took them," Kilroy said.

"Why?!"

"Because I was getting too close to the truth about Sarkesian, and he wanted to get rid of me. More important to the Maldonado family business, he wants to get rid of you. The question is, Rio, what're you going to do about it?"

FOURTEEN

Hellzapoppin'!

That was Kilroy's reaction to the firefight now erupting in the dead of night at the Sarkesian compound.

Bert Sarkesian made his home outside of town, on a ranch near the eastern entrance to Wild Horse Pass, on the eastern slope of the Tres Hermanos Mountains. He lived there with his extended family and bodyguards, about fifteen people in all. It wasn't really a ranch, not a working one, for it raised no livestock. There was a one-story ranch-type house with extended wings, a bunkhouse that now served as living quarters for the guards, a barn and stables converted to more modern home offices and work areas, and some outbuildings, all surrounded by sprawling acreage.

It was no ranch, but that was somehow fitting, for there was no Bert Sarkesian anymore either. There hadn't been for several years. The real Bert Sarkesian had died during a buying trip in

Turkey, murdered so his identity could be stolen. The man who'd assumed Sarkesian's identity was General Ali Abdul Zirani al-Tikriti, an Iraqi despot who'd been one of the driving wheels of the dictatorial reign of Saddam Hussein.

During that regime, Zirani had been doubly blessed. Not only was he a kinsman of Saddam's, but he also came from Saddam's hometown. Of course, it took more than that to rise to the top in the tyrant's power structure. It also required a single-minded ruthlessness, a Machiavellian talent for scheming, and a cold-blooded callousness toward human suffering, torture, and bloodshed on an epic scale. All these traits Zirani possessed in abundance, serving him well as a chief of Saddam's secret police and earning him the appellation of "The Hangman."

More cunning by far than his leader, Zirani had laid far-reaching escape plans well in advance of Saddam's downfall. Well before Coalition forces had moved into Iraq, he had moved out, fleeing with the members of his most trusted cadre across the border into Turkey. His flight was facilitated thanks to an alliance he'd forged with a militant Islamist faction of Turkish military intelligence, who were burrowing from within their highly placed positions of trust to subvert the Turkish government and replace it with a theocracy run on absolutist, fundamentalist principles. Their help had been key in Zirani's substituting himself for the real Sarkesian.

No less vital was the mountain of money he'd stolen during the golden years of Saddam's heyday and salted away in a number of secret foreign bank accounts. Posing as Sarkesian and using his passport and other identity documents, Zirani had easily entered the United States, establishing his new home base in Adobe Flats in Nevada, whose dry desert climate was pleasantly reminiscent of the Iraqi homeland he'd fled. It was also conveniently sited on a people-smuggling pipeline, which Zirani used to infiltrate others of his cadre across the border from Mexico and into the States. Furnished with forged ID papers, they masqueraded as members of Sarkesian's extended family. The carpet discount warehouse business he operated in Adobe Flats served as good cover for the new spy network that he soon had up and running.

Sarkesian's real identity had only become known to Kilroy in the last few days, the byproduct of a covert investigation he'd been conducting in the region during the last month. One of the Air Force's aircraft was missing, an awesome instrument of destruction whose disappearance made the service's top brass look and feel sick. They lacked the domestic operational capacity possessed by the Army. They had no equivalent to the Dog Team.

The Dog Team had gotten in on the case. Kilroy and his teammate Brand were assigned to the Tres Hermanos region, which analysts had selected as one of the most likely spots where the missing aircraft might be found. The breakthrough had come with the demolition of Greg Mayhew and his ISS. Information supplied by Elise Danner about a secret Iraqi spy

cell centered in Adobe Flats had furnished
Kilroy with the all-important lead he needed to
tie in the missing aircraft with the Iraqi cell and
accomplish his mission of finding the former
and neutralizing the latter Dog Team style.

Now he and Brand knew Sarkesian's secret
identity, that of Gen Zirani, the Hangman.
Kilroy saw no point in burdening the Brothers
Maldonado with this intelligence. Kilroy had
"proved" to Rio and Leandro that Sarkesian was
an imposter who'd launched a program of murderous attacks on them. After that, the violent
and paranoid mentalities of the Maldonados
did the rest.

The siblings saw it this way: "Sarkesian," whoever he was, was the head of a crime family not
unlike theirs. Who he really was was a matter of
indifference to them. What was important was
that he was sneaky enough to have convinced
them that he was merely a successful and
wealthy carpet retailer, a solid citizen with no
criminal ties or interests. Discovering otherwise,
that he was as much of a crook as they were, was
intensely irksome. They were galled at having
been gulled.

They reasoned that, being the head of a crime
family himself, Sarkesian could have only one
ultimate purpose, to take over the lucrative vice,
narcotics, gunrunning, and people-smuggling
rackets now operated by Clan Maldonado. This
was a logical assumption because that's what
they would do were they in Sarkesian's shoes. To
take over the town, they had to take out the
heads of the ruling family: Rio, Leandro, and

Choey. They'd gotten the kid brother and come within two trigger-pulls of liquidating the older brothers at the funeral. That made this more than a business matter; now, it was a matter of honor, a blood feud.

The only course of action acceptable to the brothers was to do unto Sarkesian before he succeeded in doing unto them by doing them in. That's why they collected a hit squad of a dozen picked killers and pistoleros to make a night raid on the Sarkesian compound and clean house.

Kilroy made sure he'd be along for the ride. "After all, I've got a personal stake in this myself. They tried to kill me," he'd said. It fitted in with the mercenary gun-for-hire persona, the legend he'd created in order to deal with the Maldonados. Too, it bought him some insurance, some valuable time before Rio put the chop on him to avoid paying the fifty-thousand-dollar bonus he'd earned. Rio would be glad to have an extra gun along for the showdown with Sarkesian; he'd delay eliminating Kilroy until the opposing crime family was disposed of.

That's why Kilroy was on board an Escalade SUV that closed in on the enemy compound at three o'clock in the morning. The vehicle held Rio, Leandro, Hector, Tony, Roberto, and Kilroy himself, along with a cache of arms and ammunition. Closely following behind it was a second SUV, an Explorer, with another half-dozen Maldonado gunmen inside.

Rio wasn't much minded to employ stealth and subterfuge on this run. The compound was bordered by a five-foot-tall stone wall; its front gates were made of black iron rails. Rio didn't try crashing the gates. He drove up alongside them while Tony jumped out of the vehicle, a bundle of sticks of dynamite in hand. Tony lit the fuse, wedged the bundle between the bars of the gate, and jumped back into the SUV. Rio threw the Escalade in reverse, backing up a fair distance from the gates, retreating to where the Explorer stood waiting.

A moment later, the bomb blew, dynamiting the gates sky-high and demolishing a good part of the adjacent stone fence. A cloud of smoke and dust mushroomed at the compound entrance, raining down debris. Rio gunned the motor and drove through the gap into the compound, followed by the Explorer.

The two vehicles punched through swirling masses of murk and dirt, charging the ranch house. Maldonado gunmen were hanging out the open windows of the SUVs, firing rifles, shotguns, and handguns at the house. Guards charged out of the bunkhouse, shooting at the vehicles.

Rio braked the Escalade to a sharp, snapping halt a stone's throw away from the front of the ranch house. The Explorer did the same. Maldonado gangsters piled out, shooting at anything that moved and much that didn't, including the big bay windows bracketing the front door.

Kilroy piled out along with them, wielding a .357 magnum handgun. A .45 semiautomatic pistol was tucked into his belt. Bullets whipped around him, spanging when they struck metal surfaces, making whiny ricochets when they struck the house's stone facing.

A round thudded into a gunman standing next to him, knocking him down. Kilroy pointed his gun at the guard who'd fired the shot and squeezed the trigger. The .357 had a satisfying report, like a hand cannon. The guard went down.

Rio shouted, "Kill them all!"

A handful of guards came into view as they rounded the house's east wing, their guns blazing. Several of the pistoleros fell to this attack from an unexpected direction. A burst of hammering gunfire sounded, felling some of the rushing guards like an invisible scythe. It came from Hector, wielding an old-fashioned Thompson submachine gun.

Kilroy darted in the opposite direction, toward the house's west wing. Roberto ran up alongside him, waving a gun at him. Roberto said, "Where do you think you're going?!"

Kilroy said, "Come on! We'll go around to the side of the house and break in through there! We'll be the first inside!"

"Good idea!"

Kilroy charged, Roberto trotting beside him. No guards or defenders appeared to block the way. They rounded the southwest corner of the house, approaching its western face. Lights from inside shone through curtained windows to cast a long yellow oblong on the ground.

Kilroy shot Roberto, the hand cannon bucking satisfactorily in his hand, muzzle outlined by a yellow, spearing flare. Roberto jackknifed like somebody had swung an ax in his midsection.

Kilroy wasn't minded to fight the Maldonados' battle, especially not when Rio or Leandro might be minded to cancel their fifty-thousand-dollar obligation by giving him a bullet in the back. Besides, he had another, more important task to perform.

Shunning the light, he faded back into the darkness, slipping away from the firefight. Trotting along in a half crouch, he made his way toward the stone fence where the gate had been. Hopping the fence, he went to the road outside the compound. Across the road, on a rise, stood a pickup truck with attached camper van, its lights dark, engine idling.

That was Brand, waiting in the prearranged spot that he and Kilroy had selected earlier that day. Kilroy put two fingers to his mouth and whistled, two short shrills and three long ones, a recognition code they had also agreed on. It would be a damned shame to have come so far only to be shot by mistake by his own teammate.

Brand, unable to whistle, responding instead by flashing the dimmers in a pattern of shorts and longs. Kilroy joined him at the pickup.

Chaos raged down in the compound, shots, shouts, screams, smoke, and dust. Kilroy said, "We've got a front-row seat for the show.

"And there won't be any repeat performances," he added.

Brand nodded. He wasn't much for talking.

A Maldonado man threw a Molotov cocktail

at the house. It burst, splashing flames on the façade and roof. The fire caught, held, thrived, and grew.

Hector stood facing the front door, firing a submachine gun blast at it, blowing out the lock. He bulled his way in, followed by Rio, Leandro, and a couple of pistoleros. Inside, Rio went one way, Leandro another. Sarkesian himself was Rio's goal; he would accept no less. Clan Maldonado's head would take the head of the Sarkesians, as honor demanded, and vengeance would accept no less.

Leandro stalked down a long corridor, looking for someone to shoot. An open door loomed on his left. He stepped inside.

Before him was Terri Sarkesian, clad only in a black bra and panties. Leandro saw for himself the voluptuous figure that the seductress had exploited so ably in her alter ego as Tammi. He should have been watching her hand, which came out from behind her back with the gun she'd been holding and shot Leandro's middle to pieces. Immediately behind him came Hector, less easily distracted. Sticking the submachine gun's snout in the room, he cut down Terri/Tammi.

Smoke curled and writhed through the house. A tendril of it brushed Rio's eyes, blurring and stinging him, causing to miss a shot at Bert Sarkesian as the latter flung open a side door and fled outside.

Sarkesian, or Zirani, to call him by his right name, fled to where a Land Rover was parked and idling. In it was Sayyid ibn-Talal, a person of importance second only to Zirani himself. Ibn-Talal was the key component in Zirani's master plan, and as soon as the shooting started, the general had hustled Sayyid out to the Rover to prepare for a getaway. So long as he and Sayyid lived, all was not lost.

This being Zirani's territory, he got behind the Rover's wheel, Sayyid sliding across the seat to the passenger side.

Rio ran outside, firing to no effect at the Rover as it fled across the grounds toward the front gate. He circled around front to where the Escalade stood. On the way, he met Hector coming out the front door, submachine gun in hand. Waving him over, Rio jumped in the Escalade, Hector climbing in the passenger side.

Indicating the Rover, Rio cried, "Sarkesian!" That was the only explanation needed. Tony ran up at the last minute and jumped inside.

The Escalade took off after the Rover, abandoning the still-raging gun battle to pursue the fugitives. Exiting the compound, the Rover drove north, heading for Wild Horse Pass, pursued by the Escalade.

A line of lights rushed up from the south toward the compound, as a row of heavily armed state police cars bore down on what was left of the firefight. Not trusting the Adobe Flats sheriff's department, Kilroy had tipped the state cops to the blazing gang war, making sure that they wouldn't arrive too soon to spoil the fun.

He'd kept his word to Sheriff Boyle, though; no federal agents had come to descend on that dirty little town. It was the state boys instead, a fast-shooting flying squad of Western lawmen acting under the orders of the governor.

Kilroy wasn't there to meet them, though. He and Brand had taken off in the pickup truck after Rio and Sarkesian. The chase was on!

FIFTEEN

Day was breaking as General Zirani prepared to unleash his secret weapon.

His Land Rover took Wild Horse Pass west through the Tres Hermanos Mountains. Rio Maldonado's Escalade SUV followed close behind, with Kilroy and Brand in the Chevy pickup truck bringing up the rear.

It was a frantic run through that narrow, winding, tortuous mountain pass, a narrow gap between towering cliff walls that rose up and up on either side. There was no paved road, only a dirt trail; no lights other than the headlights and taillights of the three vehicles. The entire pass was a falling rock area, and it would take little more than a medicine ball-sized stone fragment on the trail to blow out a tire or bust an axle and bring any one or all of the vehicles to a dead halt.

No such mishap occurred, and the Rover was first to break free of the claustrophobic confinement of the cliffs bracketing the pass. Rock walls curved outward into a bell-shaped mouth, which gave on to the flatlands of the Black Sand Desert. Zirani wheeled the vehicle hard right, following the northward branch of the trail parallelig the western slope of the mountains.

Rio followed, breaking out into the flat. It was here, opposite the western mouth of the pass, that his brother Choey, Fierro, and Gomez had been cut down in the night by sniper fire, the opening shots in a carnival of murder.

Rio drove hard, keeping the northbound Rover's taillights in view. He was reckless, lead-footed, pushing the Escalade as hard as he could, but unable to cut much distance between himself and the Rover. Zirani was pushing his machine to the limit, too.

The pickup truck swung a wide, sweeping curve out of the pass, kicking up a plume of dust. Brand drove, intent, impassive. Just before breaking out onto the flat, he switched off the headlights, relying on the wan light of the dimmers and his own acute night vision. It was a ploy to minimize Rio's and Zirani's awareness of the third vehicle in the pursuit. For the past week or more, he'd done extensive driving in the area day and night, searching out its hidden byways, box canyons, hollows, and arroyos. He had a feel for the landscape and drove with authority.

On the far side of the mountains, the sun was rising over the eastern horizon, but here the bulk of the range blocked the ever mounting light, leaving the trail and the flat thick with shadows. Overhead, the sky was lightening from plum purple to a rich royal blue in whch stars and moon were clearly visible.

After ten miles, the northern trail opened on to the vast shallow basin known as Dead Lake. An oval depression whose long axis ran east-west, it had once been an extensive lake. But that was long ago, and its last drops of water had dried up thousands of years before the coming of recorded history.

The lake bed was smooth and hard-parked. Like similar sites in the arid Southwest, it had served as a race track and playground for local speed enthusiasts to race their custom cars, dirt bikes, and all-terrain vehicles, but the takeover six months ago by a private company of the seemingly defunct gypsum mine bordering the basin had led to its being declared off-limits to outsiders, a prohibition that was strictly enforced by private guards who patrolled the area 24/7.

The gypsum mine had been a going concern through the 1950s, when the last deposits of the mineral played out and the mine was shut down, shuttered, and abandoned. So it had remained until a half year ago, when the property was acquired by a private company. Since then, little had been done except for the installation of new, massive slab doors barring the cave mouth, the construction of some shedlike outbuildings for the minimal maintenance staff, and the establishing of underground fuel tanks and aboveground pumps. No mining activities had taken place. No geologists had surveyed the holdings or taken drill samplings in search of new, previously undiscovered deposits of the mineral. As far as the folk of Adobe Flats knew, not a single truckload of gypsum had been freshly excavated from the mines.

They did know that the guards were a bunch of mean SOBs who issued a single warning to interlopers; if that warning went unheeded, the offenders were apprehended and turned over to the sheriff's department, subject to arrest, trial, and heavy fines for the crime of trespassing on private property. In the West, trespassing is dealt with with a severity unheard of in other parts of the country, in some cases allowing property owners the legal right to shoot intruders on their posted domains.

The mine and outbuildings were located at the east end of the dry lake bed, butting up against the foothills of the mountains. Now, with the sky lightening, lights still blazed in the cluster of structures grouped around the cave mouth.

Nearing the southern edge of the lake bed, Zirani's Rover left the main trail, turning right onto a dirt road that ran along the basin's rim, driving east toward the mine. Rio followed, the Escalade kicking up dirt as it pursued the Rover.

Reaching the eastern end of the lake bed, closing on the corrugated steel sheds clumped outside the mine, Zirani began honking his horn, blaring and blatting it with obtrusive blasts of noise that echoed throughout the locale.

They served their purpose, flushing a handful of armed personnel from a guard shack out into the open. Rounding the southern rim, the Rover followed a curving dirt track northeast toward the lights and the guards.

Making the approach, Zirani began flashing his headlights on and off, alternating light and darkness in a certain set pattern of shorts and longs. It was a recognition code, a prearranged signal that identified the newcomer as authorized personnel.

Unmolested, the Rover rolled up to the sheds outside the mine, braking and sliding in the dirt to a sudden stop. Zirani and his passenger jumped out of the machine, joining the guards. Zirani barked out instructions, which the others were quick to obey.

He, his passenger, and several guards raced to the mouth of the mine. The other guards remained behind, taking up defensive positions in anticipation of unwelcome visitors.

The mine mouth, a hole bored through solid rock during the heyday of the mine's production, was fifty feet high and 150 feet wide. It was sealed off by a set of double gates thirty-five feet high that extended the full length of the cave mouth. The gates were new, having been installed since the recent takeover of the property. They were made of anchor-wire chain-link metal and were covered on their inner surfaces by dark gray green canvas tarpaulins that screened the cave mouth's interior from view. Set into the fencing at the sides were smaller, man-sized swinging-door gates that allowed personnel easy access to the cave without having to open the massive main double gates.

Portable generators with cables powered the electric lighting system inside the mine. It was ablaze with light whose glare could be seen shining above the top of the thirty-five-foot gates sealing the cave mouth.

One of the smaller side access doors was opened, allowing Zirani and his passenger to enter the mine.

The Escalade skimmed east along the southern rim of the lake, following the course taken by Zirani. Rio had a kill-sized mad on. Tonight's action had already put the taste of blood in his mouth; as if that weren't enough, family pride was also involved. He was pulling out all the stops.

Coming down off the rim road, he pointed the Escalade at the area to one side of the cave mouth where Zirani had stopped, a cluster of flat-roofed, corrugated metal sheds. Unlike Zirani, he flashed no recognition code with his headlights to identify him as friend, not foe. In any case, Zirani had already made it clear to the guards that here was no friend approaching. As the Escalade bore down on them, they opened fire with assault rifles and handguns.

In the SUV with Rio were Hector and Tony. They leaned out of the side windows, returning fire. Hector had a submachine gun and Tony had an Uzi-style machine pistol.

Bullets shot out the windshield, spraying the interior with broken safety glass. Rio steered with one hand, firing a semiautomatic pistol with the other. He rested his gun hand on the dashboard, firing through the open space where the window used to be. The muzzles of the guards' weapons flashed spear-blades of light, giving the Escalade's occupants something to shoot at.

Rounds zinged and spanged the SUV. Rio took evasive maneuvers of a sort by whipping the steering wheel left and right, throwing a weaving motion in the Escalade's oncoming charge in hopes of confounding enemy fire.

A tire blew, either from a well-placed shot or from a stress-induced blowout. It was the left front tire, and Rio had to do some fancy handling to keep from losing control. He tossed his pistol on the seat to free both hands for the steering wheel.

The SUV was upon the guards, who were scrambling to the sides to get out of the way. One moved too slow and was tagged by the vehicle's front, rocking the machine with the impact before dropping out of sight under the SUV.

The blown-out front tire caused the SUV to slew around toward the left. Rio fought to compensate. The SUV ran over a concrete platform about twelve inches tall, jostling its riders out of their seats; none were wearing seat belts. It took another hard bump coming down off the platform's far side.

Suddenly, a metal-sided shed loomed up in front of the SUV. Rio swung the wheel hard right and braked to avoid it, but too late, the Escalade careened sideways into the shed, broadsiding and knocking the wall down. The roof collapsed on top of the SUV, whose motor had stalled out.

Rio's chest impacted the steering wheel, delivering him a stunning blow. Hector, in the backseat, took a hell of a bouncing around.

The headlights were still on, illuminating dust clouds that rose around them.

Hector, that bull of a man, was the first to react. He still held his submachine gun. He opened the side door and tumbled out, engulfed by dust clouds. A metal support beam dropped from overhead, narrowly missing braining him.

Wrestling open the driver's side door, he hauled out Rio. Rio, stunned, was still able to stay on his feet, thanks to the support of Hector's strong right arm. Tony wasn't going anywhere. He'd broken his neck in the crash, and now his face was twisted over his shoulder at an unnatural angle.

Hector started to drag Rio away, but the latter had presence of mind to remember his gun. It lay on its side on the front seat and he snatched it up. His chest was a zone of numbness and he was having trouble breathing. He couldn't get his chest to fully expand to take deep breaths; the best he could do was take quick, shallow puppy-dog breaths. This weakness alarmed him.

Hector half dragged, half carried Rio away. The figure of a guard loomed up in front of him. Hector shot first, cutting him down with a burst of submachine gun fire. An impressive feat, done one-handed; the recoil would have been too much for the average man to handle.

A dozen paces away stood a concrete cube, housing some kind of pumping apparatus and control wheel. It looked like good, solid cover. Hector hustled Rio to it, rounds fired by guards zipping past them but not scoring. The guards' firepower was noticeably diminished, their ranks having been thinned by the invaders' assault. Rio took heart from this; he wasn't done yet, not by a long shot!

He and Hector dropped down behind the pump housing, momentarily shielded from enemy fire. Rio sat on the ground with his back to the wall, gasping for breath. His free hand, the one not holding a gun, felt around his chest to see if anything was broken. The hell of it was, he couldn't tell for sure, one way or another. The numbness prevented him from gauging the seriousness of the injury. He told himself that it was nothing more or less than a mammoth bruising from which he would presently recover. His arms and legs still worked, he could hold on to a gun and see straight; shoot straight too, he hoped.

A guard darted into view, shooting at him and Hector, but missing. Hector shot the other's legs out from under him, and when he hit the ground, finished by shooting him dead.

A shot hit Hector's shoulder, spinning him around and knocking him down. Rio popped up his head to see where it came from. The shooter was covering behind a boulder to the right of the cave mouth. Zirani!

Rio pumped some slugs at him. Zirani returned fire. Three other guards were scattered nearby, each taking cover and zeroing in on the pumping house.

Hector wasn't done yet. Using his good arm, he raised himself up out of the dirt into a sitting position, back propped against the wall. He sat next to Rio, protected by the pump house, bullets whipping harmlessly overhead.

Rio dumped the empty clip, slapping home a fresh one into his pistol. Hector's submachine gun was empty with no spare magazines, but he still had a long-barreled .44 holstered under an arm, which he now filled his hand with. Rio said, "We'll get these bastards yet!"

They grinned at each other.

Then came the roar of the Beast. The damnedest unholy racket, it came from inside the mine, the bellowing of a dragon in the cave. A mechanical beast, venting a full-throated howl of power. The shrieking noise did not abate, but continued increasing in volume and power, echoing off the mountainside.

The massive double doors of the mine mouth were open now, slid back to the sides to unseal the cavern mouth and loose the beast on an unsuspecting world. An ungainly beast, a dragon, yes, but a flying dragon.

It showed a squat, snarling snout topped by a bubble cockpit, a bulky fuselage with massive wings, and a pair of oversized humped cylinders in tandem just forward of a tail assembly featuring sharklike twin fins.

Quivering with latent power, shrilling, shrieking, the monster machine lurched forward and began creeping out of its lair.

On a high spot on the the dry lake bed's southern rim stood the pickup truck. Kilroy and Brand had dismounted and now stood watching as the flying dragon rolled out of the mine and onto the dry lake bed. Rolled, because it was mounted on wheels.

This was what it was all about, the missing plane whose mysterious disappearance some weeks back was the root cause of the murderous machinations that Kilroy had unleashed on Adobe Flats.

It was an A-10 Warthog, an awesome weapon of destruction that had been stolen from the United States Air Force. A veteran combat flyer that had been in service since the Vietnam War, it was a product of Cold War thinking, the West's only fixed-wing aircraft designed for close air support of ground operations.

Under its nose was its primary piece of firepower, a multibarreled cannon whose controlling gearbox and ammo housing was the size of a compact car. What it was, was a tank-buster, equipped to wreak battlefield havoc on enemy armored forces. Its high-explosive incendiary and armor-piercing rounds could sieve a tank like a shotgun blast shredding a tin bucket.

Here was General Zirani's secret weapon for exacting a terrible revenge for the U.S.'s overthrow of Saddam Hussein's regime.

The seed was planted when Zirani had learned from Greg Mayhew's ISS the timetable and route of the toxic train scheduled to deliver its hellbrew cargo of chemical weapons to the incinerator in Red Mesa, right here in the state where he had assumed a new identity with his cell of high-level fugitives escaping the U.S.-authored downfall of Saddam's dictatorial domain. Red Mesa was less than a few hundred miles away.

Surely no coincidence. This was the Hand of Fate, the workings of a heaven-sent destiny.

Such was the opportunity; what was needed was the instrument to carry it out, the avenging angel. And everything was for sale in America, even a machine of divine vengeance and retribution, so long as you had the dollars. Zirani had the funds, millions of dollars in ill-gotten gains he'd looted from the Iraqi people during the golden decades of Saddam's hegemony. He'd managed to salt them away in secret numbered Swiss and offshore banking accounts before the roof fell in on Iraq and he and his cadre had had to leave on the run.

Safely established in the States with a new cover identity, Zirani was already in the process of establishing a deep-cover spy network whose goal and purpose was to bring terror and woe to the Great Satan U.S.A. Always on the lookout for those whose vices made them potentially useful tools, his wide-ranging net swept up the very creature he needed: Captain Pete Peters, Jr., USAF.

Peters was a pilot whose personal flaws ensured that his military career was headed for a swift and ignominious end. He was profligate, a gambler, drinker, and woman chaser. Zirani had just the bait needed to lure Peters to the hook. She was Tamika Rasheedi, one of his trusted agents and a member of his entourage, a sex lure extraordinaire, an adept of sexpionage. Here in Adobe Flats, she posed as his niece Terri Sarkesian, hiding her good looks with a mousy hair color and unflattering hairstyle, no makeup, and a gauche and awkward persona. Layers of unattractive, ill-fitting clothing helped to mask her outstanding physique.

But as Tammi, barely legal Las Vegas good-time girl, she was free to maximize her devastating female assets. Platinum blond hair, glamorous makeup, provocative form-fitting outfits all did their part in fashioning a formidable honey trap. Once the skirt-chasing Peters saw her, he was hooked. Once she got him in bed, with her uninhibited sexual techniques, he became mere clay to be molded to the purpose at hand. To impress Tammi, he'd gone wild at the gaming tables in Vegas, running up a debt of fifty thousand dollars to the casinos that had taken his markers.

So besotted was he, and so corrupt, that he'd jumped at the lifeline she'd offered him. His current service posting was as an instructor at Nevada's Burpleson Air Force Base, where he regularly flew training missions in the A-10. Tammi introduced him to a man who was willing to pay one million dollars for the delivery of such an aircraft. The man was Zirani himself.

Not sex, but the power of money proved to be Peters's ultimate undoing. They didn't call it the Almighty Dollar in this country for nothing. Zirani offered to pay Peters half the money in advance and half on delivery. As a gesture of good faith, Zirani deposited five hundred thousand dollars in an offshore island account solely accessible to and by Peters. No tricks, no catches, the money was his. Zirani had no fear that Peters would keep the half million and fail to make good on the delivery of the A-10. Not that he had faith in Peters; his faith in Tammi was his surety. Peters was besotted with the girl; he wanted her more than he wanted the money. He couldn't have her without the money, but he could have her and a cool million.

The plan was set in motion. Zirani acquired the rights to the Dead Lake gypsum mine. The mine was as dead as the lake and he secured the rights for a pittance. Now it was up to Peters to fulfill his part of the bargain. The theft was absurdly easy. The squadron at Burpleson was scheduled to go on manuevers. For the sake of realism and verisimilitude during the exercises, the A-10 was armed with live ammo. One morning, Peters arrived at the base hangar with forged flight orders courtesy of one of Zirani's craftsmen. Climbing into the fully fueled aircraft, Peters took off alone. Deviating from the flight plan, executing a series of tricky evasive moves, he flew low, under the radar, dropping off the monitoring screens. The nature of the A-10 lent itself to low-altitude flight. He flew west, into the mountains and out of the ken of the Air Force.

The hard-packed dry bed of Dead Lake served as a perfect impromptu landing field. The abandoned mine was pressed into service as an airplane hangar. Once the landing was made and the plane taxied into the mine, Zirani's men went to work on the lake bed, erasing all traces of its use by the aircraft. The screened mine gates and the omnipresent guards posted there around the clock ensured the plane would be safe there until needed.

As for Peters, he was no longer needed. Zirani's chief executioner, Hasan, eliminated him as soon as the plane was safely in possession. Peters's blind spot had been the money. With him dead, the half million would be irretrievably, irrevocably lost. He'd been unable to conceive that Zirani was willing to sacrifice the sum to achieve his ends.

To Zirani, the money was nothing and the ends were everything. And of course, Peters had believed Tammi and her blandishments, believed that she was in love with him and desired nothing more than to go off with him and spend the money on a nonstop love feast. Hadn't she proved her devotion the most tangible way possible, with her enthusiastic, orgasmic bedroom performances? How simple were these American fools!

Still, Peters remained close to the heart of the enterprise. His remains were buried in a desert grave covered by rocks not far from the mine. Zirani had his own pilot, Captain Sayyid ibn-Talal of Saddam Hussein's Iraqi Air Force, retired. Sayyid was a loyalist with a deep craving for martyrdom. He could be relied on to see the holy mission through.

As for Tammi, her current assignment done, she dyed her hair back to a mousy brown color, scrubbed off her makeup, hid her eyes behind thick-lensed glasses that were made of real glass because her vision was perfect, hid her figure of passion under layers of dowdy, frumpy clothing, and resumed burying her real identity behind the mask of Terri Sarkesian, Bert Sarkesian's clumsy, ungainly, ill-favored niece.

The truth of the saying that only God is perfect had recently been brought home to Zirani by his current troubles. His plan was flawless; not so the imperfect human tools through which he had to work. First there was Mayhew of ISS, who'd sold him the information about the toxic train and its Red Mesa run. Why, the man was no better than a crook, selling the same information to the Iranians! And not just any Iranian but Darius, an accomplished agent and dangerous man. It had been only through luck that Zirani had learned of Mayhew's treachery and Darius's possible involvement, at least alerting him and putting him on his guard.

After that, his troubles had multiplied. There was the murder of Choey Maldonado at a site not far from the mine, which had created all sorts of difficulties, culminating in a bloody falling-out with Rio and the rest of Clan Maldonado. There was the American Kilroy, that sower of discord and ill will, whose infernal snooping had led to the unmasking of Zirani's double life here in Adobe Flats and the decimation of his cadre of trusted advisors, enforcers, and spies.

But all was not lost. God was good, delaying the debacle of Zirani's downfall long enough to assure the success of his master plan. Even now, the toxic train was on the final lap of its run, having entered the state this very day, as dawn was breaking. The A-10 was armed, fueled, and ready to go. By the grace of God, he, Zirani, had survived the night of blood, living long enough to deliver pilot Sayyid to the takeoff point.

The A-10 was exiting the mine, preparatory to taxiing across the launching strip of the dry lake bed and becoming airborne. Soon, it would be winging its way east across the mountains, then flying below the radar on a course that would inexorably bring it to its rendezvous with destiny in the shape of a train hauling twenty boxcars filled with some of the most virulent and lethal poison gases and nerve agents known to man.

The A-10 would fly its final mission against the train, cutting loose with its lethal nose cannon and strafing the line of boxcars, shredding them, ripping them apart, and loosing their noxious contents in a death cloud that would rank as one of the most horrendous eco-catastrophes of all time.

With any luck, the winds would blow the death cloud into Las Vegas, smiting that modern day city of sin on the plain as Sodom and Gomorrah had been once felt the fury of divine wrath. What was it the Americans called the A-10 in the popular vernacular? Ah, yes: "The Warthog." The Hog, a swine, an unclean thing forbidden to the believers. Set a hog to destroy a city of sin. Here, truly, was the dreadful symmetry of divine justice!

On the rise on the southern rim of Dead Lake, Kilroy unlimbered the weapon that he'd just taken out from where it had been stored, in the camper section attached to the back of the pickup. He'd had it with him ever since undertaking the mission to seek and destroy the strayed A-10, as the ultimate insurance if and when it came to a showdown.

Now the showdown had come. The weapon: a shoulder-launched Stinger antiaircraft missile.

Hefting the launcher, making final adjustments, he sighted it in on the ungainly A-10 just nosing out of the cave mouth and onto the lake bed, getting ready for takeoff. The aircraft's engines emanated an infrared profile that would serve as an irresistible guide path for the weapon's heat-seeking missile.

He fired. A jolt, a whooshing back-blast of exhaust gases and rocket propellant, and the missile streaked across Dead Lake to dart itself into the A-10.

The initial blast was ferocious; the successive series of blasts as the aircraft's fuel tanks and ammunition exploded was cataclysmic. The explosion beat the surface of the dry lake like a hammer striking a gong.

The fireball that erupted into being was a multipetaled orange-red rose of heat and force that grew and expanded like time-lapsed, fast-motion footage of a flower unfolding itself and spreading out in all its sun-fire glory.

The inferno swept across the eastern end of Dead Lake, oversweeping sheds and outbuildings, scouring the depths of the mine itself. The firestorm touched off the fuel stored in the outdoor tanks, multiplying the hellfire.

Later, when the flames had died down, Kilroy and Brand edged closer to the site for a look-see, as close as the heat allowed.

By some freak of chance, the first shock wave had scooped up Rio Maldonado like a giant invisible hand, tossing him out of the basin and onto some rocks above the dirt road rounding the lake bed's southern rim.

There wasn't much left of him, but what there was was still alive, conscious, and aware. Staring eyes narrowed in recognition as he saw Kilroy's face looming over him. Kilroy didn't know how much time Rio had left, and he wanted to get it in before the other clocked out.

Kilroy said, "I killed your brother. That's right, me. I killed Choey and his two pals. I came across them while doing some night hunting looking for the missing plane. The two girls that survived were taken to a safe place. They told me plenty about your outfit that helped me get a line on you.

"I hired Barker and Deetz to kill you. They were killers and had it coming, too. I crossed them and killed them to get in with you. Just thought you'd like to know. Take that to hell with you."

Rio formed the words: "Finish it . . ."

Kilroy raised his gun, put a bullet in Rio's head.

"It's done," he said.

SIXTEEN

But it wasn't done, not quite.

The long trail that had begun in a Virginia suburb with the murder of Colonel Millard Sterling and had wound its way across the country was nearing its end. The toxic train that was traveling south along Nevada's eastern border now neared the town of Brigade, a junction point about twenty miles north of Las Vegas, where it would take the western branch into the central wastelands and the final destination of Red Mesa, where the CW-destroying incinerator complex awaited.

At mid-morning, as the train neared the junction, Steve Ireland and Fred Osgood were on roving patrol in the killer Klondike SUV, making a sweep of Brigade and the roads leading into and out of it. Earlier, the train had paused so the vehicle could be offloaded from the flatcar ramp and set in motion.

Steve drove, Osgood rode in the front passenger

seat. A variety of weapons and ammo was ready to hand behind the front seat.

Brigade sat amidst a vast, sprawling flat cut by roads and wrapped in immensity. There was a sameness to the landscape, a sandy tableland sprinkled with a scattering of isolated land-forms, rocky knobs, and outcroppings that rose like reefs and islets in a sea of sand.

Some miles further south down the line, closer to Las Vegas, immense tracts of suburban sprawl with hundreds of thousands of residents had developed around Sin City, which had been one of America's fastest-growing metrop-olises before the housing boom went bust, and was still one of most populous areas in the Southwest.

But not here. Here was undeveloped wilder-ness, hundreds of square miles of tan and sandy wastes studded with myriads of cacti, mesquite, and sagebrush, home to snakes, lizards, mice, gophers, coyotes, small swift birds, and high-flying buzzards.

The sun had started making itself felt shortly after dawn, and now, hanging midway between the eastern horizon and the zenith of the cloud-less blue sky, it broiled the empty land beneath it with relentless fury.

Steve gladly abandoned his usual practice of driving with the windows open to get a feel for the surroundings, in return for keeping the SUV's interior coolly air-conditioned. It further amplified the vehicle's gas-guzzling proclivities, but it wasn't Steve who was paying to fuel the tank. He and Osgood took turns driving; it was

Steve's turn now. He liked to drive, and it was a
pleasure to be out here in the wide-open spaces
where the speed limit was as fast as you could
go, except when passing through the sparsely
spaced small towns.

The highway was a straightaway stretching
out to the vanishing point. Heat waves shim-
mered on the asphalt, creating the illusion of
quicksilver ponds and lakes dotting the road
ahead, mirages that ceased to exist in an eyeblink, only to be replaced by fresh phantasms as
the road ahead unwound.

A small town that could rightly be called a
whistlestop, Brigade was a crossroads around
which had sprung up a community of several
hundred souls. Its secret: water. Below the surface, the ground was permeated with subterranean springs and artesian wells. From frontier
times to now, in this arid land, water meant life.
In the days of steam-powered locomotives, the
underground springs had put Brigade on the
map, where it stubbornly continued to cling to
existence.

Brigade was centered around a clump of food
and fuel outlets, gas stations, truck stops, diners,
and fast-food chains. A commercial district
featured several blocks of small businesses and
modest office buildings; it was ringed by a belt
of residential neighborhoods, mostly single-
family homes.

The branch line to Red Mesa ran east-west
straight through town. The imminent passage
of the toxic train had shaken up the sleepy little
town, crowding it with officials, state police,

and Department of Homeland Security types. Unlike most of the towns along the toxic train's route, the inhabitants of Brigade were aware of the nature of the cargo that was passing through town. Trains traveling west on this branch were bound for the incinerator at Red Mesa. The state of the economy being what it was, most of the citizens were damned glad of the extra business and revenues brought by the train's facilitators.

The Klondike's dashboard was fitted with a scanner that monitored the frequencies used by railroad personnel, traffic control, the state police, and all the rest of the protective phalanx cocooning the train. Steve and Osgood also had their personal handsets keeping them in communication with the train's defenders, including Mantee and Webber's M.P.s

The train was proceeding on its slow, stately, measured course through the center of town when somebody hit the panic button.

The crisis blazed into being with the roaring rush of a prairie fire, its course being charted by the ever increasing, ever more frantic signal traffic crackling over the Klondike's scanner.

It began with a state police unit reporting suspicious activity in a gas station a few miles north of town. The officers were going to investigate. That was their last message, after which they ceased to communicate. Five minutes or more passed with the state police's central dispatcher radioing repeated and ever more urgent calls.

The crisis escalated with a cell phone call made by a civilian, a citizen who was driving in the area. Monitoring the action on the Klondike's scanner, Steve Ireland and Fred Osgood pieced together the picture from the information exchanged between the Brigade police department and the state cops.

The citizen phoned the Brigade P.D. to report a crime. He'd pulled into a gas station, the same one the state police vehicle had gone to before ceasing to communicate. The citizen had stumbled into the aftermath of a massacre. The gas station attendants had all been shot dead, along with some luckless innocent bystanders who'd been getting gas at the time. Both state police officers in the vehicle that had stopped to investigate had also been shot. One was dead, the other seriously wounded.

The wounded officer was unable to radio in, but he managed to convey to the citizen that a large armed gang had hijacked a fuel tank truck. The state cops had come along while the hijacking was in progress. The hijackers had opened fire, gunned down everyone else at the site, and had fled the station with the fuel tanker. They were proceeding south toward town.

Because of the chaos and confusion entailed by the event and the inevitable delays caused by the town and state police in communicating the information, more valuable time was lost in responding to the incident.

The Klondike had been returning to Brigade when the alarm broke. It was so close that Steve and Osgood could see the long horizontal line of the slow-moving train worming its way through the crossroads, virtually cutting the town in two. A couple of state police cars with their rooftop flashers on and sirens howling zipped past, heading northbound.

Steve didn't need to be told what to do. Seeing that the oncoming lane was clear, he made a quick U-turn, crossing the highway's centerline and heading northbound in the wake of the speedy state police cars, which were already dots in the distance.

Osgood got on the scanner, using the hand-held mike to radio in that they were joining the pursuit. His use of the day's password codes established his bona fides; he made sure to describe the Klondike, too, to prevent their becoming a target for trigger-happy cops in the heat of battle. When police hear the "officer down" alert, their general tendency is to shoot, not talk.

Steve said, "Looks like the other shoe finally dropped!"

Osgood said, "Darius?"

"Who else?"

Out of the south flew a helicopter, streaking northward, flying low over the highway. It overflew the Klondike, bulleting ahead, swiftly overtaking the state police cars.

Steve lead-footed the accelerator, feeling a palpable surge of power as the SUV's mighty-muscled V-12 engine kicked in and started showing what it could do. The machine coursed forward, rocketing along the ribbon of road, a four-lane highway with two lanes on each side of the centerline.

Ahead in the far distance, a dot of motion indicated the approach of the opposition. They came barreling along the center of the highway. The fuel tanker was heralded by a wedge-shaped vanguard of three black SUVs. The tanker was all highly polished metallic finish, gleaming like a prize piece of silver cutlery.

Inside the SUVs were gunmen armed with assault rifles and submachine guns. They were hanging out of the windows, weapons in hand. One SUV took the point, using the highway's centerline as its course marker. Behind it were two more SUVs, paired in tandem, the three vehicles forming a flying wedge to clear the path of all opposition.

Behind them came the tanker truck, basically a muscular cab hauling a cylindrical tank on wheels. That cylinder was filled with highly combustible gasoline, a gargantuan firebomb in the making, winding out on a high-speed collision course with the toxic train.

The helicopter reached it first, overflying the mark, then wheeling around in midair to reverse course and continue the chase.

Three police cars were fast closing with the kamikaze convoy. The suicide squad of SUVs and the tanker hogged the road, taking up all four lanes. On they came, neither side slowing or switching course.

It was a high-speed, high-stakes game of "chicken," that roadway version of Russian roulette once practiced by hoodlum hot-rodders back in the old days of black leather jackets, switchblades, and zip guns. Two drivers at opposite ends of a straightaway point their cars at each other and floor it, speeding headfirst on a collision course. The first to break off the engagement is "chicken," the scared loser. Of course, when two real hardheads joust in like manner, with neither one inclined to back off, mutual assured auto-destruction may result . . .

The lead police car was about an eighth of a mile ahead of its two fellows. It rode the outside northbound lane, edging the shoulder. The southbound flying wedge of three black SUVs neared. The SUV in the second row, the east-ernmost of the duo in tandem, swerved into the same lane as the oncoming police car.

The state cop blinked first, cutting hard right at the last second to avoid a head-on crash. It slewed off the shoulder into the land bordering the roadside, kicking up a brown dust plume, sideswiping tall saguaro cacti, and mowing them down before hitting a ditch and losing control. The car went into a roll, pinwheeling sideways, turning over three or four times before flopping to a stop upside down, its underside with its four crazily spinning wheels turned up and facing the sky.

The second police car changed course, swerving for the gap between the SUV at the point and the one that had just run the first car off the road. The lead SUV moved to intercept, its trajectory curving to meet the newcomer. It hit the police car at a tangent, its left front fender plowing into the driver's side of the other.

Metal crumpled, tires burst, windows disintegrated in both vehicles. Locked together, the SUV and the police car both blew sideways off the road, like two balls in a bank shot in a game of pool. Only, they were not billiard balls but machines. There wasn't much left of either one when they finally came tumbling to a halt.

Osgood said a dirty word under his breath.

For an instant, it looked like the third police car was going to hit the fuel tanker head-on, but at the last instant it managed to squeeze between the truck and the second SUV, the easternmost one. This was accomplished primarily because the tanker gave ground, swerving west to allow the police car room to get through.

Why not? The tanker wasn't looking to end its run yet, not before reaching its primary target of the toxic train, Steve Ireland told himself.

The police car flashed a few hundred yards further up the road before skidding to a halt. It turned around, pointing southbound and giving chase.

The two remaining SUVs and the tank truck kept on coming, their speed unabated. The helicopter flew low over the tanker, buzzing it. A dragonfly hovering over a silver tube on wheels. Garbled noises sounded as the copilot used a public-address loudspeaker system to order the aggressors to cease and desist.

Gunmen hanging out the windows of both SUVs opened fire on the helicopter, blasting away at it. A sharpshooter aboard the copter returned fire with an assault rifle, streaming lead into the cab of the SUV in the northbound lane, riddling the roof, blowing out the windshield and side windows.

The SUV fishtailed crazily, running off the

side of the road and nosing into a ditch. It fell on its side.

The gang in the other SUV kept pouring their fire at the helicopter. A chopper can be a delicate thing, its rotors, fuel lines, and hydraulics susceptible to lead poisoning. The shooters must have scored because the copter suddenly veered off, up, and to the west. It gained height but lost forward motion, hovering and making distressed machine noises while smoke began pouring out of its underside.

Its nose dipped, pointing earthward. It descended fitfully, by leaps and starts, the pilot fighting to keep some kind of control all the way down. The last fifty or sixty feet or so, it just quit, plummeting like a stone. It came crashing to earth in a heap, the tail assembly breaking off, its rotor blades flying. It didn't burn or blow up, though.

The last surviving SUV speeded up, pulling ahead of the tanker and taking the point. Now it and the Klondike were about to come to grips.

The Klondike had something the police cars hadn't, though: a secret weapon. Mounted under the headlights were twin recessed pods, each containing automatic shotguns. The weaponry was controlled by a kind of joystick rising vertically out of the top of a boxy extension of the dashboard.

Closing for the kill, Steve Ireland flipped a toggle switch, which opened the panel lids of the pods, exposing the snouty twin muzzles of the auto-shotguns. Steering with his left hand, he wrapped his right around the joystick's grooved handgrip. The stick was gimbal-mounted, allowing for the gun muzzles to be elevated to a maximum of thirty degrees or so above the straight-on horizontal.

He thumbed open the hinged top of the joystick, exposing the firing stud. He flashed on the thought that this was like one of those old-time World War I aerial dogfights, the kind fought by the likes of von Richtofen, Guynemer, and Frank Luke, only instead of being waged with canvas-and-wire Spads and Fokkers with machine guns, it was between well-armed, souped-up ground vehicles.

Then there was time for nothing but the combat at hand as the Klondike and SUV's game of chicken neared its end. Lead spanged and smeared off the Klondike's armor-plated front as SUV gunmen hanging out of the windows fired at the machine.

Steve's thumb depressed the firing stud, triggering twin bursts from the front-mounted auto-shotguns. Their yammering blasts were slightly terrific. He fired short bursts, pouring them into the front of the SUV, unleashing tremendous firepower. Finding the range, he used the joystick to elevate the angle of fire, raking the front of the SUV, ventilating engine and cab.

Grabbing the wheel with both hands, he broke off the engagement and the collision course, swerving right to avoid the SUV and the tanker truck.

The vehicles whooshed past each other. Behind the tanker, the police car that was chasing it swung into the outside western lane to steer clear of the Klondike.

Steve threw the emergency brake, whipping the wheel around to send the Klondike into a sliding, screeching bootlegger's turn. The wheels burned rubber, laying down a cloud of gray-black smoke, as the Klondike executed a 180-degree turn.

Fred Osgood swore again, not under his breath this time but out loud. Steve released the emergency break and stomped the gas pedal, the south-pointing Klondike leaping ahead to resume the chase.

The tanker was experiencing difficulties. The SUV had turned from a vanguard striker to a corpse-wagon, courtesy of the Klondike's twin auto-shotguns. It was just so much deadweight, no longer a road-clearer but a roadblock.

The tanker cab nudged the SUV to its right, bumping it, nudging it off the side of the road, clearing the way for the final assault on the toxic train, perhaps no more than a mile away.

Steve floored the Klondike, rapidly overtaking the tanker. The police car was trying to pass the tanker on the right. The tanker swerved right to block it, running it off the road into the field.

But the maneuver gave Steve the opportunity he needed to pass the tanker on the left. Overhauling it, he flashed past it. The V-12 engine showed its mettle, winding up and out on the rpms, widening the distance between it and the tanker.

All the while, though, the distance between

the vehicles and the town and train was steadily decreasing. No more than a half mile separated them now.

Steve had been reluctant to rely on the auto-shotguns' firepower, formidable though it was, to take out the tanker from the front, head-on. He wanted a sure thing. Now that he had enough of a lead, he readied his big move. Working the wheel and brakes, he swerved the car so that it glided sideways down the road, a move known to Nascar drivers and street racers, a variation of the technique sometimes called the Tokyo Drift.

The result was that the the Klondike squealed to a halt on the shoulder at right angles to the north-south road, with its front facing west.

The tanker came rushing past in the south-bound lane, exposing its left flank to the Klondike's auto-shotguns.

For a flash, Steve glimpsed the man in the driver's seat, a long-faced fanatic whose distinguishing mane of high, wavy silver hair marked him unmistakeably as Khalid Khan, Tehran's ace international executioner:

The man called Darius.

Steve thumbed the handgrip's firing stud, unleashing stuttering bursts of auto-shotgun blasts that sieved the side of the cab and tore searing white-hot lines of force through the cylindrical tank loaded to the brim with inflammable gasoline.

He held down the stud for one final continuous blast, the recoil from the twin auto-shotguns rocking the Klondike on its framework.

The guns fell silent, empty, only to be followed a few heartbeats later by rising crescendo of man-made thunder that seemed to announce the heavens were coming asunder.

It was the crack of doom as the contents of the tanker truck ignited and exploded in a titanic fireball that obliterated all but the outlines of the truck in the incandescent fury of its purifying inferno.

Roiling, expanding like a genie loosed from a bottle, it thrust skyward, climbing into a pillar of fire of biblical proportions.

Chunks of flaming debris rained down from the sky, while the skeletal framework of what had been the tanker rolled to a halt a quarter mile from the toxic train, which was still poking along in its sluggish way as it lumbered through Brigade to continue the final lap of its westward trek to a different kind of purifying inferno, the incinerator at Red Mesa.

Once he'd caught his breath, Fred Osgood let loose with a string of obscenities whose general theme was the mad recklessness of a certain so-and-so named Steve Ireland.

Steve grinned and took it, letting Osgood go on until he'd gotten it out of his system. He couldn't blame him for it.

When Osgood was done, Steve shook his head in mock sadness and said, "Oh, ye of little faith! You should've known I wouldn't come out second best—in a dogfight."

THE RIG WARRIOR SERIES BY
WILLIAM W. JOHNSTONE

DECIPHER

"A rocketing adventure . . . Stel Pavlou's debut novel bursts with marvels of scientific chitchat and towers above most recent science fiction."

—The Philadelphia Inquirer

"Few debuts are as ambitious as *Decipher*. Exhilaratingly imaginative."

—Sunday Times (UK)

"A wide-screen special-effects Technicolor blast; perfect for a Hollywood blockbuster."

—The Times (London)

"Deep, smart, and well-researched."

—SFX

"A fascinating blend of science, mythology, language, and much more."

—The Independent (London)

"If Michael Crichton isn't nervous, he should be. Not only has Stel Pavlou written a scientific thriller that's as tautly plotted a roller-coaster ride as anything Crichton's ever written, but he's done so using intelligent characters, and a clever, synergistic premise. The weaving of scientific detail with imagination is superb and unparalleled."

—ZENtertainment.com